THE Corpse WITH THE Iron Will

CATHY ACE

FOUR TAILS PUBLISHING LTD.

PRAISE FOR THE CAIT MORGAN MYSTERIES

"In the finest tradition of Agatha Christie…Ace brings us the closed-room drama, with a dollop of romantic suspense and historical intrigue." – *Library Journal*

"…touches of Christie or Marsh but with a bouquet of Kinsey Millhone." – *The Globe and Mail*

"…a sparkling, well-plotted and quite devious mystery in the cozy tradition…" – *Hamilton Spectator*

"…If all of this suggests the school of Agatha Christie, it's no doubt what Cathy Ace intended. She is, as it fortunately happens, more than adept at the Christie thing." – *Toronto Star*

"Cait unravels the locked-tower mystery using her eidetic memory and her powers of deduction, which are worthy of Hercule Poirot." – *The Jury Box, Ellery Queen Mystery Magazine*

"This author always takes us on an adventure. She always makes us think. She always brings the setting to life. For those reasons this is one of my favorite series."
– *Escape With Dollycas Into A Good Book*

"…a testament to an author who knows how to tell a story and deliver it with great aplomb." – *Dru's Musings*

"…perfect for those that love travel, food, and/or murder (reading it, not committing it)." – *BOLO Books*

"…Ace is, well, an ace when it comes to plot and description."
– *The Globe and Mail*

Other works by the same author
(Information for all works here: **www.cathyace.com**)

The Cait Morgan Mysteries
The Corpse with the Silver Tongue
The Corpse with the Golden Nose
The Corpse with the Emerald Thumb
The Corpse with the Platinum Hair
The Corpse with the Sapphire Eyes
The Corpse with the Diamond Hand
The Corpse with the Garnet Face
The Corpse with the Ruby Lips
The Corpse with the Crystal Skull

The WISE Enquiries Agency Mysteries
The Case of the Dotty Dowager
The Case of the Missing Morris Dancer
The Case of the Curious Cook
The Case of the Unsuitable Suitor

Standalone novels
The Wrong Boy

Short Stories/Novellas
Murder Keeps No Calendar: a collection of 12 short stories/novellas
Murder Knows No Season: a collection of four novellas
Steve's Story in "The Whole She-Bang 3"
The Trouble with the Turkey in "Cooked to Death Vol. 3: Hell for
the Holidays"

For David,
and Charlotte

Be It Ever So Humble

I like Saturday mornings at home; there's something about the prospect of the whole weekend stretching ahead that makes a Saturday morning sparkle with promise, and glint with possibilities. This one followed a bit of a late Friday night; late for Bud and me, anyway. We'd been binge-watching a Scandi-Noir television series and had decided to watch the last two episodes of the season, rather than go to bed. Now I had a telly-hangover; I was a bit bleary-eyed and worn out – from all that being stretched out on the couch nibbling salty snacks, no doubt.

As I looked out of our bathroom window my spirits lifted. The light as September becomes October is magical here in our little part of beautiful British Columbia; long shadows were reaching across the glittering grass toward gold-green trees, glowing through the dazzling mist, and I could hear a loon calling in the distance – such a mocking, yet mournful, sound. It certainly conjured Keats's season of mellow fruitfulness, but a Canadian version.

My phone rang in my dressing-gown pocket. Marty – our ever-helpful black Lab – barked to alert me to the fact, just in case I hadn't heard it. I answered as I petted his head.

"Cait, are you up yet?" Bud's voice sounded strange – guttural.

"Bathroom. Teeth. Just a minute." I rinsed my foamy mouth, tied my robe around my ample midsection, and headed for the kitchen, praising Marty along the way. He stayed close beside me, just in case I was unexpectedly set upon by stealthy marauders.

"You okay, Bud?" I hoped for a reassuring response from my husband, but the silence that followed made my tummy clench. "What's wrong?"

Bud's tone was grave. "I'm sorry, Cait. I'd have preferred to not tell you this on the phone, but I've got no choice. It's Gordy. He's dead. I can't leave his property until the authorities get here."

The news hit me like a physical blow. "What? How? When?" I could feel tears snag the back of my throat.

"I don't know, exactly. He didn't answer when I phoned him this morning, so I popped next door to see if he was okay. I found him on the floor beside his bed about fifteen minutes ago. Cold to the touch. No pulse. I've made the necessary calls. I'll have to make statements. Not sure how long it'll take, and I didn't want you to not know what was going on. Sorry it has to be this way, Wife. You okay?"

I wasn't. "Did he fall?"

Bud and I had been taking it in turns to phone our next-door neighbor around eight-thirty every night and every morning, and we'd made sure to drop in on him at least once a day for the past couple of months. We'd also shared the responsibility for taking him to the doctor for his appointments, and on trips to the pharmacy, the grocery store, and bank – then that had morphed into us making the trips on his behalf. Gordy Krantz was ninety-three, quite frail, and recently diagnosed with Parkinson's disease; I'd been worrying about him falling for some time. I'd hoped we'd been doing enough to ensure his safety. It seemed not.

Bud's tone shifted to the professional; in his years as a homicide detective before his retirement, he'd observed many scenes of death. "He was in a vest and pajama bottoms, supine on the floor beside his bed, almost as though he'd slipped out of it, rather than falling. I checked his head – no obvious signs of trauma, no visible blood or bruising. His comforter was a twisted mess, pushed against the bedside wall, so he hadn't tripped on that, and I couldn't see anything on the floor that might have sent him tumbling, or slipping. But the medics are more likely to know what to make of it all, I dare say. Sorry, Cait. I know you liked him. And he liked you."

"And I know you felt a great deal for him too, Bud. You'll miss him, and your chats." Marty's wet nose pressed against my hand; he seemed to sense my distress. I stroked him; the shape of a Labrador's head is incredibly soothing. I was rewarded with two warm licks and the sound of Marty's tail beating against the wall.

I could hear a sad smile in Bud's reply: "We'll both miss him."

I sighed. A deep, heartfelt sigh. "I'll even miss the way he used to joke about my Welsh accent. I'll let Marty out to do his necessaries, then how about I bring a couple of thermal mugs of coffee over? I can wait with you. Marty'll be fine indoors."

There was a slight pause before Bud replied. "The coffee's a good idea; it's a chilly morning, and not much warmer inside – Gordy's woodstove is just about hanging in there. And maybe something to nibble? This could all take hours. And wrap up warm. See you when I see you. I'll go back to his house now, but give us a wave first, eh?"

I looked out of the kitchen window toward the split-rail fence which marked the boundary between our five acres and Gordy's fifteen; Bud was standing beside the gate we'd added not two months earlier. He raised an arm, I waved back, then he turned and strode off toward Gordy's place.

I picked up the kettle to check if there was water in it and pulled a ratty old tissue from my dressing-gown pocket to wipe the tears from my chin. There was a bitterness in my throat that had nothing to do with hours of salty snacks the night before, and everything to do with the loss of an elder I had come to know, and had grown to respect, over the past year or so. Gordy Krantz was gone, and the world would be a poorer place for him no longer being in it.

I filled the next twenty minutes with as much activity as possible, and when I got to Gordy's house Bud was sitting on a stump of wood that acted as a makeshift seat outside the front door. We hugged, and I cried a fair bit, then my curiosity got the better of me.

"I'd just like to see…" My voice was thick with tears.

"Why on earth do you want to do that, Cait?" Bud pulled back from our embrace and looked at my pink, puffy face with amazement.

"I can't get any more upset, and I think it would settle my mind to not just always imagine how he looks." I was being as honest as I could be.

Bud sighed and opened the door. "Go on then, see for yourself." He rubbed my back as I moved forward. "Here when you need me," he added, his voice softening.

I stepped into Gordy's small home. He'd been a hoarder, no question about it. Most of his possessions were books; I'd always believed it would be impossible to own too many books…until I saw Gordy's house. I suppose it was arguable that he didn't have too many books, but rather too small a house. However, they had rather taken over the place. Where there weren't shelves filled with books, or stacks of books, there were items made of wood – tiny, whittled figures, bits of furniture, and everything in between. Gordy found wood as irresistible as books.

Of course, the fact that his house was filled to the rafters – literally – with stuff that collected dust, meant it was far from what one might call "clean". Gordy had favored a corn broom, which was just fine for sweeping away largish chunks of whatever ended up on the floor, but was pretty useless for any other purpose. I had no idea how long he'd owned his broom, but the head was wedge-shaped, and worn almost to the part where the bristles joined the wooden support.

Inside the smell was overwhelming; it wasn't unpleasant, it was just "Gordy's house smell". Decades of woodsmoke engrained in thousands of books; dust that danced in shafts of weak autumnal sun, that had somehow managed to filter through the grubby windows; remembrances of hard-boiled eggs, and his ever-present pots of soup simmering on the woodstove. There was one strange element my nose picked up in an instant; I'd been washing Gordy's clothes for some time and had returned a pile to him a couple of days earlier, so there was a hint of fresh-laundry fragrance as a counterpoint to the staler aromas – an incongruity, to be sure…but not as incongruous as seeing Gordy's body.

What Bud had told me was correct – it looked as though poor Gordy had slipped out of his bed onto the floor beside it. His facial expression was peaceful, his limbs and extremities lay easily. I hoped it meant he'd died without pain, or anxiety. Bud and I have seen more than our fair share of corpses, and I took comfort in the knowledge that Gordy had at least met a natural end. I reasoned the only way it could have been better for him would have been if he'd died in his bed, rather than on the floor beside it.

The bedroom was cooler than the main living area, where the warmth of the woodstove was still managing to keep the chill off the air – which surprised me, because ours has often gone out by the time we get up in the morning, no matter how full we stuff it with logs the night before. I put it down to the fact

Gordy had decades more experience of managing his woodstove than we did.

"I wonder how long he's been dead," I mused aloud.

Bud put his hand on my shoulder. "Cait, it really doesn't matter, does it? We knew...we might have expected...you know, maybe it's better for him this way, rather than becoming more and more reliant upon others as his disease developed. He wouldn't have liked that. You know how fiercely independent he was."

"Are you suggesting he might have taken his own life?" The thought hadn't occurred to me until that moment.

Bud shrugged again. "Well..."

A question insinuated its way into my brain. "Is this something you and Gordy have talked about? Did you know he was planning to do this to himself?" As I spoke my eyes searched the room; I couldn't see anything that might offer a way of killing oneself, nor could I see anything that looked as though it could be a final note.

Bud gripped my arm. "No, Cait, we only ever talked about it in the abstract. I didn't mean to suggest Gordy killed himself. I was just saying this might be for the best, in the long term."

"Good." I felt annoyed by the idea that Gordy might have chosen to leave us...then had a quiet word with myself, because I knew I had absolutely no right to feel that way.

The sound of a vehicle crunching along the drive meant Bud and I gathered our wits and headed out to greet whichever service had managed to arrive first. I wasn't looking forward to the process we were about to embark upon, but felt it was the least we could do to honor Gordy's memory.

And I Shall Dwell

"I'm exhausted." I threw myself onto the sofa and gave Marty a jolly good cuddle. It was seven in the evening. It had been a long day.

"Me too," replied Bud, looking it. "Pizza for dinner?"

I nodded. "There's a stash in the chest freezer in the garage. I'll get two – I think we're going to need them." I hauled myself up, knowing it would be lethal to relax.

"I'll get the oven sorted," offered Bud.

By eight o'clock we'd demolished a large, thin-crust pepperoni and mushroom special – the special bit being that I always add double the amount of pepperoni – and were halfway through a questionable thick-crust Hawaiian, which needed the accompaniment of beer to make it acceptable. We'd hardly spoken as we'd eaten, which wasn't surprising because we'd been talking all day, it seemed. Talking to sadly unnecessary paramedics, then Gordy's doctor, then the cops, then each other as we'd put Gordy's house in order – to the extent we could – and locked it up safely for the night; we were the only keyholders the cops knew of, so they'd been fine with the arrangement. Besides, Bud was Bud, so both cops who'd come to Gordy's house knew of him, and his reputation.

The silence hung heavy as neither of us spoke the words we were thinking, then was pierced by Bud's phone warbling and vibrating on the kitchen counter; we'd set an alarm to remind us to phone Gordy each evening.

"Night, night, sleep tight" was how I'd closed our conversation every night, sure in the knowledge Gordy would reply with: "Mind the bugs don't bite". Just the way my father had done when he used to tuck me in. I dissolved into floods of tears as the knowledge I'd never hear Gordy's voice again hit home.

When we'd moved into our house, Gordy had been the first to greet us, and had shared his passion for, and incredible knowledge about, gardening with us as we'd struggled to understand what was growing on our acreage. Rural novices both, it was thanks to Gordy we'd found someone to help with our septic and well pumps, a reliable lumberjack, the best plant nursery in the area, and even a handyman who was able to fix gutters, siding, and all manner of electrical problems. Both Bud and I happily acknowledged we didn't know how we'd have coped without Gordy and his phenomenal knowledge of our community, and specific locale. Indeed, he'd literally saved our lives by telling us to get our water checked right away; the E-coli readings were off the charts, and he'd then gone on to save us a fortune by putting us in touch with a local couple who'd supplied us with an upgraded filtration and water purification system. Gordy always came to the rescue when you needed him.

When we'd first viewed our house, Bud and I had suspected it was too big for us; five bedrooms and five acres sounded ridiculous, but it was generally in good order, and looked appealing with its yellow wooden siding and cream trim. I'd loved its rambling arrangement on one level – they call them ranchers around here, though I still think of it as a bungalow, albeit on a massive scale. We'd quite quickly agreed that both Bud and I could do with our own, separate office spaces, and we'd set one bedroom aside for overnight guests – not that we'd ever had any. The final "spare room" was just that –

completely without use, which meant it inevitably became a dumping ground for things that had no other obvious landing spot, because we'd managed to fill the entire house with the possessions we'd each brought from our old homes into our joint home, and Marty, of course.

Right now, our home was toasty, because Bud had stoked the woodstove when we got in. I'd turned on the TV, but hadn't watched it for a moment; my thoughts were all about Gordy. I allowed Marty to snaffle a bit of pizza crust from my hand, which he held in his mouth like a great prize, retreating with the trophy to his bed in the corner.

"The paramedics and Dr. Ahmadi didn't seem…comfortable with the scene, did they?" said Bud.

He'd expressed something that had been niggling at me for hours, and the look on his face resonated with me.
"No, they didn't," I agreed. "But nobody said anything specific to me. You?" Bud shook his head. "Maybe they wouldn't. Not until they've done the post-mortem. Dr. Ahmadi – by the way, she told me to call her Safiya – said she was requesting one."

"We don't really have any standing as far as Gordy's concerned, though, do we?" Bud sounded miserable. He picked up my empty plate as he passed me, which meant Marty stood and stared at both Bud and the plates, with a look that suggested he was starving.

He continued, "Do you reckon they'd they say anything to us, even if there *was* something to say? Medics can become pretty protective of their patients when there's an unexpected death. Trust me, I've tried to get early insights many times, and some of them won't say a word. But this is different – today I wasn't a cop trying to pump a doctor for information, I was a concerned friend of the deceased, someone who's been in Dr. Ahmadi's office with Gordy many times. She might have felt able to say something – if there were something to say. But she seemed…"

"…a little puzzled by something."

Bud nodded. "Gotta be honest, nothing looked wrong to me. Except that Gordy was dead, of course." His expression was grim as he popped the plates into the dishwasher, then he forced a weak smile. "Need another beer?" He waggled his empty bottle in my direction. "There's nothing we can do until we go back to his house tomorrow, to clear out the fridge and so forth, and I think we both deserve it. How about a Guinness?"

"Okay, a Guinness it is." I pushed myself away from the dining table. "I'll get the glasses, you can pour."

"Ah yes, patience…not your strong point, is it, Cait?"

We met beside the fridge and hugged – a snuggly, comforting hug. Marty wagged his tail as he joined us. It had been a long day, yes, but it had also been a sad one.

"I love you, Cait."

"And I love you, Bud."

"It's a terrible thing to know that someone you care about died alone."

I wondered if Bud was thinking only of Gordy, or whether he was recalling the day when his first wife had been murdered. Marty slurped at us happily, and the ragged edge of his ear – injured by the same gun that had killed Bud's wife, Jan – was the first part of his head that I touched, seeking comfort.

I eventually settled on the sofa, with Marty and a Guinness. I must have dozed off, because my phone woke me.

"Who can that be, at this time?" said Bud groggily. "I think I'd dropped off for a moment."

I grabbed the phone before it vibrated off the coffee table, and didn't look at the number. "Hello?"

"Is it true? Is Gordy Krantz really dead? What was it? Heart? A fall? Poor thing. Wonder who'll get the house. Not that it's worth anything. Tear-down, I should think."

I knew immediately who was speaking; Colleen White was known for her ability to utter a stream of consciousness – half of it frequently totally unrelated to the topic at hand – often leaving those she was "having a conversation with" open-mouthed and confused.

I sat upright as I said, "Hello Colleen, how are you?"

"I'm just fine, of course, thanks to a good diet and a fair amount of exercise, but Gordy never was one to take advice, was he? And now it's come to this."

"Yes, Colleen, I'm sorry to say Gordy is dead. But he was ninety-three, and still climbing trees to limb them a few years ago, so he wasn't exactly a slouch." I immediately regretted snapping at Colleen; she was well-meaning, generally speaking, but she was also quite a sensitive soul.

Her tone was sharp. "I've never had a bad word to say about Gordy, not in all the years I've known him. I'm a good Christian, and I'm surely not going to speak ill of him now he's passed."

I'm always annoyed by the euphemisms people use when they really mean "dead" or "died". Why does saying someone has "passed" make their death more acceptable, or palatable? I understand why Bud often refers to someone as being "deceased", because it's professional parlance for cops and first responders, but "passed"? Nope.

I bit my tongue, literally, then replied, "How did you hear?"

"Tom told Jack, Jack told Sheila, and Sheila phoned me."

Of course! Tom White had arrived at Gordy's house around eleven that morning and we'd told him what had happened; he'd been due to have coffee with Gordy, he'd said, which had surprised me, because I had no idea the two men even knew each other. Apparently, they'd bonded over mushrooms; Tom was eager to learn all he could from Gordy about foraging, to be better able to offer seasonal foods at his still-relatively-new restaurant just ten miles or so along the highway.

"Luckily that nephew of mine is a good boy and passes on critical information," added Colleen, "and it's a good thing he did too. We'll have to make an announcement at church, in the morning."

I couldn't imagine why that needed to happen, and said as much, before I realized that was probably quite a bad idea. Bud hauled himself out of his recliner and made "do you want another beer?" motions. I nodded and waggled an empty bottle – to signify I couldn't manage another Guinness – as I listened to Colleen.

"Gordy used to be our church warden at St. Peter's. Many years ago, maybe, but he was still an important role model, in so many ways."

I was surprised. "But Gordy never went to church."

"He didn't have to attend to still be an influence," snapped Colleen. "Colin Evans, who's the church warden now, often told me it was Gordy's example he wanted to follow…he even said that to my Auntie Ann when she was visiting from Scotland. She can't come any more, because it's a bit too much for her now, but she managed to make the last trip when she was eighty-seven, if you can believe it, so that must be quite a few years back, now, because she'll be ninety-six this year. Oh – I mustn't forget to get a card for her. With flowers on it. She likes flowers on cards, and cats, does Auntie Ann. Anyway, Colin watched Gordy when he was a young man, and it made him want to grow up to be just like him. And he has, in many ways; Colin credits Gordy with having helped him find his way in life."

I had no idea who Colin Evans or Auntie Ann were, and managed to stop myself from asking. Bud placed an open bottle in front of me, and smooshed Marty's face in his hands as they both settled into their respective spots. "Lovely," I said to Bud, and hoped it was the word that might shut Colleen up. It didn't.

"*How* did he pass? What happened? Tom didn't know, or, if he did, he didn't tell Jack, or, if he told him, Jack didn't tell Sheila, so she couldn't tell me. It would be most helpful if I could inform the reverend in the morning, before the service. Tom said you found Gordy. Is that right? Did you? Where was he? How did he look? Poor thing, he must have been in a bit of a mess. Was there much blood?"

Colleen's tone told me she was desperate to be *the* person in her congregation to have more knowledge than anyone else, so I decided to be charitable and tell her all I knew, which – to be honest – really wasn't that much.

Her diagnosis was instantaneous. "Must have been his heart, then he fell out of bed, dead. Poor thing. Still, only to be expected. He'd had blood pressure for years, I know. Colin told me. Thank you for that, I'll tell the reverend."

I couldn't let that pass. "No, Colleen, no one has said it was Gordy's heart and – while he might have had high blood pressure – we can't know how or why he died. Please don't go spreading rumors." I sighed. "He was ninety-three, Colleen. There might have been many things wrong with him, but we don't know why he died." Bud made calming signs at me, and suggested I took a swig from my beer, which I did.

"Well, I guess at least he didn't go missing. We wouldn't want another one of those around here. One every few decades is quite enough, thank you very much."

"Missing? Who's gone missing? From where? When?" Colleen's wittering was grating on my frayed nerves.

"Oh, it was a long time ago. Back in the nineties. Oh no, the eighties. Or was it the seventies? I don't know, they all seem to blend into each other. Anyway, it was a local. A girl. Well, I guess she was a woman, really. A dentist, maybe? Long red hair. I'm a natural redhead, you know. I remember I dyed it brown at the time. You can't be too careful, right? Besides she wasn't an old man. Old men don't disappear, unless they walk off into the brush, like cats."

"Gordy didn't wander off, Colleen. He just died."

Colleen's tone told me she felt wounded. "Well, I'll ask the reverend to not say too much tomorrow, but please let me know what they tell you as soon as you can. Who'll be organizing the funeral? Do you think they'll want it at the church? We can do a very nice funeral, even if I say so myself. The hall's a good size, thanks to Gordy himself – he oversaw the extension we built some years ago – skookum, he was, back then. We could have up to two hundred in there for a tea afterwards. We could organize a pot-luck, or we could use Max Muller to cater; he's a bit nervy still – he would be after his breakdown, of course – but he's very good."

I could feel myself getting sucked into a bottomless pit of conjecture. "I don't know what the arrangements will be, nor who will make them, Colleen. Gordy had no family, so we're not even sure who his next of kin might be. I dare say it'll all get sorted out, in due course. Now, if you'll excuse me, Marty's telling me he needs me to let him out. I'll get in touch if we hear anything more."

"Promise?"

"Promise. Good night, Colleen." I hung up before she could reply.

Marty didn't need to go out at all, but sometimes it's handy to have a dog to use as an excuse.

"That was Colleen White." I announced, unnecessarily. "She wanted to know how Gordy 'passed'."

"I gathered as much," replied Bud. "It's amazing how different the White siblings are. Jack's got all the qualities he needed when he was a cop – patience, attention to detail, he's steady and thoughtful, and just plain inquisitive. Then there's his younger brother, Tom's father, who's part hippy, even to this day, and there's Colleen, their big sister, who's…well, she's pretty unique, you have to give her that."

"The spinster sister who stayed at home to look after their father when their mother died, while her two little brothers went off and built lives for themselves in the big world."

Bud nodded. "Jack always said it was what she wanted, but I guess there weren't many choices for women back in the day – at least, probably not around here. She's got to be almost eighty by now, I reckon. Big gap between her and Jack, then his brother's just a year younger than him. Life's a funny thing, eh? Why was she talking about people going missing, by the way?"

"Goodness knows why she says what she does half the time. Wittering on about some girl, or maybe a woman, possibly a dentist, who definitely had red hair, having gone missing at some point between the seventies and the nineties. She said the victim was local – I assume she meant local to here, as opposed to local to where she lives, which is Harrison Mills, isn't it? Ring any bells?"

"Yes, Colleen's still in the old family home out that way. Nice spot. But no, no bells ringing about a redheaded dentist, or otherwise, going missing in any of those decades. But I wouldn't have necessarily known of such a case; I didn't pass my RCMP entry exams until the early eighties, then I was in training and stationed all over the place. We're all only too well-aware of the terrible tragedy of so many women having gone missing in BC over the years – but part of the problem was that the various law-enforcement agencies didn't connect very well with each other until relatively recently, so anything happening out this way might have been either before my time, or just simply beyond my purview."

Thinking back to Colleen's words I added, "She said Gordy had been a church warden. I can't picture him as a church warden, can you? Doesn't seem to fit with the man I knew."

Bud stretched, at almost exactly the same moment that Marty extended himself to his full length beside the woodstove. "Gordy, a church warden? Hmm. Well, I guess he was ninety-three after all, which doesn't just mean his body was old, it also means he'd done a lot of living. We've only known him for – what? – less than a couple of years? That's ninety-one years of his life we never witnessed. And I know for sure that when he and I chatted it wasn't just a list of 'when I did this' or 'when I did that', it was more about what we were looking at, or doing, at the time, you know?"

"And when he and I talked it was usually about art, or what he was reading, or maybe something he'd heard on the radio. It's odd, given how keen he was to learn new things, that he never wanted a TV. It opens a window onto so many parts of the world. Always found that a bit weird. I know he told me he thought TV was like a drug, but he could have rationed himself – been selective in his viewing."

"Says the woman who overdosed on chips last night as she watched six straight hours of a gruesomely dark crime drama." Bud chuckled.

I smiled back. "Speaking of which, I don't suppose you fancy watching just one episode of the second season, do you? I could do with something soothing for an hour."

"Soothing? Good grief, if we'd had that many grisly deaths to cope with around here, the powers that be would have swooped in, telling us exactly how to do a better job."

"But it's so enjoyable when there's an inadequate police presence, comprised of people who can barely function – or effectively communicate with each other – let alone apprehend a ruthless 'unknown subject' who's come up with the most devious ways possible to kill seemingly random people, don't you think? And you're from Sweden – so it should resonate for you even more."

"Born there, not brought up there," said Bud wagging his finger at me. "Swedish blood but Canadian raised, that's me. Besides, you know very well they were Norwegian, not Swedish. That's a significant difference."

I reached for the remote and plumped a cushion behind my head. As the now-familiar theme tune began, Marty flicked an ear then sighed as only a warm, comfortable dog can.

"You should probably turn off the reminder on your phone to call Gordy in the morning," I said sadly, before my mind began to wander along deserted snow-covered roads bristling with broodily threatening inhabitants and psychologically scarred, monosyllabic cops.

"He'll be missed by more people than just us," said Bud heavily. We reached out and touched fingers, then settled into an hour of joyfully bloody unreality.

Cleaning House

It's not unusual for it to rain in our little south-western corner of British Columbia – we live in a temperate rainforest after all – but the truly heavy stuff doesn't usually arrive until mid-October, which means that by the end of September we're all exhausted by the stress of living with a high risk of forest fires for months, and are hoping the rain comes sooner, rather than later. Given how much of it we get through the winter, I realize that's more than a little ironic. However, I reckoned it must have bucketed down overnight, because there were ducks waddling about in a brand-new pond in a part of our front acreage that has a bit of a dip in it. They seemed happy enough, and I was pleased to spend a few moments watching them splash about as I allowed my brain to wake up properly.

With a couple of mugs of coffee inside me, I got dressed so Bud and I could head over to Gordy's to empty his fridge, and find out when his bills were due to be paid. Though we'd taken him to his bank, and had even got cash out of the wall for him on a few occasions, we knew little about his financial arrangements, so we'd also steeled ourselves to having to wade through his belongings to try to find out what we needed to know.

And that resolve would be required; I was in no doubt that sorting through Gordy's possessions was going to be difficult, and dirty, work.

I was just getting a snack out of the treat-cupboard for Marty when Bud's phone warbled. I wasn't really listening to Bud, but could tell he wasn't happy about the conversation he was having. I focused on telling Marty how handsome and clever he was; I can't give him his snack until we're literally walking out of the front door, because he'll just demolish it and expect another before we leave. He was bouncing up and down with excitement by the time Bud finished his call.

"Let's go," he said curtly, which Marty took as his cue to lunge toward my hand and snatch the treat from me. I didn't hang about; Bud and I bustled through the front door, and Marty trotted to his bed beyond the laundry room to relish his treat.

It was chilly outside, though the shredding clouds above the towering hemlocks, firs, and cedars allowed the odd glimpse of blue skies, and suggested the possibility of sunshine later in the day. I locked the front door and asked, "Who was on the phone?"

"Dr. Ahmadi. Safiya. She wanted to know how Gordy had been feeling the past couple of weeks, since you took him for his last appointment. She seemed concerned about his medication – asked if it had been disagreeing with him."

"He hadn't said anything to me about it. And I didn't notice anything. I'd have got in touch with her if I'd thought there was an issue."

"I know." Bud fiddled about, trying to push his phone into his jacket pocket with a gloved hand. He was nibbling his lip. "She asked how he'd been in general terms. Had he been good at taking his meds on schedule? Experiencing much dyskinesia? That sort of thing. Mentioned some broken china in the bedroom."

"That period when he'd had uncontrollable spasms every time he took his meds stopped a few weeks ago, when she changed his dosage. She said it would, and it did. Doesn't she know we'd have told her if it didn't?" I was beginning to wonder if Dr. Ahmadi thought Bud and I were less than capable of looking out for Gordy – then realized he'd died, somehow, on our watch, so wondered if she had a point.

"It was scary to see him moving so uncontrollably back then, but she altered his dosage and it seemed to work." Bud seemed to be speaking to himself as much as to me.

"To be honest, it doesn't surprise me there was broken china in Gordy's bedroom, but you and I know it could have been there for months. That said, I didn't see any. Did she say where it was?"

"No, she didn't, but we didn't exactly go poking about when we were there, did we? Could have been under the bed, or even under him, to be honest." Bud's tone was flat. "There's something she's not telling me. *Us*. I couldn't draw her on it. Do you think she's following the same train of thought we did? That Gordy might have killed himself."

I stroked Bud's back. "I don't know. Your mind went there, then you took mine along for the ride – maybe she's had the same thought. But maybe she won't, or can't, say more. Not quite the same as interviewing a suspect, is it, Husband?"

Bud managed a wicked smile. "Not at all. Sometimes I miss the good old days." He flashed me a broad grin, and I even got a wink.

Despite this bit of levity, I knew Bud's spirits needed lifting. I forced a smile. "Tell you what, let's go over to Gordy's, get done what we need to, then we can take a bit of time to have a good look around the place. It might put our minds at rest. Somehow."

We strode through the gate with fresh determination and made our way next door. The padlock, which was the only form of security on the outside of Gordy's front door, put up its usual fight, but finally succumbed.

"Right, let's get this done," said Bud.

We both removed our jackets, pulled on rubber gloves, grabbed black plastic bags from the roll we'd brought with us, and began by emptying the fridge. We'd agreed we wouldn't fancy eating anything from it ourselves, because it was an ancient model, badly rusted, and it dripped pretty heavily – but Gordy hadn't wanted a new one, so that had been that. The freezer box worked well enough, though, and that was where Gordy had kept the meals we'd arranged to have delivered by a local service; their menu was quite limited, but they prepared decent food without lots of salt and flavorings added, which we knew was important because of his elevated blood pressure. They were also reasonably priced, which was good because we were as careful as we could be about any money we advised him to spend, as he was living off a state pension.

Not knowing how things would play out as far as ownership of his house would go, we thought it best to remove only items that would perish quickly; we also checked the cupboards and the other rooms for detritus or leftovers. Next, I washed up the dirty dishes we found scattered about the place, as best I could. Gordy only had cold water in the house; there was a water heater, but it hadn't worked for years, apparently, and he hadn't wanted it fixed. He'd at least allowed Bud to do some repairs to the kitchen sink when that had backed up, but, otherwise, he had one working cold tap in the kitchen, and a flushing toilet. That was it. The bath was full of bits of furniture and various other "precious" objects. I'd been told by Bud – because it wasn't something Gordy would ever have shared with me – that Gordy's idea of personal hygiene was to have a wash with warm water and a flannel in the kitchen, the warm water courtesy of a pot that was always on the woodstove. To say he lived a simple life would be understating it somewhat, and I'd been shocked when I'd first visited his home. However, over time I'd become accustomed to it, and even felt comfortable sitting in the seat opposite his beloved armchair without squirming, despite knowing that the holes in all the soft furnishings had been made by mice.

We'd brought thermal mugs of coffee with us and stopped for a breather after about an hour of clearing around the place. We'd done almost everything we could, under the circumstances. Gordy had no cable service, no gas supply, he got his water from a well and had a septic field, like us, so it really was only the electricity we had to worry about – we just had to find out when his bill was due to be paid, to make sure the power wasn't cut off. They could disconnect his phone whenever they wanted.

Bud put his arm around me. "You look sad."

"I hope he was happy." I said. "He told me once that he chose the life he lived. He was a good, kind man, with a wealth of knowledge about so many things. But…is it odd to say I hope there'll be more people than just us who'll miss him? He never seemed to interact with other people very much. Almost never had visitors. I hope we won't be the only ones at his funeral. Or memorial. Or whatever."

Bud stretched out his back. "Well, it looks like at least two members of the White family will miss him – Colleen and Tom both seem to know him, which I'll admit came as a surprise to me."

"Me too," I agreed.

"Come on, let's haul that pot of vegetable soup off the stove and chuck it into the bush somewhere; the local fauna can make the most of it. It's going to be a job for both of us; I'll carry it, you hold the door open."

As Bud carefully carried the pot through the front door, trying to prevent a soupy tsunami, a thought occurred to me. "How did you get in yesterday morning? Hadn't Gordy bolted this door?"

"Nope, he must have forgotten."

I couldn't help but shake my head. "That's not like Gordy; good grief, anyone could walk into the place at any time."

Bud placed the pot on the ground beside the six-foot-high pile of wood chippings that had stood along one side of Gordy's house ever since we'd arrived. "What about over there – further away? We don't want to invite vermin into the house, do we?"

I agreed; we each took a handle of the pot and tipped it carefully and slowly when we got to a clump of bushy undergrowth a good way from the house itself.

I picked up the empty pot; it was crusted inside with yukky stuff, the base blackened with age and use. "I don't see any point washing this, Bud. Why don't we just leave it outside for the rain to rinse it."

"Good idea. Whoever gets to be responsible for this lot can decide if they want to keep it, or chuck it."

"Well, whoever that is I can't say I envy them having to clear out the house. We've got a couple of bags for the dump from just his fridge and a few cupboards. What on earth will they do with it all? Good grief, it'll be one heck of a job."

"Luckily, not our problem," said Bud. "But what we *can* do is see to it that the place is well looked after until someone is given the eventual legal responsibility for it. That desk of his, in the living room?" I nodded. "Let's start to look for bills and bank statements and so forth there, okay?"

"Agreed."

We entered the house again and I looked at the desk. It was barely visible, buried beneath piles of books, wooden figures, and a massive carved wooden bowl. I squeezed between the desk and a bookcase, while Bud pushed back a couple of old electric heaters to be able to attack it from the opposite side. We began our search.

In the days when I was contracted by Bud to consult for his homicide squad as a victim profiler, I'd spent hours – sometimes days – working through the *minutiae* of people's possessions to try to establish the nature of the life they'd led, and to extrapolate from that how they might have come into contact with someone who had done them harm. I hadn't done that – officially – for some time; searching through Gordy's desk took me back to those days, but without the cloud, or urgency, of malice aforethought hanging over my endeavors.

"Bank statements, all filed in date order," exclaimed Bud. "That's a good start. This drawer here seems pretty well organized. Good for Gordy. Hydro bills too." He fell silent as he read the papers in his hand. "Paid directly from his bank account. Wonder if he did the same for the phone. Why are you so quiet, Cait?"

I'd discovered an old photograph album wedged into a shelf beneath the desktop. I flicked through the first few stiff pages, and was taken completely by surprise. I dare say it showed on my face.

"Look for yourself." I handed the album to Bud and watched his expression change. His mouth opened into an O. The photographs of a young boy, then a couple of formal portraits of a teen – all of whom I assumed were Gordy – were to be expected; then there were a few of him in plaid shirts, his sleeves rolled up, leaning on a shovel in a somewhat bleak-looking landscape. It was the photos that followed that were surprising; they were of young women, naked, lolling about in woodland areas, looking quite lascivious. Their clothes were scattered about the ferns and logs. Some were in color, some in black and white, all of them were Polaroids.

Bud's eyebrows shot up. "Hmm…they look like snaps, not posed porn shots. Girlfriends?"

"Well, I'm guessing they weren't passing strangers."

"Wonder when he took them, if he did. Polaroid cameras haven't been around that long, have they?" Bud's brow furrowed.

"Launched in 1948. In fact, in the late 1960s they gave free cameras and film to people like Ansel Adams, Andy Warhol, and Helmut Lang to build a collection that would cement the role of the camera in modern art. The cameras weren't cheap, but Gordy could have owned one as early as the 1950s, if he'd had the money. Looking at some of the clothes that have been divested in these I'd say they were probably taken in the 1960s and 1970s…that's when those patterns were in fashion."

Bud looked as though someone had asked him to suck a lemon. "Not what I'd have expected of Gordy," he said, then shut the album.

"Any other photos in there that might give us some leads about Gordy's life?"

"I guess we could take this home with us and have a look later. Maybe over a sandwich?" Bud flashed me a "cute" smile, and I flashed one back. "In fact," he continued, "I'll pull all these papers together to take home, and we should both try to find something – anything – that might give us a clue about Gordy's wishes…you know, for his remains."

I agreed, and we continued with our tasks.

I eventually waggled a piece of paper at Bud. "Letter from a law office here. Oishi and Singh, in Mission. Accepting their role holding Gordy's last will and testament, and as executors of said document. Dated just nine months ago."

"That's about the time he got the first tentative diagnosis that he might have Parkinson's, wasn't it?" Bud looked up from the sheaf of papers in his hand.

"Yes. I remember it was January when Dr. Ahmadi first referred him to the specialist. It took a couple of months to get in to see him, of course, but it was during that dreadful snow that she first mentioned her suspicions to us. Maybe that spurred Gordy to sort out his affairs? Mind you, there can't be that much to settle. Shall we take this with us, and give the law office a ring in the morning?"

Bud shuffled away from the desk, trying to avoid all the tripping hazards surrounding him. "Let's do that. And let's just have a quick look around to see if there's anything we've missed."

It didn't take long to work our way around the four rooms and small bathroom. I'd picked up Gordy's watch from his bedside table, and – for some reason – I'd popped four pairs of his spectacles into my pockets as well; Gordy kept losing his glasses, so had to keep buying more. They were only the reading cheats you can pick up at most drugstores, but they did the job. Well, some of them did; I was testing out the glasses to see how badly they were scratched, when I came across a dog-eared notebook on a low bookshelf. Intrigued, I plucked it out to see what it was, and I knew I'd struck gold; it was a diary, neatly written in flowing cursive.

I added it to the pile on the desk we were taking home with us, then looked around for something other than a garbage sack to pack everything into. An old vinyl bag was stuffed under a chair; it had been red and white at some point during its life, but now? It had certainly seen better days, however, it looked sturdy, and the zip across the top still worked. The side was emblazoned with a CP Air logo, which I knew was a long defunct Canadian airline. As I pushed the paperwork and album inside, I wondered if Gordy had flown somewhere exotic when he'd purchased it – he'd never mentioned leaving the country to me. I supposed it might have been a domestic flight – Canada is so huge that flying is the only reasonable way to cross it…unless you have a few weeks to kill.

"I know we're only next door, but I have to admit I don't like the idea that people might think the house is empty," said Bud. "How about I nip back here later with one of those timer things we have for the Christmas lights, then set up a lamp to come on when it gets dark, and turn off again when it would be bedtime."

We made our way to the front door. "You do realize that everyone hereabouts already knows the house is empty because Gordy's dead," I said. Kindly, I hoped.

Bud nodded. "Sure, but I'm thinking about the passing opportunists."

I looked into Bud's lovely blue eyes. "Darling Husband, we live on a dead-end road, halfway up a little mountain, where the nearest street lamp is two miles away – and even then there's only one. Do you really think there'll be any 'passing opportunists' out this way?"

"Now, now, ma'am, we must always prepare for the unexpected, especially when it comes to the prevention of crime. We can never know what's in the mind of the opportunist thief, so we should make our homes as secure as possible, at all times. Plan for the worst, hope for the best. Which is why we always check that our house is properly secured when we leave it or go to bed. Right?" He saluted and smirked.

"Yes, officer," I replied, as Bud waved me out of the door, and snapped the padlock.

My mind wouldn't stop churning that night in bed; Bud was sleeping as though he were dead, but Marty snored loudly, and his furry backside was stuffed into my middle, with me wrapped around him. I thought I'd never sleep.

It was about three in the morning when I woke with a start. Marty was standing on the bed, growling, fully alert.

"Good boy," I said, trying to both calm and thank him for having warned me of the fact that something was happening over at Gordy's place. The area where we live is absolutely silent at night – unless the bats and owls, or the coyotes, are making a fuss – so alien noises are easy to hear. I shoved Bud's back, and Marty helped by pushing his nose into Bud's ear. Bud made groggy noises, which I assumed were his way of asking what was going on.

"I can hear clanging over at Gordy's," I hissed. I had no idea why I was whispering, it just seemed the right thing to do.

"Waah?" Bud lurched over to look in my direction, fending off Marty's licks.

"Listen! Can you hear that? It's as though someone is hitting metal against metal over there. Do you think someone's trying to break into Gordy's place?"

Bud pushed himself up onto his elbows. "I'll call 911," he said without hesitation, swinging his feet out of bed. "While I'm doing that, turn on all our outside lights. That might scare them off…stop them achieving whatever it is they're trying to do. Maybe you can get out the binoculars, too – see if you can spot anything useful."

We each fulfilled our tasks – Marty helped me with mine, but I was a bit annoyed and puzzled that he didn't bark, because I suspected a barking dog would add to our somewhat lackluster scare tactics. Bud was still on the phone when I got to the dining room and grabbed the binoculars. I opened the window, hoping that would help me see more, but neither the binoculars nor the open window helped, because Gordy's property was completely dark.

I caught a flash of something, and a noise that sounded like breaking glass. I rushed to the switch for the lights at the side of our house closest to Gordy's and flipped it off and on several times, hoping it would make more of an impression if whoever it was out there believed someone was actively interested in what they were getting up to. Then, in the distance, I heard a siren. Given the way sound can travel up the mountainside from the valley below, the siren might very well have been miles away, but the combination of me flashing the lights and the suggestion of cops arriving must have worked, because I heard something, or someone, moving along Gordy's drive; I couldn't hear a car or truck engine, and there were no lights showing, but there was a sort of swooshing sound. Not footsteps. Maybe a bicycle? I couldn't identify it, which was extremely annoying.

When Bud presented himself, fully dressed, I wasn't convinced it was a good idea for him to venture through the gate to Gordy's, but that nervousness was tempered by my belief that whoever had been there had already left. In his best Bud-like manner, my husband pointed out it would be sensible for me to stay indoors, taking care of Marty, while he went to meet the cops when they arrived. Given that I needed to visit the bathroom, I didn't disagree, so I headed off as he left the house; I just managed to catch a glimpse of the lights on top of a police cruiser through the trees as it wound up the mountainside.

I pulled on some "house clothes" in case I had to go out, then peered through the window trying to see and hear as much as I could of what was transpiring next door. We don't have a clear view of Gordy's house from our place – it's too far away, beyond some trees which offer both homes privacy, but we can see his driveway, and I spotted flashlights bobbing about beyond the treeline.

I could also tell that two cops had responded; one voice carrying through the silence of the night was female, the other male. I worked out that all the possible entry-points to the house, including windows, were being examined. Radios crackled and popped; I could tell things were winding up when the lights inside the car parked on the drive went on, and one of the officers sat down to enter data into their computer. Eventually Bud came through the gate, waving his flashlight about until he was within the pools of illumination created by the exterior lights on our house. Marty was desperate to join in all the fun, so I went to the front door and allowed him to greet Bud.

"I'll walk him around the house so he can pee," announced Bud. "The cops will do a few passes, as and when they can, until it's light, then we're on the lookout for potential intruders until we're stood down."

It wasn't surprising news, but it didn't fill me with glee. I put the kettle on, in case we fancied a cuppa before trying to settle down again. I wasn't sure I'd get back to sleep; it was five in the morning and I was wide awake – not a good thing on a Monday, especially a Monday when I was due to meet with my department head at the university at ten, sharp. Oh joy!

Home Away From Home

I knew I needed a lot of coffee inside me before I headed off to the University of Vancouver, because I'd only managed to snatch a couple of hours' sleep. I was dreading the meeting. I hadn't taught a course for a year – due to my time in Budapest, then my recuperation period after the disaster there – and I wasn't scheduled to deliver any this semester, either. No one, myself included, had been prepared to say I'd be up to teaching in September when the timetabling had been done a few months earlier. Yes, I had a "secure" job, but I had no tenure, so they could dump me if they wanted and, similarly, I could walk away from them if I chose.

Bud and I had been discussing my decision for months, and I knew what I was planning to say at the meeting, but – even as Bud and Marty waved me off from the front door – I still wasn't absolutely certain I'd go through with it. We were financially secure: the compensation Bud had been paid after his wife was murdered, because she was mistaken for him, had been generous – if such a calculation can be made – and I'd just earned more money than I could have imagined by using my eidetic memory to help the publisher of one of the world's best-selling series of books. No money worries. Amazing.

I had to be honest with myself and admit I'd much rather have stayed at home to know what was going on next door than traipsing all the way to the university to sit down with someone who really didn't want to meet face-to-face with me at all. However, I'd agreed to do it, so I had to go through with it.

I enjoyed the drive out through the sprawl of Maple Ridge, the Golden Ears Mountains showing that the recent rain we'd had at our elevation had fallen as snow on their peaks. Port Moody was as welcoming as ever – its village atmosphere always lifts my spirits, despite the way the traffic clogs up between what seem to be a ridiculous number of traffic lights. When I arrived at the campus I parked where I'd always parked, and took the pedestrian route I'd always taken to my office. I'd hardly been there in the past year, but – universities being what they are – it had been kept for me, because it was still "mine". At least, that was what I'd believed until I arrived at it, when I discovered that my nameplate had been removed, and all my personal belongings – dozens of books, a few mugs, and a dead pot plant – had disappeared. The shelves were empty, the desk drawers bare.

The sight should have made me feel less stressed about the meeting I was about to have, but it didn't. I was livid. There was no way they were going to dump me; I had come prepared to dump them. I'd even written the letter to Professor Frank McGregor – the man who'd been elevated beyond his abilities to become head of department because he could be easily swayed by our dean.

I stomped toward Frank's office and found myself caught up in a flood of students rushing about at changeover time. As the eddying crowds dissipated, I finally knocked on Frank's door at exactly ten o'clock. I didn't wait for him to respond, but flung the door open, marched in, and reached into my bag for my carefully worded letter. He didn't even have time to look up before I spoke.

"I'm leaving," I said without a hint of a quiver in my voice. "I've found my time here most rewarding, and have always done my best to fulfill the requirements of my position, as well as take every opportunity afforded by it. I'll always be grateful to the university for hiring me, which allowed me to migrate to Canada, and for granting me my professorship. And you know I met my husband because of my role here, so thank you for that, too. But now? Now it's time for me to leave. I imagine you guessed that's what I'd be saying today, so thank you too for arranging to have my office packed up; Bud promised to come with me in the truck to take everything away, but was needed at home. Our next-door neighbor passed a couple of days ago, and there are…well, things to be done." I was angry with myself for having said that Gordy had "passed". What was I thinking?

I finally drew breath, and the face that had been one of the first to speak words of welcome to me upon my arrival in Canada over a decade earlier broke into a smile. I interpreted it as a sign of relief.

"You don't change, do you, Cait?" Frank motioned for me to take a seat, but I declined, so he continued, "We'd be sorry to lose you. Very sorry. We'd taken the decision to move your office up to the fifth floor, where you'd be able to focus on your research far away from the corridors where students wait for appointments with their tutors. But, if it's your decision to leave…well, what can I say to dissuade you?"

They were *moving* my office? I *wasn't* being kicked out? I felt my tummy tighten, my breaths shorten, and my face get hot.

I took a deep breath. "My mind's made up."

"But what about the research plans you had, Cait? You're giving up research too? Or have you…" Frank stopped making eye contact with me. "Maybe you've found another university that wants you, and your research? I can imagine you'd be in great demand."

One of the things I've learned since Bud and I have been together is how to allow myself to take a moment before I speak in anger; Bud's helped me realize how powerful it can be to compose my thoughts. I counted to ten, then said simply, "No, I haven't been approached."

Frank nodded and removed his glasses. In slow motion. It was a thing he did in every meeting, just before he was about to utter some words of great import. I braced myself for some sort of weighty observation, but that's not what I got.

"You saying you want to leave makes this an extremely sad day for me, Cait. The research you were working on before your necessary hiatus was particularly promising, and it could prove to be a real breakthrough. Please, sit. Let's talk."

I could feel my knees wobble, and my resolve shift. He was right, I'd been hugely invested in my project before I'd left for Hungary. "No, I can't stay at the moment, Frank. I'm needed at home. Gordy Krantz – our neighbor, who died – was a dear man, and I promised Bud I'd be back at home with him as soon as possible to—"

Frank leapt up from his seat. "Gordon Krantz is dead? That's terrible news. I must call the chancellor's office." He picked up the handset of his desk phone.

"You know Gordy Krantz?" It seemed most unlikely.

It was Frank's turn to look confused. "But of course." He blushed a little. "Well, I never actually met him. It was the chancellor who had most dealings with him, and the dean attended a few of the university-wide meetings early on, I know. But that would be the case when such large amounts are involved, of course."

I was at sea. "I'm sorry, Frank, I've no idea what you're talking about."

Frank put his glasses back on, which – in his case – signified he was losing his temper. "Krantz Hall? Our Center of Excellence for Environmental Research? Behind the swimming pool? Gordon Krantz is the man whose name is on the building because he's the one who financed it."

It was clear to me that Frank and I were talking about two entirely different Gordon Krantzes. "No, that's not *our* Gordy Krantz, Frank. Our Gordy Krantz lived on Red Water Mountain, eking out his government pension every month. Though he was the sort of person who'd have laughed to know there was someone with pots of money who had the same name as him."

Frank peered at me over his glasses – something I knew he did to try to intimidate people, but he looked so unthreatening I had to have a sharp word with my face about not laughing. Then he beamed almost manically at me.

"There are some lovely, airy offices available in Krantz Hall, Cait. They might be persuaded to allow you to use one. As a favor to me. Krantz Hall is very much a carrot on a stick for folks considering studying, researching, or even teaching here."

Frank had managed to bring the conversation back to that issue. "Well, yes, Frank, I'm sure it works wonders. After all, why wouldn't anyone want to study or work here?"

"Does that mean you'll pick up the keys to your new office on the fifth floor before you leave?"

I drew a few deep breaths. Maybe a semester of pure research, in an office far from the maddening hoards of students, would allow me to be *absolutely* certain I was ready to leave academia behind.

"I'll drop by the admin office on my way out," I said. "Goodbye, Frank. All the best."

I turned and left, but not before I heard Frank put a call through to the chancellor's secretary; another reason he'd done so well for himself was that he lived by the rule of covering his backside, and he wouldn't want an opportunity to talk directly to the chancellor to pass him by, especially if he might be able to illustrate his love for the university by alerting his superior to a potential death in the U of V "family" – even though I knew he was barking up the wrong tree.

By the time I got to my car, with the keys to my new office safely tucked into the zippered pocket inside my bag, my hands were shaking, and I was breathless; my visceral reaction to not having resigned surprised me, then I allowed myself to acknowledge the fact I wasn't actually ready to say goodbye to the last twenty-odd years of my life after all, and all that entailed.

I finally stopped snivelling, but was still bunged up when I phoned Bud. He answered his cellphone on the second ring.

"How did it go? How are you?" His voice was gentle. Wonderful to hear.

"I…I didn't do it. It didn't feel right. I can think about it during this semester. I feel a bit…you know. You don't mind, do you?"

"No, I don't mind. We agreed it's entirely your decision. But I can tell by your voice that you're upset. Promise me you won't drive if you're crying, it's not safe." Concern. Warmth.

"Promise." I wiped my nose. "You're sure you're not cross?"

"Oh Cait, why would I be cross? I know how hard you've worked to achieve what you have at that place. I'm not truly surprised by your decision. I'm with you one hundred percent, whatever you choose."

Relief washed over me. "Any news your end?" I ventured.

"Don't worry about what's going on here, just come home, when you're ready." The word "home" filled me with joy.

"Come on, you promised to keep me updated."

"Cops arrived. I've been with them. We chatted and explored. Nothing taken, no entry made, though there's evidence it was attempted via the front door, and a window was broken – Gordy's bedroom window. I called the lawyer's office as we agreed, and told them what had happened; they asked me to cover the window with a plastic sheet, as a temporary measure, and they'll send someone to board it up as soon as possible, and to fit some better locks. Should be here this afternoon. Will you be back by then?"

I hoped he could hear the smile in my voice. "Yes, I'm just leaving. I, too, have news about Gordy."

"News about Gordy?"

"Well, sort of. You'll have to wait, sorry. I'll be there in an hour or so, with a treat. I feel like eating cake."

Bud chuckled. "You know I'll eat whatever you put in front of me. And, on that note, I'll let you take a few moments, and get on your way. Come home, Wife, Husband's waiting to hug you."

"Love you."

"Love you most, Professor Morgan."

Hearing Bud use my title warmed my heart; he was right, I'd worked for so many years to earn and acquire that title…had I been mad to think of throwing it all away?

That chapter of my life wasn't quite finished.

All the Comforts

Marty was at my feet, beneath the dining table, peering at my cake with one eye. I'd bought lemon and cream, rather than chocolate, because I'd convinced myself it would be "lighter". It was certainly refreshing, but the second piece had probably been a poor decision on my part.

I'd fended off Bud's requests to tell him whatever it was I'd heard about Gordy until we were both stuffed with cake, then I told him what Frank had said about the other Gordon Krantz. His monosyllabic reply was: "Weird".

I like it when Bud's pithy, and nodded my agreement. "Coincidences happen all the time, in real life. *Never* during a criminal investigation, of course." Bud and I shared a knowing smile as I referenced his total and immediate suspicion of any coincidences happening within any case he'd ever investigated.

"It's funny to think of another Gordon Krantz having pots of dosh. It would have given our Gordy a good laugh, I reckon," I said, dropping a few crumbs to Marty. "I've no idea how much this other Krantz must have given the university to get his name on a building; it's a pretty big one...all built from sustainable materials, green roof, solar energy, fancy lecture hall with lots of tech stuff built in to manage the climate and so forth. The work being done there on environmental matters is making an impact around the world. Our Gordy would have been proud. I know he felt he was the richest man on earth, he told me that more than once, and he'd certainly surrounded himself with everything he loved, but I always got the impression he'd have liked to have been able to – I don't know, do more for humanity, I suppose. He had a generous soul. Maybe he and this other Gordon Krantz had that much in common, at least."

Bud pulled his phone from his pocket and started tapping it.

"If you're about to Google 'Wealthy Gordon Krantz', don't bother," I said, "I've already tried that. There's the mention of his name in connection with the building, and that's it. He's only referred to as a benefactor – no illumination or information at all."

As I was speaking, Bud continued tapping, and nodded. "As you say," he mumbled, "and a few other entries about people with the same name too…one Gordon Krantz has been a mayor in Ontario forever, it seems; there are movie characters named Gordon and Gord Krantz; dozens of them on Facebook using every version of the name Gordon you can imagine, and some guy who was a bit of a legend with the American rhododendron people, it seems. I guess I'd always thought of 'Gordon Krantz' as being an unusual name. Seems that's not the case at all."

"My own Googling tells me the name Krantz is an ancient one, from the Old High German '*cranz*' meaning 'garland'. I thought it was apt, because Gordy loved being at one with nature. We could get some sort of garland made up for his memorial, maybe?"

Bud was distracted by his phone. "I sometimes wish I could access all my old systems."

"Google's a great place to start looking. We could do a deeper dive, later on, if you like. I'd find it fascinating." I stood to clear our mugs, the remainder of the cake, and our plates. Marty followed me to the dishwasher, sulking as though we'd never fed him. *Ever.* I moved toward the treat cupboard and he perked up significantly.

"Any idea when they'll be here from the lawyers' office, to secure Gordy's place?" I asked.

Bud checked his watch. "No, but Tom called. Tom White. Asked if he could help with anything over at Gordy's place. I told him we were sorting it all just fine, but invited him over later today – he said he'd come around four, when he's cleared up after lunch service."

Bud wandered to join me at the kitchen counter, and we snuggled. He patted my back, then his whole body tensed. "There's someone coming up Gordy's drive."

I pulled back; Bud had been looking over my head out of the window, and he was right – a dark sedan was driving slowly toward Gordy's house. "Reckon it's the lawyers?" I asked.

Bud was heading for the front door as he replied, "Hope so, or I'll be sending them packing. Can you stay with Marty?"

I managed to shout, "Of course," before Bud was out of the house. I petted Marty, grabbed the binoculars, and noted the car's licence plate number, just in case we needed to know it later.

I'm not good at being on the sidelines of something, and felt a bit left out as I watched Bud greet the tall, thin man who alighted from the car which parked a good way from Gordy's place. He pulled some sheets from a clipboard and handed them to Bud. Bud signed something, then they both headed toward the house. They seemed to be out of sight for an age, though my watch told me it was only twenty minutes later that Bud waved the car away, and headed back to our home.

"So?" I asked eagerly, as he pulled off his jacket.

He tugged some papers from his pocket. "The guy from the lawyers' office fitted a new latch and padlock, but someone else is coming to board up the window; he took the measurements. And we've been summoned to their office at eleven o'clock tomorrow. Sit-down meeting. Connected with Gordy's will.

Couldn't tell me any more than that. Said, 'All will be revealed at that time.' Young guy. Pale. Spotty. Don't think he's very high up the food chain."

"'All will be revealed?' Sounds like a magician's show."

"Should we wear cloaks…or sparkly onesies?" mugged Bud. I shoved him, lovingly.

The afternoon dragged a little; I had some university emails to deal with, but I hate the feeling when I'm waiting for someone to arrive – I just can't settle to anything. I was relieved when I heard Marty's excited barks announcing Tom's arrival.

I greeted him as Bud put the kettle on to make a pot of tea, and was delighted when Tom presented me with a box of blueberry scones at the front door.

"I know you like these, Cait," he said, as he loomed over me. At six feet tall Tom always makes me feel that my five-three – five-four on a tall day – is diminutive, and he's broad-chested too, with the ruddy complexion many freckly redheads have. He's recently chosen to grow facial hair, though his beard, and carefully twirled and waxed moustache, don't really suit him, in my opinion. He's got a great background – lots of folks know him because of the young chef knock-out show on TV he won, and all those rave reviews for his food in Vegas were well-deserved. I knew he was doing something significantly different back here in BC, very much a field-, farm-, and tide-to-table set up. I reckoned he'd make it work, if anyone could.

"The blueberries were a bit later than usual this year," he continued, as he removed his boots and jacket, "so now there's a bit of a glut. Did you know that BC produces almost all of Canada's highbush blueberries, and Canada's one of the biggest sellers of blueberries to the world? Blueberries make a seven-billion-dollar impact on the BC economy every year…though I might not buy that many" – he flashed a cheeky grin – "but I'm happy to do my bit, so I'm using as many as I can while they're fresh and bursting with flavor. Lots of jam-making to be done, and I'll freeze as many as I can get at a good price. As long as they're in good shape when they're frozen, they'll be excellent for baking all year."

I'd warmed to Tom upon first meeting him at Jack and Sheila's place, and we'd spent many hours with him, over the years; the dreadful time we'd shared in Las Vegas when we'd all been locked in a private restaurant with a killer was something that further bonded us – though neither he, nor Bud, or I, ever mention it.

We settled at the dining table with tea and scones. They were delicious – just the perfect amount of crumbliness and butteriness to let you know you were enjoying an indulgence, and the blueberries were flavorful…and heathy, I told myself.

"Terrible news about old Gordy," said Tom, after petting Marty and exchanging greetings with Bud. "I'll miss him. Taught me a lot. Such a shame he won't be able to teach me more." He didn't make eye contact with either of us as he spoke; he toyed with his teacup, twirling it in its saucer.

"We didn't even know you knew him," I replied. "Bud mentioned foraging?"

Tom nodded, still not looking at us. "He was great. Knew all sorts of places to find wonderful things. The ostrich fern fiddleheads on his property alone allowed me to do some great dishes right through May. And mushrooms? Boy, did he know how to find them. All sorts, almost year-round. Wonderful variety he had, with all the woodland and wetland areas on his property. The best season's starting up about now. He'd promised to take me to one of his secret spots this morning."

I wondered how on earth Gordy had been planning to do that – his shuffle had worsened recently, and his acreage was anything but level. Maybe the place he'd meant to take Tom had been close to his house.

"We've never seen you coming and going next door," said Bud, brushing crumbs of scone off his chest and onto the floor, where Marty's tongue found them in an instant.

Tom grinned. "Not like you two to miss something, eh? An eagle-eyed pair, always interested in what's going on around them." He winked at us. "Uncle Jack and Aunt Sheila told me all about Jamaica, and – of course – you know…"

He finally took a mouthful of tea – to avoid mentioning Vegas, and Tanya, I suspected.

"Maybe you have a point; we're not always here, at home, so I guess we've just kept missing your visits," said Bud, whose expression told me he'd spotted Tom's discomfort.

"That, and the fact I usually park at the base of the mountain, by the river, near Gordy's old cabin. I'd leave my truck on the bottom road and walk across the lower part of the property, you know, around the little lake? I'm stuck in the restaurant so much of the time I like the excuse for a good stride out now and again. And it was always very early in the day – morning twilight's the best time for foraging for mushrooms, a few days after heavy rain. And you know what the weather was like a few days ago."

Bud and I nodded. His birthday had seen a deluge, but we hadn't had any plans to go out, preferring to celebrate quietly at home with a good dinner. As I recalled Bud blowing out the candles on his cake – I'd spent ages sticking in fifty-seven of them, to make him laugh – it occurred to me that we'd been celebrating his birthday in Vegas with Tom two years earlier when Miss Shirley's murder had kicked off that particular nightmare. I decided to not mention Bud's birthday, knowing how it would upset our guest.

"Did you ever go into the cabin?" I asked. "I never did, nor did Bud, right?" Bud shook his head. "I often wondered what he kept in the place, if anything."

Tom put down his teacup. "Nope, never went inside it. I didn't ask, and he never offered. Can't imagine you could keep much of anything in there at all. Kinda tiny. Hard to imagine he once lived in it. Just one room, he told me. With an outhouse." He scrunched his face.

"Yes, that's what he told me too," said Bud. "He never spoke of it, but I guess he must have cut down the trees and prepared the logs himself. All that bottom area would have been wooded when he moved here."

"I guess," replied Tom, staring out of the window. "That bit of land down there offered wonderful opportunities for growing stuff, and he told me all about what he and Terry achieved with it."

"Who was Terry?" I asked.

Tom looked surprised. "He didn't tell you about Terry?"

Bud and I shook our heads.

Tom picked up his tea again. "Friend of his. Business partner, too. They used that area as their first nursery, back in the 1960s, I think. Before they set up all the others."

"What nurseries?" Bud and I spoke in unison.

"Terry Dumas. You know, the K. Dumas Nurseries?"

Bud and I nodded; the chain covered Greater Vancouver, all of the Lower Mainland, and stretched across the whole of southern British Columbia.

Tom said, "I believe Gordy Krantz was the K in the name. I heard he and Terry built the business together." He paused, put down his cup and pulled at the waxed point of his moustache. "I'm surprised you didn't know."

So was I. I couldn't imagine why Gordy hadn't told us – we'd spoken so often about plants, and he'd even recommended the local K. Dumas nursery to us when we'd decided to invest in a lot of new trees and shrubs. It seemed a bit…odd.

"Maybe that's where he got all his money," said Bud, winking at me. I glared at him.

Tom chuckled. "If Gordy had money, he kept it well hidden. No one with any sort of cash would live like he did. No, I reckon something went awry with the business and Terry ended up with it all. Why do you say Gordy had money?"

Bud explained about the building at the university; Tom looked as amused as we'd felt when taking in the news.

"Well, that's a real funny coincidence," he said, smiling broadly. "Or maybe old Gordy was slyer than I'd thought. Ha! That being said, I bet his property is worth a few dollars nowadays. I wonder how much it would cost to buy fifteen acres? Way beyond anything I could afford, that's for sure. The land alone would cost a fortune, even if the house is a tear-down."

We discussed the horrific price per acre that land was fetching locally, and we all agreed Bud and I had been fortunate to find a bargain when we'd bought our forever home: the couple who owned it were getting divorced and, frankly, couldn't wait to get out of it – we'd come along and everything had fallen into place very nicely…for us, and them.

"Did the people you bought it from build it? This place, I mean," asked Tom. "It's big, a real family home. I wonder how kids got on living next to Gordy."

"Yes. Gordy told me they bought the five acres from him and built it themselves, but they didn't have any children," I replied. "He told me he hadn't really wanted to subdivide the acreage, but he made enough money from selling these five acres to be able to build his own house. I believe both homes were built around the same time as each other, in 1995, with Gordy and his neighbors sharing construction services and so forth."

"Great way to do it," said Bud. He pointed out of the window. "The utilities companies bring services to the property line for free, but it's the home-owner's responsibility to bring it from there. Gordy and the people who built this place shared those costs. See where our power comes to our place, and then goes over to Gordy's? Each party only had to shell out for a short installation run on their own."

"Good thinking," replied Tom.

"It's great of you to drop by, of course," ventured Bud, "but I got the impression there was something specific you wanted to talk about. Is there?"

Tom was staring out of the window, then – finally – looked directly at Bud, then me. "It's a bit awkward, really. I wondered…well, you know what the local rumor mill is like, and Aunt Colleen's been on at me to find out what happened to Gordy. What *really* happened. She…she can be quite persistent, and she knows all about Vegas, of course, so thought you might tell me because of what happened to us there, even if you won't tell her. And now I can see there's police tape around Gordy's place. So…well, what does that mean?"

I'd given my full attention to Tom as he'd been speaking. His darting eyes told me he felt uncomfortable; I suspected it was because he didn't like to use our friendship as a way to ask questions on behalf of his aunt. I probably sounded a bit sharper than I meant to when I said, "I understand your Aunt Colleen is desperate to know what happened next door, but there's not much we can tell you, I'm sorry."

Bud snatched a glance at me, then backed me up, but in a much warmer tone than I'd used. "Tape's there out of an abundance of caution, Tom. Word gets out about an empty property and folks might think it's easy pickings. Tape signals to any interested parties that the cops are keeping an eye on the place. We might know more tomorrow, though. We've been asked to go to Gordy's lawyers' office."

Tom grinned. "Funny, that. Me too. And Aunt Colleen. She was hoping for the inside scoop before we got there; I guess she'll just have to wait, like the rest of us."

Bud and I exchanged a look. "It might turn out to be an interesting meeting," he said.

"There speaks the retired cop," said Tom. "Just like Uncle Jack. You guys never really stop being cops, do you? I guess you just can't help yourselves."

"More tea?" I offered, as I picked up the pot.

Tom shook his head and pushed back his chair. "Thanks, no. Gotta go. Time to get back to the kitchen and get going with the jam."

We all wandered toward the front door. "Any plans to start opening up on weekday evenings yet?" I asked.

"Couldn't cover the costs of the wait staff," said Tom, suddenly looking a bit gray around the gills. "I mean, it's all going pretty well, but I don't have room for many covers, and in any case there's only so much money folks want to spend on a meal out, and they only want to do it so often. If I could only have afforded a place in Downtown Vancouver, then I could be full-on, open all hours. But out here? Not the same market at all."

"Your Uncle Jack was telling us you've been getting rave reviews online, and that quite a few folks are driving out this way just to eat at your place. Destination dining, he called it." Bud handed Tom his jacket as the young man bowed his head to stub his feet into his boots.

Tom paused, took the jacket and smiled. "Vegas was a heck of a place to be a chef, but I could see people burning out pretty fast there – it was so easy to work hard, and play hard, and I knew a few people who did both *too* hard. Me? I knew pretty quickly it wasn't exactly what I wanted, not long term, though it was a fabulous experience, and then…Tanya…all of that…" Bud and I nodded, and I rubbed Tom's shoulder for comfort, reaching up to get at it. He straightened his back, and wiped away a tear. And it was there, in our entrance hall, that he finally crumbled.

He began by trying to swallow down a body-wracking sob. "I was more of a mess than I let on to anyone, when I got back from Vegas. Tanya really…well, it really freaked me out. I could hardly believe what had happened. I couldn't concentrate in the kitchen any longer, my knife skills deserted me, and I almost injured someone with some hot oil one night. So I quit. Ran back here to lick my wounds. Couldn't even face Mom and Dad, so I kinda shut myself away in Uncle Jack and Aunt Sheila's basement suite for a while. I was lost."

Standing there with one boot on, and his jacket clutched in his hand, Tom looked like a very tall six-year-old boy, with a fake, waxed moustache stuck onto his sad, little face.

He sniffed. "That was when I met Gordy. I guess I was trespassing really, down on that lower meadow of his, but he didn't mind. We got talking and he began showing me all the things growing around us that we could eat. We pulled salmonberries off the massive bushes that grow down by the road, and he asked if I would make him some jelly. That day – the day we almost made ourselves sick by eating so many salmonberries – was the day I realized there's enough here, in British Columbia, to make great food. Gordy saved me, gave me encouragement, and direction." He sobbed, wiping at his eyes angrily. "I'm gonna miss him so much. But I'm doing it – what Gordy and I talked about for so many hours. Because of him, now I'm doing what I really believe in, and I'd rather take it slow and get it right. It means something to me, so it's worth doing well. I'll…I'll honor his wishes, and I'll keep going."

We beamed at him. "Good for you, Tom," said Bud, with feeling.

Tom finally pushed on his second boot, pulled on his jacket, and gave Marty a parting pat on the head. "See you tomorrow. And thanks. I know I can talk to you about this in confidence."

"Total confidence," replied Bud. "See you tomorrow."

Tom waved as he headed to his car, which was tiny, and proved to be almost silent as he pulled away – those electric vehicles just hiss and scrunch the gravel as they move.

We waved as he headed past the bend in the drive, sharing our hopes that Tom was now finding his way – personally and professionally – then, when he was out of sight, I said, "That noise I heard last night, when whoever it was headed away from Gordy's place in the dark?" Bud nodded. "The noise Tom's car just made – silently moving yet scrunching and sort of hissing – that's what I heard, I'm certain of it."

Bud tilted his head. "An unsuccessful thief in an electric car? Well, I guess they've got to get about some way or another – environmentally considerate thieves must exist, I suppose. Food for thought."

"And time to walk Marty, before it gets dusk and the bears become an issue," I observed.

"I'll do it – just once around the perimeter, and I'll take the stick with me, just in case the beasties are on the prowl," said Bud, kissing me on the forehead.

"And I'll get going with dinner prep – those scones won't hold us for long, and we've got lamb chops on the menu. I know it's nowhere near as sweet as proper Welsh lamb, but we do enjoy it, don't we?"

Bud rolled his eyes and said, "I'll fire up the grill for you," and headed for the back deck. He makes fun of my longing for real Welsh lamb, but I'm at least happy knowing we're supporting BC's young people who raise animals well, and without antibiotics, by taking the time to go to the Maple Ridge agricultural fair each year to meet the animals, and the families who raise them, then bidding at the 4-H auction at the PNE. Small-scale farming was something else Gordy and I had talked about on many occasions – and there I was, back to thinking about how much I'd miss my times with him.

A Room Full of Surprises

We arrived at the lawyers' office just before eleven: I hate being late for appointments, but we'd got stuck in traffic. Heavy traffic isn't something we're used to encountering in our neck of the woods, so we never really make allowances for it, which can turn out to be a problem. We only have a choice of two routes to get from our house to Mission, and there was a bad accident on the Lougheed Highway so we had to wiggle along a few backroads to get to Dewdney Trunk Road, then drive the long way around. Normally I very much enjoy the sight of the mountains clothed in evergreens kissing the shimmering sheet of the reservoir, and it's always a joy to marvel at the bald eagles – they love the municipal dump we pass on that route. However, we were in a rush, and Bud was driving, so I gave my full attention to the twisting road…as though my watching the way ahead made Bud's driving safer. I'm a terrible passenger; I even twitch my foot when I think Bud should brake.

Despite the fact we were cutting it fine, I had to pop to the loo as soon as we arrived, because I knew I wouldn't be able to concentrate if I didn't. By the time I came out of the washroom the entryway was deserted, except for an extremely young receptionist who told me to go ahead and join everyone else in a meeting room at the end of the corridor.

The office was in a building stuffed to the gills with periodontists, chiropractors, accountants, and other lawyers. The décor was standard office "meh", with beige tones playing a leading role. Dried grasses mixed with faded silk flowers in some poorly selected vases added to the underwhelming impression being made by Messrs. Oishi and Singh. The slightly dinged mobility scooter parked in the dimly-lit hallway added to the general air of abandonment.

The meeting room itself was surprisingly full; a large oval glass table was surrounded by people, only some of whom I knew.

Tom White and his aunt, Colleen, were there, as expected. I recognized a woman by the name of Louise North I'd seen several times at the local feedstore where I buy Marty's food; she's around eighty or so and known to be vinegar-tongued – I suspected the scooter outside the door was hers. There was a woman sitting beside her who was probably only ten years Louise North's junior – though it was clear she'd spared no expense to give the impression she was ten years younger than that; she was dressed in tone-on-tone layers of caramel and cream cashmere, which almost exactly matched her high- and low-lighted bob. I'd never seen her before, but noted her expensive jewellery, perfect manicure, and haughty air. Then there was a man who looked to be about the same age as Tom White – in his early thirties – sitting one chair beyond Bud; he was smiling at everyone, and looked like an exceedingly healthy swimmer, with a big neck, broad shoulders, and a ruddy complexion.

Immediately I'd taken my seat beside Bud, the young man whispered, "Nice to see you again, Cait. I hope the twin at the top of that old cedar is hanging on alright?"

The familiarity in his tone surprised me, then I realized who he was – Dayton Woodward, the lumberjack who'd helped us out with a large tree that had lost its top in a windstorm about a year earlier; in my defense he looked considerably different in his smart navy suit than he had in his tree-climbing safety gear, goggles, and hard hat. I found it quite endearing that he'd dressed so formally for a meeting with lawyers.

I nodded at the man and woman in their forties sitting opposite me; their body language, and matchy-matchy wardrobe choices, suggested to me they were a married couple – they seemed somewhat puzzled by everything going on around them. She looked tired, and he looked vaguely familiar, but I couldn't place him; I struggled to picture him in his correct setting. Having an eidetic memory is all well and good, but sometimes it's annoyingly uncooperative.

Finally, the man and woman at the front of the room stopped fiddling about with their laptops and settled into the two vacant seats at the end of the table. The woman cleared her throat dramatically, drawing the attention of us all; she was probably in her early forties, whip thin, long-bodied, and sat so upright in her seat that I, also, straightened my back.

"Thank you all for being here." A surprisingly deep voice, but annoyingly – to me, anyway – with one of those strong, local, West Coast accents, where an upswing in tonality means every statement sounds like a question. "I'm Mahera Singh, and this is my colleague Rylan Oishi." Rylan – wizened, bald, bespectacled, and looking as though he might be well past normal retirement age – nodded. "We're the executors for the estate of Mr. Gordon Krantz, late of Red Water Mountain Drive. You all knew Gordon, so you'll understand when I tell you he insisted I called him Gordy when we had dealings, so I shall refer to him that way today, to honor the man who always knew what he wanted, and usually told you so."

A ripple of half-chuckles worked its way around the table; I noted a range of expressions from angry, though bemused, to puzzled.

"I dare say you're all wondering why you're here," Ms. Singh continued, and heads nodded. "Well, of course we all mourn the loss of such a vital man as Gordy, and I can tell you immediately that we'll be making all the arrangements to ensure his final wishes are fulfilled. Gordy made a highly detailed, and extremely precise, last will and testament. As part of our fulfilling his final wishes, we've invited you all here to receive personally addressed letters from him, which were to be delivered under these specific circumstances, with the instructions that you all open your letters, read them, and then make it known to us – before you leave – if there are any requests being made of you in said letters that you are unwilling, or feel you are unable, to undertake."

The energy in the room shifted a little.

"There's one more point: we were instructed to make it clear that this gathering must be treated by everyone in attendance as completely confidential. If you agree to this absolute confidentiality, we ask that you sign the agreements Rylan is now passing around. If you do not want to sign the agreement, that's just fine, but that will mean we are unable to give you the letter Gordy prepared for you."

There was a general wriggling of bottoms on chairs as Rylan Oishi laid a basic non-disclosure agreement on the table in front of each person. I noticed that Colleen and Tom White exchanged a few whispered sentences, as did the married couple.

A few minutes later, Rylan was able to collect a full set of signed documents.

"Thank you, on behalf of Gordy," said Mahera as she tucked the papers into a leather binder. "Rylan will now give each of you your letter."

Having seen Gordy's shopping lists over the past several months, all written in arduously formed block capitals, I could tell he was the one who'd written the envelopes. Each one was opened in a way specific to the addressee; some, like me, took care with their envelopes, others just ripped them apart.

Gordy's block letters filled the page of lined paper that he'd torn from a pad.

Dear Cait

I don't know what I'd have done without you and Bud coming to be my neighbors. It was just the boost I needed when you arrived, and it turns out you were just the folks I could rely upon in my time of need. To be honest, I never thought I'd get to be this old. It's been one heck of a life and, now that I'm facing the end of it, I want to say two things to you.

First, I want you to know you've made an old man very happy by treating me like a normal human being, with interests and opinions, and a continuing desire to find out new things, rather than just coddling me, or treating me like some used up old thing.

Second, I want to tell you that you're *not* always right. I can imagine you're bristling about now, but you have to admit, even if only to yourself, that you're not. Don't get me wrong, you're bright alright, about the brightest woman I've met (and I've met a few real bright women in my time) and you also have a real talent for understanding people. No, that's not what you're wrong about. You're usually right about people, but sometimes you're wrong about the way you act towards them.

I've watched you and Bud together; you're good as a couple. You balance each other. But you don't seem to have any real friends, or mix with our community and – trust me when I tell you this – that's not good. Maybe think about how you can do a bit more of that. It's the most rewarding thing a person can do – to build connections, to be an active part of the fabric of local life.

Now, I have a specific request: I want you to write and deliver my eulogy. When you're done talking, I'd like folks to know about my life. My entire life. I won't be around to hear what you say, so speak freely. Truthfully. Find out about me. Dig deep. Please. Find the truth, and bring it out into the light.

I know you're diligent, and I know you're good at research – that's why I'm asking you to do this. Get Ms. Singh to allow you access to whatever you want from any part of my estate.

In a way, I wish I could watch over you as you dig into my life. You're in for a few surprises, I reckon. I might not turn out to be the man you thought I was.

By the way, the first thing I want you to 'discover' is that I always used to throw away those seeded buns you bought for me. Terrible things…got stuck in my teeth all the time, but – for some reason – you seemed to think I liked them. The birds enjoyed them very much.

Seriously, thanks for all you did for me. I enjoyed our talks. I hope you like the gift I've asked them to arrange for you.

And, by the way, I still think Hemingway was a terrible writer, praised only by those who think that a person with a bloated ego, writing bloated, misogynistic, testosterone-fuelled prose is somehow to be admired.

Gordy

I raised my head with tears in my eyes. Bud was staring at me, open-mouthed, which worried me a bit; I couldn't imagine what Gordy had written in his letter to him, but certainly had the feeling this wasn't the time to ask.

Seeing my distress, Rylan Oishi rushed to my side with a box of tissues, then took another to Colleen White who was reading her letter with tears streaming down her face; she had one tissue of her own, but it wasn't going to be enough for the job.

Gradually every head came up, and the atmosphere of general curiosity that had been present when we'd all arrived had been replaced by a tension that almost fizzed around the table.

Once all our letters were folded closed in front of us, Mahera Singh spoke. "So, is there anyone here who is unwilling, or feels unable, to do what has been asked of them in their letter?"

The question hung in the air like that "speak now, or forever hold your peace" moment does at every wedding.

The woman I judged to be in her seventies, whom I didn't know, tentatively waggled a finger.

"Yes, Mrs. Dumas, you have a question?" Mahera's voice was warm.

All eyes turned to the woman I now suspected – after our conversation with Tom the previous day – was the "Dumas" of K. Dumas Nurseries. She fidgeted in her chair and twirled one of the numerous rings on her right hand – diamonds sparkled in the sunlight filtering through the blinds.

"I might have a question," she spoke hesitantly. "But…are we supposed to keep our letters a secret? If we are…then I can't really ask the question, you see."

Mahera replied, "That's entirely up to you, Mrs. Dumas, and everyone else, too. Gordy made it clear we were not to 'force' anyone to reveal anything they don't want to – which we couldn't anyway – but I would remind you that you've all promised to not divulge any facts or opinions expressed at this meeting outside this room, ever, to anyone, with the exception of those present today. Thus, you are free to mention the contents of your letter if you wish now, or to any of these persons, at any point in the future."

Mrs. Dumas touched her letter with a perfectly manicured fingernail. "When my darling Terry left us, he also left a room full of papers that I've never had the…energy to sort through." Her choice of the word "energy" left me in no doubt it was a euphemism for "inclination". She quickly added, "Maybe I should introduce myself? I'm Janice, Janice Dumas, of K. Dumas Nurseries, I dare say you've all heard of them?" Everyone nodded. "Oh good." She didn't seem terribly surprised. "Well, Terry never, ever threw away a piece of paper that passed through his hands, and – though all the business stuff got sorted out by the accountants and lawyers – his personal stuff is still…well, a bit of a mess. Now, in Gordy's letter he's asked me to…um…find some particular papers, and…um…do something with them. But I'm not sure I'd know where to start looking. I mean, how long have I got? I'm supposed to leave on a cruise to Australia next month."

By the time Janice Dumas had finished speaking, she was pink in the face and had given everyone in the room the impression she was more than a little dithery, even if she clearly believed she was a cut above the rest of us.

Mahera replied, "Our client's instructions were that all requested tasks be completed within two weeks. It is at that time that we are able to release the items listed in his will to each person."

Janice Dumas seemed to be somewhat mollified and settled back into her seat. "Two weeks? Oh, dear. Well, I suppose I can probably manage it, somehow." She didn't seem to be awash with confidence.

I took the chance to raise my hand. "Yes, Professor Morgan, you have a question?" Mahera turned her attention to me, and smiled.

I followed Janice Dumas' example. "Hello folks, Cait Morgan, Gordy's next-door neighbor. My husband Bud Anderson." I waggled a hand at Bud, and nods were exchanged around the table. "I've been asked to deliver Gordy's eulogy, so I have a few queries: first, with whom should I keep in touch about the funeral, or memorial arrangements, please?"

"That would be me," said Mahera. "We'll be organizing a cremation, without attendees, and Gordy's ashes will be scattered – as he requested – in a certain location on his property."

"I'm doing the scattering, according to this letter," piped up Bud, "so Cait and I will keep in touch with you on that score."

Mahera nodded, and I continued, "The letter asks me to request access to all of Gordy's 'estate' in order to carry out my research to be able to write the eulogy. Is that you too, Ms. Singh?"

"No, that would be me," replied Rylan Oishi. His voice was as arid as his aged skin.

"Thanks. And finally," I continued, "I don't know everyone here today, but I'm guessing you all knew Gordy well enough to have a tale or two to tell about him, so would it be alright if I get in touch with each of you to gather some insights for the eulogy? Maybe I could get all your phone numbers, or email addresses? I already have contact details for Tom and Colleen" – I nodded at them – "and for you too, Dayton, but it would be most helpful if I could get everyone else's today. If you're happy to talk to me, of course."

"I have nothing to say about the man," snapped Louise North. "I shall not be giving you any 'contact details', Professor Morgan, so you can give up on that idea for a start. Nor shall I tell anyone what he asked of me in this ridiculous letter." She sounded as though she gargled with hot asphalt every morning, and still had traces of an American accent.

I hadn't expected such a response, so simply replied to the octogenarian: "Thanks anyway." I turned to the lawyers and finished with: "Thanks, that's all I had."

"I have a question," continued Louise, staring daggers at the lawyers. "Do you two know what we've been asked to do in these letters?"

Mahera and Rylan nodded their heads.

Louise's cheeks puffed out, and she waved dismissively toward the lawyers. She said nothing else.

"Anyone else have any other queries?" asked Mahera, forcing a smile. Rylan's eyes scanned the room. "No? Very good then…"

I took my chance, and shot my hand up again. "Just one more thing. No one has asked, but I think we'd all like to know – have you any information about Gordy's cause of death?"

"I dare say it was his heart," sniped Colleen White.

I tried to not glare at her.

Tom patted his aunt's hand and whispered, "We don't know that, do we, Auntie? We talked about this." He beamed around the room and added, "Tom White, and my aunt, Colleen White. Both friends of Gordy, in my aunt's case for some considerable time."

"Knowing Gordy, he was halfway up a tree trying to limb it, and fell out," said Dayton Woodward brightly. "By the way, I'm Dayton. Dayton Woodward. Lumberjack. Gordy always made fun of all my safety gear."

The female half of the married couple opposite me raised her hand, and Mahera nodded. "Hi, Ann Evans, wife of Colin Evans. Colin originally knew Gordy from church, though Gordy had left before I joined the congregation, so I hardly really knew the man, but – well, here I am anyway. Thing is, I work at the hospital up the road, at reception in the emergency department, not as a nurse or anything like that. Colin's a nurse, I'm not, but I do know quite a lot about how these things work, and it really shouldn't be too long before they release the report on Gordy's death, should it, Colin? But maybe it's a bit early yet." The woman beamed broadly at her husband, who shrugged.

I immediately recalled where I'd seen her husband before – he'd visited Gordy as one of the nurses who'd checked on his general health, on a weekly basis, and examined his meds to make sure he was taking them as directed.

Mahera Singh stood, and patted the air with her hands. "It's only natural that you'd all like to know how Gordy passed, but we are not at liberty to comment. All we can say at this time" – she glanced almost imperceptibly in Rylan Oishi's direction – "is that the authorities are treating Gordy's death as having been from natural causes. However, we received word this morning that the coroner is carrying out some further investigations into exactly what those causes might have been. This might lead to a minor delay in the remains being released."

"You're saying he wasn't killed? That he just *died*?" Everyone stared at Louise North, and she bathed in the attention. I noticed a cruel crinkle at the corner of her purplish lips, and a gleam of satisfaction in her hooded eyes.

"No one would kill Gordy, everyone loved him. Why would you say that, Miss North?" It was the first time I'd heard Colin Evans speak, and was surprised by how rounded his baritone was.

Probably got a lovely singing voice at church services, I thought, because I suspected he was the Colin of whom Colleen White had spoken as being the current church warden for her congregation. What I said aloud was, "Yes, why do you suggest he might have been killed, Miss North?" I couldn't resist.

The octogenarian's eyes slid around every face at the table. "He was the sort of man who was likely to end up being killed. That's all."

A general twittering broke out around the room, and I was puzzled – along with most of the others present, by the sounds of it. I couldn't imagine what Gordy could have done to make Louise North speak of him in such a manner.

Mahera Singh was looking slightly panicked. "My words about the additional tests being done by the coroner were not meant to alarm you – they are normal investigations, under the circumstances. I don't know any more than I have told you." The lawyer regained her composure somewhat, and added, "And I would remind you that you've all signed a contract relating to confidentiality today. Now my colleagues and I will get on with the work we have been assigned regarding Gordy's wishes. I'm sure you can all make your own way out. Thank you for coming. We're here if and when you need us, regarding your allotted tasks."

We'd been dismissed, and rather abruptly at that.

Decked Out

Bud and I had just enjoyed a delicious spread of local cheeses, with some excellent herbed bread, and were lingering over a bottle of inexpensive, yet delicious, BC sparkling rosé as we watched the trees on our mountain turn from green, to gold, to amber, then ink. It was going to be a clear night with a full moon, and there was talk of a possible ground frost in low-lying areas. I suspected the coyotes would be noisy later on, as – no doubt – would Marty, who hated to be left out of a good howling session.

The cheeseboard had been my choice; when we left the lawyers' office in Mission I'd persuaded Bud to head out toward Harrison Hot Springs so we could enjoy the views on such a beautiful day, which I knew would give me at least half an hour to think. It's a stunning drive on a road that winds around, then over, the mountains alongside the Fraser River. My favourite part is cresting the last hill before swooping down to the plain, where dairy farms nestle and hazelnut trees thrive. I've driven it many times since I arrived in British Columbia. On this particular day my musings had been about Gordy Krantz, of course, and Bud had known better than to try to engage me in conversation.

We discussed the coroner's desire to conduct a more thorough-than-normal investigation into Gordy's demise over a coffee in a little place on the banks of Harrison Lake, and we'd immediately agreed it reeked of his death having happened under some sort of suspicious circumstances. Then we'd both agreed to not jump to conclusions. We both knew we were lying to ourselves, and each other, but we'd entered into a pact, of sorts.

On the way home, we stopped at a local *fromagerie* we both adore, where we get to meet the sheep, cows, and goats whose milk is made into the wonderful variety of cheeses they make there. Finally, we picked up some specialty loaves at a tiny bakery in Mission – we were fortunate they had a couple left so late in the day. And so we'd enjoyed a hearty meal without having to do much more than open a few packages and plop ourselves at the table on the back deck…the wine was a treat we felt we deserved.

It was idyllic, though we both needed light jackets; a pair of hummingbirds peeped with delight as they paused to sip nectar from the remaining blossoms on the honeysuckle which scrambled over the railing on one side of our deck. However, I was somewhat preoccupied; despite promising Bud I wouldn't make any inferences from the lawyer's words, I had, and suspected he had too. One of us needed to break our pact, and I threw myself on my sword, to save our sanity.

"Is there anyone you can phone to find out what's going on at the coroner's office?" I asked bluntly.

Bud placed his wine glass on the table. "I knew you wouldn't be able to resist," he said, with a smile. "Truth be told, I've already sent a couple of texts. But no word yet, I'm afraid."

We both chuckled at each other.

"While we wait for news, would you like to tell me what was in the letter Gordy wrote to you?" I asked. I adopted my "cute smile" face, to show him I was serious about finding out.

"Want to swap?" he replied, slyly.

I gave his proposition a moment's thought; Gordy's remarks about my lack of friends and my judgmental nature when assessing people tallied pretty much with Bud's comments to me over the years, so I certainly couldn't see the harm in his reading them. And I desperately wanted to know what Gordy had written to him, so my answer was a cavalier: "Okay then, I'll show you mine, if you show me yours."

I left the table to fetch my bag. Marty jumped up from his position beneath the table, hoping I was about to give him a cheesy plate to lick, but we weren't quite finished with our human meal so I fended him off with a slice of rind from a very good blue cheese I was saving until last.

Bud and I exchanged letters when I retook my seat. He'd topped up our glasses, and I settled back to read what Gordy had written to him.

So, Bud, I'm gone. I hope you miss me. I've enjoyed our times together. As soon as I saw you two drive up on the day you moved in, I could tell you were a good guy. Asked around about you – and found I was right.

First, let me say something I never said to your face: thank you for your service to the community. It must have been terrible to lose your wife the way you did, and I bet you feel guilty about it every day – that she was shot by a guy who thought she was you must prey on your mind. They call it "survivor guilt", which is a terrible thing. But I guess you know that. Cait will have talked to you about it, and I guess they sent you off to some sort of professional after it happened. I'm glad I met you when you were happy with Cait – it just goes to show that second chances can work out just fine.

I've got a couple of favors to ask of you, and I hope you'll do them for me – in remembrance of our times together.
First of all, I want you to scatter my ashes along the riverbank down in the meadows, below the house; I want my remains to find their place in the world…maybe I'll stick around the

streams, or find my way out to the Pacific Ocean, who knows. I want you to be the one to send me on my way – a good, safe pair of hands to help me start my final journey.

Then there's the cabin. I know you've seen it, but I also know you've never been inside it. Few have. I want you to take everything you think is worth saving out of it, then burn it to the ground. Burn it until it's ash, that's what I want. I guess you'd better talk to the lawyers about the best way to do it without causing alarm in the community, or any danger to it. But it's my wish that you do this, as and when you can, and I trust you will. As for what to save and what to burn? Well, Bud, that will be up to you.

You might want to take that wife of yours along with you when you go exploring – I'm guessing she'll have her own opinions about what's worth saving. In fact, I'm going to guess you've both agreed to tell the other one what's in these letters, or you're even reading each other's, which is just fine by me. You're both good people, and you've both had your share of hardship and loss. That ex-boyfriend of Cait's the cops thought she might have killed? Terrible. She actually shrank in front of my eyes when she told me about him. Awful. Men should respect women, not treat them like some sort of pawn in their desire for power. Your wife's a strong woman, Bud, but I could see how deeply she'd been affected by that relationship. Like I said, I'm glad you two are happy together. You both share a love of life.

But the other thing you both have? A good nose for what's right and what's wrong…and I'll say no more than that. By the time you get to do this for me I'll be gone, so nothing will matter to me anymore – but you'll have to consider how what you find out about me will impact others. Every plant, animal, insect, and fish might all be just a jumble of chemicals, but we humans also have will – and it's what we do with that when we're alive that matters. I won't have left this world without stains upon my soul, but I've done my best to make reparations. I've tried my best to take care of anything and everything I could in many ways, some of which were probably a waste of time, but I did it anyway. Maybe some will endure. I hope so.

It's important to live every day as though it's your first – seeing the wonder around you, but knowing that every decision, every act, impacts everything and everyone around you. Unless you believe you're going to have to live with the consequences of your actions you'll act without thought for tomorrow, and that's not a good thing. But now – if you're reading this – I have no more tomorrows, only yesterdays, and there's nothing I can do about them. I hope fate is kinder to me than this damned disease is being.

You know, since you two arrived, I've rallied, and your actions and kindnesses have been a real pleasant surprise, so thank you for that. It was a joy to spend time with you, despite this diagnosis. I won't miss you, because I'm gone. I hope you miss me.

Your friend, Gordy.

I'd been dabbing at my eyes as I read, and finally blew my nose, trying to regain my composure. "They're really quite different letters," I observed, "yours and mine."

Bud smiled. "We're quite different people, Cait."

I nodded and reached down to pet Marty's head. "So, we're going to explore his cabin, by the looks of it."

"I thought you'd want to come."

I stabbed at my blue cheese. "Absolutely. Though him wanting it to be burned until it's ash is a bit...well, 'scorched earth' smacks of being just too much on the nose, but it *is* a literal request, in this case. Don't you think that's odd?"

"The cleansing nature of fire?"

I shrugged. "He loved his philosophy books, and used to enjoy our metaphysical discussions a great deal. Fast reader, too – until quite recently."

"Were they your favorite type of discussions? You know, 'heated debates'?"

"Not really heated; Gordy was pretty cool-headed, though his take on panentheism as opposed to pantheism was something he was passionate about."

"And yet Colleen White said he'd been a church warden. Wonder how that squares."

"From our conversations I know he was a man who believed he was on a spiritual journey, and that means he might have tried out different organized religions to see if they really suited him. He was an interesting subject."

"Person, Cait," snapped Bud, "Gordy was a person; he wasn't ever, and isn't now, a 'subject'."

I felt heat rush to my cheeks. "Sorry, just a slip of the tongue. Is there any more wine?"

Bud waggled the empty bottle in front of me.

"Okay then, I'll put the kettle on and make a pot of tea," I said, and stood to do so – accompanied by a hopeful-looking Marty.

"Good idea – we always regret opening the second bottle, don't we?" Bud winked, and we both knew he was right.

This Old House

My day had begun far too early and had been horribly busy. I'd had to drive to the university to sort out my parking pass for the semester – which involved hanging about in a stuffy office for ages, surrounded by other exasperated people, all of us being "helped" by folks who moved at the speed of a glacier. Finally able to wield my pass with pride, I went to my new office and gave it my all for a couple of hours. When I left it was far from perfect, but I was exhausted; the repetitive actions of picking books out of boxes and placing them on shelves had made my back ache, and I felt sticky and dusty. It was – as promised – a delightful, quiet office, with an enviable view down the mountain to the inlet below, but the wi-fi signal was anything but reliable, and the five phone calls I'd made to various tech support people resulted in a "tentative" promise that they might be able to speed it up, or at least ensure it was stable, by the end of the next week – just in time for the Thanksgiving break.

I got home in time for a lovely lunch of cheese on toast and Bud insisted I put my feet up for half an hour. I didn't argue, and the next thing I knew I was being woken from a nap by Marty's wet tongue, which told me he needed to get outside, urgently. I had no idea where Bud was, then I spotted a text from him; while Marty sniffed about looking for the perfect spot to relieve himself, I craned my neck to look toward Gordy's house where the text had told me Bud would be.

I couldn't see my husband anywhere, but I could see a car. I wandered back inside our house accompanied by a satisfied dog, and decided to put the kettle on; I knew a pot of tea would refresh me. Bud wandered through our front door about ten minutes later and was happy to see the teapot and mugs at the ready.

"It might be sunny, but there's not a lot of warmth in the air," he commented as he hung up his jacket.

"Whose car was that?" I asked.

"Yet another member of what seems to be a pretty big team of people at the lawyers' office who're working on Gordy's estate."

"It's probably a cunning plan on their part to be able to charge for a huge number of hours' work when they submit their invoice – to themselves," I replied.

"Glad to see you're not getting any less cynical in your dotage, Wife," quipped Bud, settling on a chair at the end of the table with his mug of tea steaming in front of him.

"I'm fifty, Bud. Fifty. Just wait until you see how I can ramp up the cynicism through this decade of my life." I raised my multi-purpose eyebrow to make sure he understood my warning was sincere.

"Almost fifty and a half, now," he replied, mock-shielding himself from a potential thump.

"Hmm," was the only reply his observation deserved. "What did they want? The unnamed person from the lawyers' office, I mean," I pressed.

"I sent an email this morning telling them about Gordy wanting me to burn down the cabin. I got a phone call from Mahera Singh almost immediately, then this guy showed up. I had to take him to the cabin, and he checked some maps of Red Water Mountain he had on his tablet to make sure he knew which structure I meant. He said he'd have to look into whether the cabin had any historical significance before I could set fire to it, and I assured him we weren't going to pour gas over it any time soon. Seems Ms. Singh had skipped past the part of my email where I explained I had to completely clear the place out before I did anything else."

"They might have a point – about the cabin's significance, locally. Do we know when Gordy built it? Might someone want to move it, and rebuild it somewhere else? You know, save it for posterity."

Bud blew across his tea, his brow furrowed. "I seem to recall Gordy telling me he'd arrived in BC in the mid-1950s. Even if he'd built the cabin right way that wouldn't make it old enough to be of real historical importance, would it? I know we're just across the Fraser River from Fort Langley, and that's been there since the Hudson's Bay Company built it in the early 1800s, but the area where Gordy's cabin is located would have been forested until he felled the trees to build it. It can't mean anything to anybody, except Gordy, surely?"

All I could do was shrug; my concept of "historical significance" differs so widely from anything understood by most residents of my little bit of BC that I rarely comment upon it. I grew up in Swansea, where there's an eleventh-century castle in the middle of the city that most people who live there totally ignore.

"Did you venture into the cabin itself when you were there?" I suspected I would have done.

Bud answered thoughtfully. "I didn't think it appropriate. What Gordy asked me to do was private. I think we should be alone when we go inside for the first time."

I acknowledged he made a fair point. "When do you want to do it? Today?"

Bud shook his head. "I don't know how long we'll need to be there, or what 'clearing it out' will entail, but I reckon an early start would be best – we'd have a full day of natural light then, at least." He looked at his watch. "It's a bit too late to set out now. Why don't you get on with reading that diary of Gordy's, and I'll pop some pork chops on the grill; it's a nice enough evening, and we won't be grilling out on the deck for much longer this year."

Bud enjoys using the grill; there's something about the appeal of an open flame that, apparently, makes grilling feel completely different from cooking in the kitchen. To be fair, Bud's pretty good at it…and he's a dab hand at rustling up a leafy salad as well, so I retired to my office where I sat at my desk to give my full attention to Gordy's diary.

"Half an hour until it's ready," called Bud.

"Excellent," I shouted back. I decided to focus on Gordy's earliest writings for twenty minutes or so, and opened the stout, if greasy and worn, linen-bound notebook that had a first page embellished with "1st January 1954". It seemed Gordy had started off meaning to write an entry each and every day, but things had dwindled to a few lines every few days, then once every couple of weeks by the middle of the year.

I learned he'd been living in a rented room in Hope when he'd begun the diary, having arrived from Saskatchewan the previous August. He'd told us quite a while back that he'd been born and raised in Saskatchewan, but why he'd moved from there to Hope – a town about an hour away from us – he didn't say, but that's where he was. Then, in July 1955 he obviously had a Big Day, because he had written his entry in capital letters – unusual for him – and it was a puzzling one.

15th July: TODAY I BOUGHT A MOUNTAIN. IT'S JUST A SMALL ONE, BUT THE WATER RUNS RED – SO A REAL LIKLIHOOD OF IRON, I RECKON. IT WAS CHEAP, NO ONE ELSE SEES THE POTENTIAL. IDIOTS. IF I CAN RIP IT APART LIKE THE LAST PLACE I BOUGHT, I'LL DO WELL. SWEET CHARITY.

It didn't sound like something Gordy would write, or do, and I couldn't imagine what it really meant. But I knew I wanted to talk to Bud about it, so took it to the dinner table with me, to discuss it while we ate.

The pork chops were beautifully charred on the outside, and just cooked through on the inside – which is just how I like them, and the pesto-mayonnaise dressing on the salad made for a truly tasty meal, which we both enjoyed. Marty's tail thumped on the floor beneath the table as we ate, in the hope of getting two plates to lick clean when we'd finished…I think he really hopes for the bones, which he's never given, but the attention he gives greasy plates when I place them on the kitchen floor suggests he's not too bothered.

I finally got to show Bud the puzzling diary entry.

I said, "My only idea is that he's writing about our mountain, Red Water Mountain, when he says the water runs red – which we know it does in the ditches, hence the name, I suppose. But he writes as though he bought the entire mountain, not just his original twenty acres of it. And as for the idea of ripping it apart…do you think he envisaged an iron ore mine? Here?"

Bud nibbled his lip. "There's certainly iron ore to be had in BC, but I don't know of any mining that ever went on near this area. And I can't see Gordy wanting to mine this place, anyway; he loved it. This is the Gordy who talked to me for hours about the delicate balance of our ecosystems here, about the wonders of nature."

"And don't forget he believed strongly that the divine is in everything; he'd rattle on about Ralph Waldo Emerson, the transcendental movement, the concept of panentheism found in Buddhism, Sikhism, Gnosticism, and lots of other 'isms', for as long as I'd let him. Gordy planning to tear open a natural phenomenon like a mountain to mine its innards makes no sense. And he mentions he'd owned land before buying this property, too. I wonder where that was. Saskatchewan, probably."

Bud shrugged. "Maybe you'll find something else in the diary that'll allow this specific entry to make more sense."

I knew Bud was right, which meant I found it difficult to settle to the final episodes of the second season of the dark serial-killer drama we were still watching. Maybe it was my preoccupation that meant I couldn't suspend my disbelief enough to allow the ending of the second season to hang together, but I stomped off to bed grumbling about how thrillers on TV often seemed to disappoint, and frequently left unanswered questions about something that had happened in an earlier episode. I can't stand that – every single red herring and subplot needs to be dealt with for me to feel at ease when the adventure is over. Bud rambled on about how annoying it was that none of the cops with deep emotional problems were told to attend counselling by their bosses, but I didn't follow up on that line of discussion; I know better.

I had horrid dreams that night, and at one point found myself being carried off by a flood of blood that overwhelmed our jolly yellow house as it thundered down our mountain, which itself looked like something out of a steampunk fantasy, replete with towers belching smoke and skeletal children dragging massive iron boulders across cobbled streets. Weird.

In a Cabin Made for One

I was up at five, and at my desk with a mug of instant coffee beside me by a quarter past. Somewhere on our property, hidden by what was either a mist rising from the ground or a cloud descending from the mountaintop, was a lone frog, singing his heart out. I felt sorry for him – he was woefully out of step with the mating cycle, and destined to remain single until after he'd been buried in mud through the winter.

I allowed my fingers to do what they love most: tap away, taking me along paths which branch from the main thoroughfare of my initial inquiry, until I'm able to get a bird's-eye view of the issue at hand. I love the thrill of researching a topic this way and find my ability to speed read, and have dozens of screens open at once, to be exhilarating.

By the time Bud emerged I'd made a pot of proper coffee, Marty had been dragged around the perimeter of our acreage, and I'd showered and dressed, having got myself thoroughly soaked while traipsing about in the unexpected rain. I was raring to go, but it took Bud a little while to gather his wits.

While he slurped coffee, I shared my fresh insights with him, though I found myself having to report a poor harvest.

"The nearest iron mine to us – to Red Water Mountain – is a very long way away, so I don't know what made Gordy think he'd found a mountain ripe for mining, other than the red water, of course."

"So, nothing new, then?"

I slurped my coffee. "Not a lot, no. I really enjoyed finding out more about BC and Canada's phenomenal history of mining, but relating to iron, here? Nope. However, sometimes finding out negative information can be as helpful as finding out positive information. His diary entry still makes no sense, but we could ask the lawyers about other property or land he owned in the past, before he arrived in BC; they might be able to tell us something."

"Why not send them an email? But let's not hang about waiting for a reply, let's go down to the cabin and have a looksee," said Bud, standing.

"You know we'll get soaked, right?"

"Skin doesn't leak, Cait, and if we take Marty with us he can have a good old run about – you know how he loves that." He smooshed Marty's face in both his hands. "Love doing zoomies in the puddles, don't you, boy?"

Bud's "talking to Marty" voice always makes me feel warm inside, because it allows me to see his purely sentimental nature out in the open – not a place it's displayed very often. It wasn't a tone of voice I imagined any of his colleagues from his cop days would have heard at all, which made it even more special.

"That might not be such a good idea, Bud. Who knows what we'll find there, and we don't want to have to wrangle Marty as well as explore an old cabin. Besides, he's already had a good run around – he might enjoy a nap."

Bud agreed, just as Marty yawned, so – fully swaddled in waterproofs and wellies – we set out to walk down to Gordy's cabin, unaccompanied by Marty. At the bottom of the mountain the meadowland was saturated, and our feet squished into the waterlogged soil beneath the long grass. There were no paths, except for those made by the local wildlife; I suspected deer and coyotes had made most of the noticeable trails, and bears too, because there was a good variety of telltale scat about the place.

I studied the cabin as though I were seeing it for the first time; yes, I'd been to this part of Gordy's property before, but visiting the cabin hadn't been the reason – Gordy's invitation to wander had been our spur on that occasion, and the walk had been more casual.

The cabin was small – about twelve feet by sixteen – and the walls were about six feet high, the apex of the cedar-shingled roof rising to about twelve feet. The entire rectangular box was made of large logs laid on top of one another, crossing at each of the four corners. There was one small door, made of planks with peeling red paint, and one tiny, square window, now covered with a plastic sheet. There was a chimney made of large, rounded rocks, probably hauled from the stream which ran close by. Overall, it seemed to be in pretty good condition, but we encountered our first challenge when Bud approached the door.

"Padlocked! But of course. Why didn't we think of that?" I said.

"One of us did," replied Bud, beaming. He triumphantly pulled a key from his pocket. "Got it from the guy yesterday – it was on Gordy's keyring. We worked out which one it was, and he handed it over. Made me sign for it."

Bud wrestled with the padlock for a moment, then pulled the door open; it took some doing.

We both stepped forward and the first thing I noticed was the smell. "Something's been living in here, and I reckon several somethings have died in here too."

We both stood back to allow the air to circulate a bit before we ventured in.

"Should have brought a flashlight," said Bud. "Didn't think we'd need one, but it's so overcast today."

"Phones," I said pulling mine out of my pocket. "But let's get inside, where it might be stinky, but at least it's dry," I added.

"Stop!" Bud shoved his arm in front of me before I had a chance to step inside. "Look, possible footprints." He pointed his phone's bright white light at the floor, and I could see what he meant: there were patches in the thick dust that weren't shoe-shaped but were definitely marks. Whoever had made them had scuffled about the place; there wasn't so much a pattern of prints but more of a sort of criss-crossing of dust-disturbances.

"Someone's been inside here," Bud spoke with certainty. "Let's take some photos before we do anything else." We both did. Of everything. There was a small, rusty, cast-iron woodstove, a rusty, iron bedstead with blankets bundled on top of a woefully stained, lumpen mattress, and a rudimentary table and chair. An ancient-looking oil lamp was on the table, beside an enamelled mug and plate. It looked as though a human had got out of bed and walked out a long time ago, then the local wildlife had moved in. Thick dust, spiderwebs, droppings from a variety of rodents, and the carcasses of all manner of insects covered every surface. Otherwise, the place was empty, which surprised me, because Gordy struck me as the sort of man who'd at least have built some bookshelves.

"I can see why he told me to set fire to it," said Bud.

I put my finger under my nose and tried to breathe through my mouth. "You're not wrong. There's not much here worth saving – if anything. That quilt on the bed might have been wonderful once upon a time, but there've been so many mice and rats living in it there's almost nothing left of it now. And as for everything else? Well, there wasn't much to start with – the place is essentially empty. About the only thing that's still in good condition is the structure of the cabin itself."

We both looked up at the roof; it was clear it had continued to do its job, despite the abandonment of the building. The only place the cabin was wet was where the plastic sheeting at the window had ripped, a patch of it flapping in the breeze.

"That plastic looks to be quite new," I noted. "Do you think Gordy's been down here relatively recently to fix that up?"

"Wouldn't put it past him," replied Bud, his eyes searching the cabin for something. "Even with that increasingly shuffling gait of his, he still managed to get about amazingly well."

"What are you looking for?"

"Whatever it is that smells so bad. I can't believe a few dead rats and so forth could smell this strong. It's like…"

"It smells like a larger creature, doesn't it?" I said. My shoulders drooped. We both knew that smell, and it was never a good sign.

We finally entered the cabin. Bud stepped toward the bed. "It's strongest over here." His nose wrinkled.

I followed him. "You're right. Do you think we should move the bed?"

"It might be something like a coyote – managed to get in, couldn't get out?" Bud didn't sound convinced. "In fact, the scuffle marks in the dust on the floor could be those of a larger animal, trapped in here for some time."

"I'm sure you're right."

I pulled two garbage bags out of one of the many pockets with which my waterproof is equipped. I'd popped them in thinking we might want to bring some items home from the cabin, without them getting wet. I hadn't expected it to be so completely bare. I passed a bag to Bud and I shoved one hand into each corner of mine, so I wouldn't have to touch the rusty iron of the bed frame. Bud did the same. We both grabbed on and tried to pull the bed away from the corner. It was surprisingly heavy. We stopped for a moment.

"This seems heavier than it should be," I said, a bit puffed.

"You're not kidding. Maybe if we take the mattress off?"

It was a good idea, though neither of us fancied touching the bedding heaped onto it, so we both used our plastic-covered hand-stumps to push it off the edge of the bed onto the floor. Once the mattress was visible, it was clear there was something amiss.

I poked at it with an elbow. "There are pointy things in there," I said. My mind conjured bizarre pictures of just what the pointy things might be.

Bud made a bold move; he stuck a couple of fingers into a tear in the mattress covering and pulled. Out popped a volume much like the diary I'd taken from Gordy's house. He handed it to me; I took it from him by its corner. It was in remarkably good condition for a notepad that had been stuck inside a mattress covered with rodent droppings.

"Are there more?" I sounded as excited as I felt.

Bud prodded around the mattress. "Feels like there's a load of them. Probably why the thing is so heavy. How about we leave them where they are, for now, and just try harder to shift the bedstead with the mattress still on top, eh?"

"Agreed." I pushed the notepad into one of the large outer pockets of my waterproof, and zipped the pocket closed.

We put a real effort into moving the bed – diary-filled mattress and all. Even so, with all our best efforts, the blessed thing only moved about a foot away from the wall, then it got snagged on something. We exchanged a frustrated glare, then both bent at the waist to peer under the bed. I was dreading what I might see – so was relieved when I saw a large, metal trunk.

There was nothing for it but to lift the entire bed to get it away from the chest, and that took some doing. We finally managed to shift the bed and mattress right up against the table, exposing the chest...and the source of the stench. Somehow a Steller's jay had managed to get into the cabin, but had never left. That explained the marks on the floor – the beating of wings as the poor bird had flapped about. Bud was incredibly brave, and managed to scoop up the remains with the enamel plate from the table; he tossed the carcass out onto the grass.

We both felt relieved we'd found the source of the cadaverous smell, and turned our attention to the tin trunk. It was about four feet long by two feet wide and high; an iron bar was screwed to its top and side. Luckily, there was no locking mechanism.

Bud flung the top open, and it banged backward. A puff of dust flew up from the floor. The anticlimax of seeing it full of neatly folded linens was a relief.

We pulled out the topmost item from the chest, which turned out to be a plastic-lined printed tablecloth. Since we both agreed it was something we'd probably end up throwing out, we cleared the table, covered it with the relatively clean tablecloth, then returned to the trunk to investigate.

"My mother was a great hoarder of linens," I said as I pulled out the fourth pillowcase.

"A tendency you've inherited," muttered Bud.

I chose to not respond to his possibly accurate comment, instead observing, "These sheets are all hand-embroidered, along the part you turn down at the top." I pointed to the white-on-white embellishments. "Some pretty fancy stitches, too."

Bud took the folded sheet from me and stared. "Jan was a great one for embroidery," he said softly.

I'd had no idea, though I knew his late wife had been an incredibly enthusiastic scrapbooker, and knitter, and quilter, so I supposed a passion for embroidery wasn't such a surprise. I remained quiet for a moment, as did Bud. He ran his fingers gently over the stitching, and examined the design.

"Whoever did this was good," he said. "Very good. And to work in the same color as the fabric is tough, so I'm guessing they were quite young when they did it – or at least had excellent eyesight. Do you think it's a *trousseau*?" He looked up at me with clear eyes. No tears, just curiosity. I was relieved.

"It could be, though why Gordy would have a trunk full of bridal linens is a mystery."

The remainder of the items proved to be table linens, and two nightgowns on which the *broderie anglaise* had also been hand-worked.

"Well, it really does seem to be a *trousseau*. I'm no expert, of course, but these items could be quite old. Maybe they once belonged to Gordy's mother?" It was the most likely explanation I could come up with.

Bud nibbled his lip. "That could make them well over a hundred years old," he said thoughtfully. "Not something we should destroy, I don't think. These should definitely be saved. And maybe even the trunk is original to them, too, so we should keep that as well."

"Do you think we could manage to haul the trunk and the linens across the lower acreage to the road, if we brought the truck around? You know, to where Tom said he used to park."

Bud stood and smoothed the nightie he'd just placed on the table. "I think we should take a look at a possible route before we plan to do that. I'm not sure exactly how it would be best to go about it." He checked his watch. "We could do that now – and moving about a bit will be good for us. Okay?"

I agreed, and we headed out, leaving the linens where they were, having folded the tablecloth over the top of them in case any rain came into the cabin through the gap in the plastic sheet on the window. We trudged through the tall, thick grass – flattened somewhat by the wind and rain – and did what we could to avoid the massive banks of brambles that had grown, unchecked, for some years. It wasn't easy to find a path through to the edge of the property; it was like trying to work out how a completely haphazard maze could be traversed. Finally, we found the fence, and the road. Not that there was much of a fence left – it had fallen into disrepair long ago, by the looks of it; there were still a good number of uprights, but the split logs that would have zig-zagged between them had almost all disappeared. Not that it really mattered – the brambles alone were enough of a deterrent to walk onto the land, if a deterrent were required.

Once we reached the road, we walked along a little way to get our bearings, and I checked my phone to see if I could get an exact location. We seemed to be in a dead spot as far as cell reception was concerned, as neither Bud nor I could get any bars on our phones at all. We worked out generally where we were, and found a long, broken branch on the ground with a distinctive Y in it. We took a little while to shove it into the ground beside a fairly sturdy upright, so we'd have a marker to guide us when we came back with the truck; you couldn't see the cabin from the road, so could easily begin a trek in the wrong spot, or head off in the wrong direction.

Then we started back toward the cabin. For some reason it seemed to take us longer, because the route back proved even more challenging than before – we couldn't see any of the tracks we'd assumed we'd have made on the outward journey, which was puzzling and annoying. We both put it down to particularly springy grass.

It wasn't just me who was a bit puffed when we got back to the cabin, so we sat on the front step for a few minutes – it had stopped raining – and discussed how best to organize our time. We agreed we'd start by getting the diaries out of the mattress and carrying them home with us in the garbage bags I'd brought – or as many of them as we could, at least. That meant we could let Marty out, and have something quick for lunch. Then we'd drive the truck around, traverse the bramble-maze, and lug the trunk to the truck together. We also agreed to bring some more bin bags for any of the diaries we couldn't manage to carry on our first trip. We had a plan – plans are good.

However, we also decided it would be best to pack the *trousseau* back into the trunk before we headed off, so it would be instantly ready to carry away later on. When we re-entered the cabin it looked much as we'd left it: the bed and mattress were back in their corner, undisturbed; the open trunk was in the middle of the floor; the plastic tablecloth was on the table...but there was no *trousseau*. Every item we'd carefully lifted out of the trunk was gone.

Welcome to My Parlor

If Bud hadn't been a retired cop, there's no way we'd have reported the *trousseau* as having been stolen. As it was, he was on the phone to the cops as soon as we got home, and he emailed Gordy's lawyers about it too. His argument was that, when put together with the attempted break-in at Gordy's house, the theft from the cabin suggested a pattern of behavior the cops should be alerted to. When it comes to matters of policing I let Bud lead, so that was why we'd packed up the diaries – they'd all fitted into the bags we had with us – and got back home as fast as we could. We'd allowed Marty a brief runabout, then I'd nipped out to the nearest White Spot, about fifteen minutes away, to pick up Double Double burgers, fries, and a side order of onion rings, which I hoped would stop my tummy rumbling, even though I knew the meal might give me indigestion.

Once we'd eaten, we were finally able to talk about what we'd found – and lost – at the cabin that day, and what it might all mean. Sadly, we just went over old ground, without any bright ideas or explanations for either finding – or losing – what was there. Which was extremely frustrating, though we were both delighted the thief hadn't taken the diaries.

I noisily drained the vat of Diet Coke that had come with my meal. "If I'm going to eulogize Gordy, the diaries will be helpful. It'll be interesting to read his accounts of his life, but there'll be far too much detail in them – all anyone wants of a eulogy is a relatively brief piece about the person they are memorializing; it's not as though I need to write up a full life profile of the man, is it?"

"Like you did for victims, when you worked with me?" Bud replied. I nodded. "Gordy specifically asked in his letter that you give a full picture of his life in his eulogy. He knew what you did for a living, didn't he?" I nodded again. "Well, I'm guessing that's exactly what he'd expect you to do – work up a full life profile of him, as you would have done if he'd been a victim."

The gauntlet was down. "I'd love to do a full work-up. No holds barred. Okay with you?"

Bud started to rub his hand through his hair – a sure sign he's feeling stress. "It doesn't need to become a big 'thing', Cait. I just meant I believe that's what he'd have expected of you. His letter did say—"

"Yes, I know what it said." I hadn't thought of profiling Gordy in the way Bud was suggesting, and I was snapping at him despite the fact that it was absolutely *not* his fault. I was cross with myself. I did my best to pull in my horns. "Sorry, I didn't mean to speak so sharply. I should have thought of this before."

Bud flashed me a smile, and I was just going in for a loving kiss, when his phone rang.

Marty dutifully barked, and Bud petted him to try to quieten him as he answered.

Listening to just his side of the conversation was annoyingly uninformative.

"Yes, it is. Yes, she is. Yes, of course we can. Do you mind me asking what it's…Oh. I see. Yes. Of course. Hang on." He turned to me. "Can you make an appointment at the lawyers' office right now?" I nodded. He said, "Yes, we'll be there. Thanks. Bye."

I was agog. "Why are we going to the lawyers' again?"

"No idea. Wouldn't say."

"They enjoy being mysterious, don't they?"

"Gotta find their fun where they can, I guess," said Bud, shrugging. "They're lawyers, after all."

"They didn't even give you a clue?"

"Not remotely." Bud raked his hand through his hair.

"You're good at picking up on a person's tone – what did that tell you?" I pressed.

Bud shoved his hand into his pocket. "I don't think it's good news. But, come on, hanging about here won't make it any better, so let's get our skates on."

The roads were relatively deserted, so it didn't take us long to get to the lawyers' place. The reception area of Oishi and Singh was deserted when we arrived, then Mahera rushed out of an office and beckoned to us to join her. She looked a lot less well put-together than she had when we'd first met her, and she had dark circles below her lackluster eyes.

"Rylan's not here, sorry. He and I agreed I'd take this meeting. Thank you for coming." We mumbled that it was no problem. "Sorry it's such short notice," she continued, her eyes darting across the piles of paperwork on her desk, "but there's been a development, and I have to tell you about it."

Bud and I exchanged a sideways glance.

"They've found something, in the post-mortem, that is worrying. More than worrying, in fact." The lawyer was constantly licking her lips, then rubbing them together. It was a bit off-putting, and I had no doubt she didn't know she was doing it. A nervous tic, like Bud and his hair.

"What can you tell us, Mahera?" Bud was using his calming voice.

The ramrod back I'd noticed at our first meeting slouched as Mahera's shoulders fell. "The coroner thinks...well, they're certain...that Gordy was poisoned." Her chin puckered, but I couldn't work out why she was on the verge of tears; was it stress, or something else?

"You mean his death was suspicious?" Bud likes to get the facts straight as soon as he can.

Mahera nodded. "Yes, that's exactly what they said. Suspicious. They found *conium* in his system. It's found – so Google tells me – in poison hemlock. It's deadly."

"Socrates!" I couldn't help myself, I just blurted it out.

Bud and Mahera both looked startled.

"Socrates drank hemlock," I said, then quickly added, "but he didn't commit suicide, like some people think, rather he was carrying out his required death penalty."

Mahera's eyes narrowed. "Do you think Gordy might have killed himself?"

There was that question again. Bud replied, "Cait and I discussed the possibility when we found him. We both agreed it was unlikely."

I added, "Gordy didn't strike either of us as being in the frame of mind that would indicate suicide – he wasn't showing any signs of depression. And there was no note – which there isn't always, I know, but Gordy was the type who would have left one, I believe."

Mahera nodded, then started licking her lips again. "I didn't know him well, I only met him less than a year ago, and we had very few in-person meetings – most of the detailed work was done over the phone, but I share your opinion. Though I understand he'd recently been diagnosed with Parkinson's disease, so maybe…"

That intangible concept hung in the air; I decided to pluck it down. "I still don't think he'd have done it. He was dealing well with his medication, was generally in good health, and certainly in good spirits. And I truly believe he was the sort of person who – had he planned to kill himself – would have left some sort of an explanation."

Mahera's eyes were darting again. "You were the first people there. You found him. Are you certain there wasn't a note?"

"Quite certain," replied Bud. His tone was grave. "If the coroner has said this is a suspicious death, there'll be an investigation."

"The theft from his cabin you emailed me about?" Mahera tapped at her keyboard. "Do you think that might be seen in a new light, given what they've just told me?"

"I'm not sure how the disappearance of what looked like an old *trousseau* could be linked to Gordy being poisoned, but it's certainly odd." As I spoke I was desperately trying to make some connections. None came to mind.

"What's the next step, as far as we're concerned?" asked Bud. "It's good of you to have told us this, of course, but why did you ask us to come here, to your office, to do so?"

Mahera seemed to focus on us for the first time. "Ah, yes, the letter."

"There's another letter?" I sounded as surprised as I was.

Mahera tapped a folder on her desk. "That's the thing, you see. Gordy gave us another sealed letter a couple of months ago. It was to be handed to you both, personally, if his death were deemed 'unnatural'. And I'd say poisoning with hemlock is quite unnatural, despite the official line being that it's 'suspicious'. Rylan and I have discussed this at length, and we are not in agreement; he thinks we should hold onto this letter until the police are certain that Gordy's death was…well, 'at the hand of another' sums it up. I, however, think Gordy used the term 'unnatural' in the way a lay person would – and that his use of it would cover the official term of 'suspicious'." It was almost as though Mahera Singh was continuing her disagreement with her invisible colleague, with Bud and myself as witnesses.

"Here it is." The decision was made; she held the envelope in the space between the two of us. "I was told to not share the news from the coroner. You mustn't tell *anyone* that I have told you."

Bud tilted his head, and said, "Agreed."

I took the envelope before Mahera had a chance to change her mind, and was sorely tempted to rip it open on the spot, but I resisted. "Thank you, Mahera," I said, "we'll read it in private, if you don't mind. Is there a room we could use, please?" There was no way I was waiting until we got home to find out what it said.

Once Bud and I were alone in the meeting room I pulled the letter out of the envelope and read it aloud.

Dear Bud and Cait,

You're reading this because I died an unnatural death. I wonder how it happened. I will selfishly tell you right now that I hope I didn't suffer, but maybe I should have done.

I'm asking this of you because it's important: don't let the cops, or anyone else, blame the wrong person…or bring them up on the wrong type of charges.

Bud, I know you always did the best you could when you served – that's what everyone says about you, in any case. But you must know of cases where the wrong person gets accused, and maybe even gets found guilty, of something they didn't mean to do. That thought haunts me. I need you two to make sure it doesn't happen now.

I trust you two to do the right thing. You're a couple bound together by a desire for justice. Well, justice comes in all shapes and sizes. Sometimes there's a natural justice, sometimes man must intervene. Sometimes the worst possible punishment – way beyond the horror of incarceration – is for a person to have to live with the weight of the knowledge of what they've done…who they've hurt…how they've hurt them. Please make sure the *right* justice is brought to bear in the *right* way on the *right* person. Please. It's important.

I've gone, yes, but I hope you'll fulfil this last wish of mine, whatever you might come to feel about my right to ask it.

Gordy

Bud's hand had started to rake through his hair as I'd been reading, and my nerves were jangling too. Neither of us said anything for a few moments.

"So…what do you think? Should we, somehow, make sure the 'right' person is brought to the 'right' type of justice for killing Gordy?" I said.

Bud glared at the desk. "It would be good to be certain he really was killed before we attempt anything like that, don't you think?"

I gave Bud's words some thought. "You're right. We need to know that. Can you wriggle your way onto an inside track on this, somehow?"

Bud sighed. "I never thought I'd have to call in favors to help out with a possible investigation this close to home, Cait. I've done it before, in foreign parts, as you know. But here? It feels different. It *is* different. This is, literally, our own backyard. If someone, somehow, managed to get Gordy to consume hemlock – either against his will, or without his knowledge – you know what that means, don't you?"

I too, sighed deeply, and nodded. "He trusted them enough to eat or drink with them, or to consume something he was given by them, or they were able to somehow get hemlock into his food or drink without his knowledge – so they'd have had access to his home. That's very, *very* few people. And they're all locals – members of our little community. Our neighbors."

"Exactly; if Gordy Krantz *was* murdered, one of our neighbors did it. That's not a pleasant thought."

Everything I'd been feeling about the loss of dear old Gordy had shifted. His diaries called to me, and I knew what I had to do.

Welcome to Our Home, Gordy Krantz

I installed myself in my office with the garbage bags full of diaries and emptied them all out onto an old tarpaulin I'd laid on the floor. Some were in a terrible state, others were almost pristine. The one thing they all had in common was that they smelled awful. Bud had offered to help me sort them out, and I took him up on his offer.

We decided right away that we'd need to use latex gloves to handle the notebooks, and that we'd have to work hard at not putting our hands anywhere near our faces after we'd been touching them. We had to shut Marty out of the office, because he was understandably interested in sniffing every book. He lay outside on the floor of the hallway, making the little whimpering sounds that tell us he's sulking.

Our first objective was to sort the diaries into chronological order – which took the best part of a couple of hours. Gordy had covered more than one year in many volumes, and had written from both ends of some of the pads. We found we had pretty comprehensive coverage from 1954 right up until 1993. A few individual years were missing, and 1988 to 1990 were nowhere to be found, but we reckoned we'd get a good insight into Gordy's life from what we had.

"I'll leave you to it then, shall I?" Bud was stretching out his back as he surveyed our work. "How long do you think it'll take you to read this lot?"

I was also trying to realign my neck – having been bent over on the floor for so long. "No idea. You can see his handwriting is all over the place. I might be able to get through the stuff he's written clearly, in biro, quite fast – but we've both seen lots of parts where his writing was very small, and in pencil. I think I'll finish up the first one then just move ahead in date order for as long as I can. I should get faster as I go, and I'll be able to give you a better idea of the scale of the whole job when I've got a couple of hours under my belt."

Bud nodded. "I'll take Marty out for a good long walk, and I'll get going with dinner when we get back. Eat at six, okay?"

We agreed, and he left me to it. It was lovely to see how happy Marty was to be going out with his human, but I knew I had to get this job done, so I focused, and settled myself at my desk.

It's true that I get lost in my work sometimes, but I could have sworn it was only about half an hour later that Bud gave me a shout to tell me dinner would be ready in a few moments. I looked at my watch. Where had the time gone?

I'd made mental notes as I'd been reading – one of those instances when an eidetic memory really does come in handy – so now I had the highlights of Gordy Krantz's life from 1955 to 1972 all sorted. And what a life it had been; I couldn't wait to tell Bud, and arrived at the dinner table in a fairly excited state.

We'd agreed that salad would be a quick fix for dinner, but my mouth didn't exactly water when I looked at the bowl of green goodness topped with an unappealing lump of tinned tuna. However, I reasoned it was just as well the food wasn't going to distract us from my recounting of what Gordy had got up to during the better part of two decades.

Marty looked exhausted as he lay beneath the table, only managing to wiggle his eyebrows as he made a feeble effort to seem interested in our meal – he was obviously wise enough to know there wasn't anything on our plates in which he was remotely interested.

After I'd eaten all the interesting bits off the top of the bed of salad greens, I poked the rest about as I said, "Do you want to ask questions, or shall I just tell you?"

Bud sat back from the table. "Just tell me. You're bursting with it, so get going."

"Okay, but I warn you, there's a lot."

"Never doubted it. Gordy must have been quite the guy in his youth."

"You're not wrong," I said. "As you know, we meet him in 1954, and I showed you that weird entry in 1955." Bud nodded. "Well, the first thing I should do is tell you I'm still none the wiser about what that entry meant. Sorry about that. But 1955 was also a big year for him because that's when he began to clear the land to build his cabin. He bought the property in the July and lived in a tent down there as he felled the trees he needed. Believe it or not he met his own deadline, and celebrated Christmas 1955 in the finished cabin. That's quite something, I reckon. To be honest, there are hardly any entries for that period; I assume he worked incredibly hard, and he doesn't mention having any help. The start of 1956 was a different story though – he took a job working at one of the cedar mills down near Stave Lake; he'd got to know the people there when he'd dealt with them for supplies for the cabin's roof."

"I didn't realize those mills had been there that long," said Bud.

"Longer," I replied, "since the 1930s, in fact. And that's all of any real interest for the next couple of years. He had paying work, and continued to clear his land. Doesn't sound like much – but it must have required a huge amount of effort. He'd have been in his prime back then, and it seems he cleared the entire area that makes up the bottom meadowlands of his property by 1960. He managed to sell the trees and made some money from that too – though not as much as you'd have thought. No mention of any sort of social life until the 1960s. Then things hot up."

Bud mugged a look of rapt anticipation. I poked my tongue out at him.

"A woman is mentioned!" I said, with a flourish.

"Good for Gordy," said Bud, and raised his glass of fizzy water in my direction.

"A certain 'Rachel' is mentioned several times throughout 1960 and 1961. Gordy's still at the mill, but is now clearing stumps from his property with an old truck he's bought; the vehicle allows him to take her on various outings – some to the 'cesspit' of Downtown Vancouver, as well as to nicer places like Stanley Park. His notes make it quite clear that he much preferred the park to the city, which is to be expected, I suppose…but he cites his great disappointment when Rachel turned out to be more impressed by the city than rural life, so he 'dumped her' – which I thought was a turn of phrase that had only come into usage more recently, but even I live and learn."

"He dumped her? Ah well, young love and all that. Fancy a cuppa? You're not going to eat any more of those leaves, are you, so I might as well clear everything away, right?"

I looked at my plate guiltily. "It was very tasty, thanks. But maybe I'm just not hungry. Probably the smell of the diaries – it's put paid to my appetite. Tea would be good, thanks."

"You carry on while I clear. I can do two things at once." Bud winked at me.

"Okay, onto 1963, which is when it gets even more interesting. It seems Gordy had always planned to turn that bottom meadow into an area where he could grow rhododendrons, fruits, and vegetables, so he scouted out plant suppliers in the area. That's when he met Terry Dumas, who had a smallholding over in Thornhill where he ran a sort of makeshift nursery – mainly selling to locals. It reads as though Gordy and Terry hit it off, and there's a lot of social time spent together, as well as all of the plant selection – then actual planting – which Terry seems to become more and more involved with. By 1964 Gordy and Terry have formed their own company – with a great deal of fanfare and more than a few beers to celebrate – and they're using Gordy's bottom meadow to sell what they've grown to the public, with younger plants being cared for up at Terry's place. From what I can work out, they had a stall on the road almost exactly where we were standing yesterday. They had built two large greenhouses 'up the mountain' by the end of 1965, which I think were located around here. Our five acres, and the bit of Gordy's land where his house now sits, are about the only flat land up here. Anyway, they must have been making a real go of it, because Gordy's no longer working at the mill…though he used shingles from his old place of work to encase the entire roadside sales-stall, which morphed into an actual store."

Bud placed the teapot on the table, beside our mugs. "Very enterprising. Attaboy."

"During this period – and I'm talking about 1965 to late 1969 now – the vast majority of entries are about work, and a general improvement in Gordy's life. He's still living in the cabin, and working hard on the propagating of plants and so forth. Sounds as though Terry did most of the sales shifts in the store, and was also doing all the books for the business at night. Reading between the lines a bit, I reckon Terry might also have put money into the enterprise in the first place, though it seems as though the greenhouses were built from the proceeds of the business itself, as was the road up the mountain by which they were accessed – our road. It's funny to think of someone creating a road, isn't it?"

Bud managed a quick: "I guess."

I pressed on. "Anyway, Gordy gets a new truck to replace his clapped-out, old banger – with which Terry had been making deliveries. The newness of the truck was a big deal for him. He also starts to write in much more detail about the plants he's raising; there's a lot of technical stuff about the cross-breeding he's doing. The broad principles are pretty straightforward, but the record-keeping was diligent, and detailed."

"What was he breeding?" Bud sounded genuinely interested.

I closed my eyes to visualize the passages. "Hydrangeas and rhododendrons. Mentioned a great deal of correspondence with the American Rhododendron Society, and notes how excited they are about what he's doing."

"Do you think that means he might, in fact, be the Gordon Krantz I found on Google who invented new types of rhodos?" Bud picked up his phone and started tapping.

"I wouldn't be surprised," I replied. "It was evidently a passion of his. Maybe Canada didn't have a similar body, so he got involved with the folks south of the border? Anyway, the hybrids he created were numerous and, especially in the case of the rhododendrons, took many years to evaluate. His records go on a bit, but they needed to."

"I've emailed you the links," said Bud, looking proud. "He won prizes, in that case," he added. "Funny to think people grow plants today that Gordy 'invented'. Quite cool, when you think they were developed right next door to us, or – if the greenhouses were here – maybe right where we're standing. Or sitting, you know."

I agreed. "The early 1970s tell me Terry wanted to spread his wings in terms of opening more stores with nurseries attached, and Gordy was becoming increasingly frustrated with him. The main gist of it is that Gordy wanted a business model where stores remained quite specialized, focusing on the plants he loved, and created. However, Terry wanted to enlarge the range of plants offered, and even buy in a percentage of plants from the USA, acting more as a retailer than a grower. And that's about as far as I've got."

Bud sipped his tea. "Not much about Gordy's life, as such, eh? Has your summary focused on his work, rather than that aspect, or was that his focus, too?"

"Honestly, other than the bits about Rachel, his friendship with Terry, and his truck, he wrote almost nothing about how he lived. I can only guess that most of his life was, in fact, plants; his fascination with breeding new hybrids seems to be it."

"I guess that fits with how simply he lived his life in the times we knew him. No social connections that I know of – though there must have been some, I guess, at some point in his life."

I shrugged. "I don't think I've found out anything pertinent in terms of who might have wanted to do him harm. Which is…well, 'disappointing' isn't the right word, I suppose, but you know what I mean."

Bud smiled. "You've got through quite a few years – well done. Any idea how much more time you'll need to put in to finish?"

I stood to clear the table. Marty didn't stir. "A lot's going to depend on how much of what's in there is stuff I can read past; when I could see he was writing notes about plants and so forth I was able to skim those bits. The meatier parts got more of my attention. I should be finished by the end of tomorrow, if I apply myself. I have to admit I'm less hopeful now of finding out something that might help us work out what happened to him. Though I do think it would be a good idea to talk to Janice Dumas. If I push on and try to work out how Gordy ended up removing himself from that business – or being ousted – then we could be better prepared to ask her some relevant questions.

I could approach her under the guise of wanting to prepare Gordy's eulogy – she knows I'm doing that, and we could try to find out if there was any bad blood between the two men. Do the Dumases have any children? Could there be a child seeking retribution for something?"

Bud gave a little chuckle. "You make it sound so dramatic. We both know that the reasons for murder can be frighteningly mundane. Retribution sounds biblical."

"We also both know that what seems mundane to outsiders can be a reason that burns with a terrible fire in the mind of a killer; what seems like nothing to you and me is all a killer is focused on – it becomes their entire world, leading them to do the most dreadful things."

"You're right, of course," replied Bud.

"And there's something else I've been thinking about," I added.

Bud tilted his head, inviting me to continue.

"I spent a little time checking out *conium*, the poison found in Gordy's system. Ms. Singh was quite clear that was what it was. It's a nicotine-like alkaloid, and there are some homeopathic treatments that use a tiny amount of *conium*, which creates *coniine*, to treat several of the symptoms Gordy had been experiencing. Did he ever mention to you that he was taking anything like that? Something that wasn't one of his prescribed medications?"

Bud looked puzzled. "Don't you think I'd have mentioned that? Besides, where would he have gotten hold of something of that sort? We've either been with him over the past few months, or else we've done all his fetching and carrying for him."

"Other people have visited him, Bud. Maybe Tom brought something, or someone else did."

"It's unlikely, Cait. You know he hated taking any meds; I don't think he'd have chosen to take more than he absolutely needed. Besides, we'd have found whatever it was at his house, when we were clearing things out. I didn't. Did you?"

I shook my head. Bud was right – Gordy had an inbuilt dislike of swallowing handfuls of unnatural chemicals, as he always called them, but he understood how well the drugs managed his symptoms, and took them pretty much on time, three times every day.

"What else did you discover about the poison they found in him?" Bud poured himself another mug of tea, draining the pot when I signalled I didn't want any more.

"*Conium maculatum* is the proper name for poison hemlock, and it occurs naturally in great quantities in many situations, often near water. Then there's water hemlock, which contains *cicutoxin*. The plants look almost identical, are just as lethal as each other, but – chemically, at least – they are quite different. And they can both grow near water…not just the water hemlock."

Bud's eyes were round. "So, let me get this straight: there are two types of plant, with similar names, which look almost the same as each other, both grow in the same places, and they can each kill you – but with a different poison?"

I nodded. "Nature is quite wonderful, isn't it?"

Bud didn't look convinced. "Do you think we're looking for someone who knew enough about plants to be able to differentiate between these two very similar ones?"

I sat back in my chair and laced my fingers behind my head. "I did think of that, but then I asked myself – would it really matter which one was used to kill him? Either one would do the job. Both have roots that look like a parsnip, and leaves that are just green. Either plant could have been disguised in anything that…" I sat upright. "Oh Bud – I've been so stupid!

Gordy's soup! The pan we emptied out into the bush. That could have contained the poison hemlock. It doesn't kill immediately – he could have eaten the soup for supper and the poison could have acted overnight."

I pushed back my chair, frightening Marty who bolted for the sitting room; I headed for the door. "Do you think we'll be able to save it? Will we have messed up the evidence?"

"Where are you going?" Bud caught up with me before I could leave.

"Over to Gordy's to see if I can save some samples of the soup." I'd thought that was obvious.

Bud used his calming voice. "You know what the rain's been like since we emptied it onto the soil. I can't imagine there's anything useful left. Besides, it's dark; how on earth would you find it now? Let's go over in the morning."

"We left the stew pot next to the spot where we dumped it; it'll be easy to find. And it could rain all night tonight, so let's at least try to save it from that."

Bud scratched his head. "Tell you what – let me make a couple of phone calls, see if I can find out who's working this case, and let them know the situation. I might have to break my word to Ms. Singh to not mention that she told us about the coroner's findings, but that can't be helped. While I'm doing that, can you go out to the shed and find the new tarp I bought at Canadian Tire last week? It's still in its packaging. We can at least protect the area from any more rain – and all that means – without causing too much more corruption of evidence."

We had a plan.

Home Cooked Meals

When I woke on Friday morning, my first notable emotion was guilt. Bud and I had possibly ruined the best chance the RCMP had of finding the means by which Gordy Krantz had been murdered. I brushed my teeth, showered and dressed, and plodded around our property behind Marty; he knew something was wrong, and kept looking back to make sure I was keeping up. The scarlet glow of the maples couldn't raise my spirits, nor could the jolly faces of the rudbeckia, but Marty did his bit, nosing at my hand whenever I caught up with him; he's a great comfort.

Bud was ready to scramble some eggs when I got back to the house. As he stood stirring, I sat staring out of the window.

"They'll be here any time now," he said, as he placed the plate of yellow lusciousness in front of me. "A hearty breakfast, if ever there was one."

"And we're the condemned, aren't we?" I sulked.

"It's not about us, Cait." Bud was trying to sound reassuring. It wasn't working. "We didn't know that soup might have contained poison when we got rid of it."

I ground some black pepper over my eggs. "I know, but the penny should have dropped as soon as Ms. Singh told us about the poison hemlock. Why on earth didn't it occur to me sooner?"

"It didn't occur to either of us, Cait. You do realize that by beating yourself up about this you're making me feel worse too, right?"

More guilt piled on top of that which I already felt. "Sorry." I concentrated on my breakfast.

I barely noticed the sun glinting on the dewy grass beyond the windows as I crunched the buttery toast beneath my eggs, and Marty had to put his paw on my foot before I realized he was hoping for my empty plate. I put it on the kitchen floor and he licked it clean in three seconds flat.

"Did they give you a time?" I suspected they hadn't. Why would they?

Bud wiped his mouth. "It's not as though they're making an appointment with us. They'll get here when they get here. Gordy's home is the scene of a suspicious death now, that means it'll be treated quite differently. They'll expect the forensics to have been compromised; it's par for the course. They won't like it – I mean, who would? But it happens more often than not, in cases where the coroner determines there's something amiss after the fact. We did what we could, with the tarp. I'm sure we'll be forgiven."

When Marty had all but taken the glaze off it, I shoved my plate into the dishwasher. "I got so wrapped up in those diaries. And they aren't much use at all. I wasn't thinking clearly. I was in Gordy's past, not focused on the present."

"Cait…" Bud's voice held a warning.

I tried to sigh away my frustration with myself. "I know we're going to have to talk to them when they arrive, but in the meantime, I think we should *do* something."

"Like what?"

"How about we make a list of all the people we know have visited Gordy's house recently – people who might have had the opportunity to poison him?"

Bud's expression told me he was thinking about going along with my idea. "It won't be much of a list. There's us, Tom, and that nurse Colin Evans, plus the female nurse who visited – whatever her name was. That's it. And I'm only including Tom because he told us he used to drop in from time to time; if he hadn't told us, I wouldn't have known."

"The female nurse is Oxana. Oxana Kowalchuk. But she's been away on holiday in Hawaii for the past two weeks. The people who delivered his meals should be on the list, too," I added.

"Good point. Hadn't thought of them. There are two of them, right? I've only ever seen them from a distance. Remind me of their names."

"She's Maddie, he's Max," I replied. "We've got the number we use to order Gordy's food, we can reach them that way, I'm sure. Oh heck, that's another thing we haven't done – we haven't cancelled his delivery for this week, have we?"

"They usually arrive around eleven, on Fridays, right?" Bud looked at the clock on the mantlepiece; it has a wonderfully reassuring tick, and sits proudly between the two urns which contain the earthly remains of my parents. It once belonged to my maternal grandmother, and is one of the very few items I own that I remember from my childhood. I feel a wave of emotion whenever I look at our mantelpiece that no one else could imagine; I had a quick, silent word with Mum and Dad, and felt the weight of guilt lift from my shoulders a little.

"They'll get a bit of a shock this week," Bud continued. "We could go down to the road to meet them, talk to them there?"

I nodded, a bit sullenly.

"Cait..."

"I'm not twelve years old." I pouted, reacting to his tone.

Bud rose from the table and put his plate on the kitchen tiles for Marty. "Well then, don't act like you are."

My tummy churned when Bud marched off toward the bathroom, so I petted Marty's head. "I'm such an idiot, Marty. Do you know that? So busy being focused on the wrong thing, sometimes."

Two mournful amber eyes looked up at me and told me Marty knew exactly who and what I was, then he padded off to lick his lips and paws. I ran the dishwasher, and finally ambled in the direction of the bathroom. On the way I gave myself a good talking to.

I stuck my head in to see Bud brushing his teeth with enormous vigor. "I'm sorry. I'll buck up," I said as winningly as possible.

Bud turned, winked, and gave me a frothy smile. "I know you will," he mumbled.

No one official had arrived by the time we wandered along our drive to the road at a little before a quarter to eleven. Bud threw sticks to entertain Marty on the front of our property, while I kept my eyes on the corner, to spot the meal-delivery truck before it turned into Gordy's place. The violently yellow vehicle arrived just a little after eleven, and I flagged it down.

The couple inside looked puzzled, and curious, as they came to a halt on the edge of the roadside ditch. Maddie was looking her usual, slightly dishevelled self – hair in a casual topknot, a sensible jacket, and a lightweight scarf covered with rainbow-colored horses wrapped around her long neck. She dressed like a teen, despite the fact she was well into her thirties – about a decade younger than her companion, Max.

I told them about Gordy's death as simply as I could.

"I'm so sorry to hear that," said Maddie. Her voice told me she meant it. "He was a good age, of course, but failing a bit. We'll miss him, won't we, Max?" Max looked devastated, which surprised me. "We used to chat, and he gave me some very good advice about some investments I was planning to make to ensure this service can remain afloat…and he made a real difference to you, didn't he, Max?"

Tears rolled down Max's cheeks, and Maddie scrambled to find a tissue in the glove box, which she handed to him. As he dabbed at his eyes Max shook his head; he sobbed aloud.

Maddie looked slightly panic-stricken.

"Would you like to come inside for a cup of tea?" I offered; it's my natural response to most emergencies, because I learned from my mother that all Welsh women are genetically programmed to believe that a pot of tea can help solve every problem. I looked around, hoping for some support from Bud, but he was busy trying to stop Marty from racing off along the road – which he knows very well he's not allowed to do.

Maddie looked at her watch, then at me. "That would be lovely, and it's very kind of you, but we have to stick to the schedule, you see. People expect us to arrive at a regular time. Older people can be very set in their ways. They rely upon us."

I knew she was right.

Max blubbed, "He saved me, you know? Saved me. I was on the edge and he helped me more than anyone else." He dissolved into floods of tears again.

Maddie leaned toward me and whispered, "Max was the captain of the Canadian chef team, and he ran a restaurant in Vancouver. Then he…well, it all got a bit much for him. He had a complete breakdown. He told me Gordy was the one who got him into practicing yoga, and that allowed him to control his anxiety better than any medications ever could." She glanced sideways at her companion and leaned closer to my ear. "He met Gordy when he was trying to find a place to live out this way – he wanted somewhere quiet. Never looked back. And now look at him – he created all these meals and menus, he gives his time for next to nothing to prepare and deliver them, and he's got a good catering business on the go too. Marvellous." She forced a smile, then said aloud, "How about I drive, Max? Give you a chance to…you know."

Max nodded, and got out of the truck. Maddie did the same, and they swapped seats.

"We should pay you for Gordy's meals," I shouted. "I'm so sorry we didn't think to phone to cancel. Can someone else make use of them?"

"You don't have to pay," sobbed Max as he struggled with his seatbelt. "Louise will have them. We'll give them to her later."

I nodded, they turned the truck in the entrance to our drive, then I waved them off.

Bud finally released Marty, who decided it probably wasn't worth the effort to run after the truck.

As we made our way back to the house, with Marty prancing around us, his huge tongue hanging out, I recounted to Bud the conversation I'd had.

"Gordy was quite the man, wasn't he?" Bud observed. "Investment advice? Yoga?"

"You're right, he obviously impacted a lot of lives."

"A bit like George Bailey," said Bud as he opened the front door and Marty bounded into the house.

"Who's he?" I asked, taking off my jacket.

Bud's mouth became a small O as he mugged shock. "The famous George Bailey? Oh, Cait, you disappoint me."

I wracked my brain – the name was familiar, but why? Having a photographic memory can be incredibly useful, but sometimes I sort of "misplace" knowledge, and sometimes I never actually possessed it in the first place. But, if George Bailey was famous, I should have known who he was. "Don't tell me," I said, as Bud's eyes glinted playfully. "I'll get it sooner or later."

He headed for the bathroom. "Going to wash the slobber off my hands," he yelled, "call me when the name rings a bell."

Trying to grasp a person's name from my memory became less of a priority when I saw the first of the official vehicles rolling up Gordy's drive.

"There they are," said Bud as he held his clean hands away from an excited Marty; I was towelling his damp fur as best I could. "I'll grab a couple of those grain bars to snack on, and head over to see them."

As I pulled the towel along Marty's tail, which he knows means I've finished with him, I replied, "I thought we could both talk to them."

"I'll throw myself on my sword as far as tossing out the soup is concerned," said Bud quite cheerily, "and I might know some folks on the forensics team anyway," he added.

So might I, I thought. "Well, enjoy yourself, then," was what I said.

Bud kissed the top of my head. "You know it's not about enjoyment, Wife, but it might be better if just one of us is there; no need to completely insert ourselves into the investigation – we just need to know anything that might be useful, in terms of our aim of trying to stay in the loop. Maybe you could make some progress with the diaries, and possibly make a few calls to the people on that list we were talking about?"

I nodded. "I can say I'm looking for remembrances, or stories, to use as part of Gordy's eulogy; that might get people talking. But I think I'll put Tom, and Maddie and Max, at the bottom of the list, for now. Colin Evans might be a good place to start – he seemed quite happy to give me his number at the lawyers' office."

"Great idea. Bye. See you when I see you. Love you most." And Bud was gone.

I dug Colin Evans's number out of my bag and settled down with the phone and a notepad; yes, I can remember a phone conversation when I need to – word for word, if necessary –

but sometimes it's easier to hand a pile of notes to Bud so he can read them for himself.

I couldn't tell if the nurse had given me a cell or landline number, but the fact that my call was answered by Colin's wife suggested I was phoning the family home.

"I'm afraid Colin won't be home until about eight this evening," Ann Evans told me. "Could he call you back then? I'll leave a note for him; I'll have left before he gets home. I'm on nights, you see, he's on days."

For a brief moment I wondered how a marriage could be sustained if the people within it missed seeing each other – awake – for days on end. Bud and I were so fortunate in that respect – with him being retired, and me being able to choose to work either at home, or at the university, at least for the time being.

"That would be most useful, thanks." I took a chance and added, "I'm phoning to talk about Gordy – I know you mentioned at the lawyers' office that you didn't know him well, but I wondered if you had any stories about him you'd like to tell me so I can include them in his eulogy."

I thought it had been a bit odd that someone who claimed to not have known Gordy was the recipient of a personal letter from him, but decided to play gently with Ann Evans, because she struck me as the sort of person who might resist if she felt challenged. I reckoned that being the first person to meet anyone arriving at an emergency department must teach a great number of life lessons, and I suspected Ann would have to be sharply perceptive to be able to tell the difference between someone seeking attention as a route to getting their hands on pain meds to assuage an addiction, and someone in real physical distress requiring rapid triage.

She proved my assumption to be correct when she replied, "I guess you want to know what our letters said, right?"

I decided to be honest. "I'd love to know every word – but having read mine and Bud's, I know Gordy might have included some specifically personal information, or opinions, so I'd be happy with an edited version."

Ann's laugh sounded surprisingly cruel. "Information? No. Opinions? Plenty. Gordy's letter was full of them."

I was more than a little intrigued. "Can you explain what you mean?" I stuck with the direct approach.

I could hear creaking in the Evans household, and pictured Ann settling into a chair. "Colin's a complete addict, and it's all Gordy's fault."

A list of possible pharmaceuticals whizzed through my mind. Had Gordy been peddling drugs of some sort? It seemed highly unlikely.

"Addicted to…?" I didn't want to commit to anything.

Ann's tone was one of surprise. "Church, of course. What did you think?"

"I just wanted to be clear."

Ann tutted. "Even the people Colin works with are starting to mention it. If he's not at church he's talking about it, or thinking about it. I'm happy that he believes, of course, but the church thing has gotten out of hand."

I had no idea where the conversation was going, but decided to follow its trail. "I got the impression you and Colin attended church together. I believe it's the same church attended by Colleen White, and the one where Gordy was once a church warden. Is that correct?"

"It is, and there you have it in a nutshell. Gordy Krantz was the perfect church warden, and Colin wants to be even better than he was. But Gordy didn't have a wife, nor an extended family in the area. He didn't even have a proper job at the time, so he had all day, every day, to do good works for the church. And Colin thinks he can do the same, but he has a demanding profession, and a family. Do you know he hasn't come to visit my parents with me for two years? Two years. They think they've done something to offend him, but it's just the bloody church. Excuse my language."

"That must be difficult," I observed.

"You could say that," replied Ann. She didn't speak for a moment, then said in a softer voice, "I'm so sorry, I didn't mean to…let's just say it's been a trying few days. Gordy's letters haven't helped."

I'd been hoping we'd circle back to them. "In what way?" I tried to sound as innocent as possible.

"Colin's parents used to take him to church, from the time he was an infant. Gordy joined the congregation when Colin was about fifteen – an impressionable age – and Colin found him to be an inspiration. He's told me more than once that he'd been on the cusp of not wanting to accompany his parents to worship, when Gordy's enthusiasm for the community of the parish inspired him. He attended Bible study groups led by Gordy, a youth club overseen by Gordy, threw himself into beautifying the church grounds as a member of working parties organized by Gordy. Honestly, to hear Colin talk sometimes you'd think he was going to church to worship Gordy, not God. Which might be pretty close to blasphemy, but there you have it."

I was still in the dark about the letters, so I gave it another go. "And the letters have exacerbated this?"

"Exactly. Brought it all back to the surface, just as I was beginning to think Colin might be getting a bit of perspective. In his letter to Colin, Gordy asked him to examine his relationship with the church. Examine it? It's his whole life. Now Colin thinks Gordy's been watching him from afar and thinking he's not been pulling his weight. Gordy hasn't even been to church since Colin turned twenty. Not once. It's ridiculous."

"And Gordy's letter to you was…?"

"An insult. He told me I should help Colin find his true path. What on earth does that mean? I let Colin read Gordy's letter to me and he took that as yet another sign that Gordy thought he'd strayed somehow."

"And what do *you* think the letters meant?" I was truly curious.

A sigh. "I honestly don't know. They were ambiguous."

It seemed odd that Bud and I had received such transparently written letters, yet Ann Evans was telling me that Gordy's sentiments in the letters to her and her husband had been quite opaque. Gordy had never struck me as the ambivalent type – you generally got a clear statement of fact or opinion from him.

"Did Gordy have any role in your lives other than years ago, at the church?" I thought it was worth delving.

"Well, I suppose you could say so. Colin saw Gordy quite frequently of late, because he visited him at his home every couple of weeks. But I happen to know it was Gordy who'd encouraged him to go into nursing in the first place."

"Really? Was Colin not convinced it was for him?"

Ann's tone was chilly. "Colin did, his parents didn't. His dad was an accountant, and thought Colin should follow in his footsteps. But Colin's not the type – he thrives with people, not paperwork and figures. He's naturally empathetic, but doesn't take any messing about. He's really found his niche with the home visiting – sees a lot of older folk that way, and he has a high regard for the elders in our community. He just gets a bit…well, it's normal to get frustrated with work at times, isn't it? And he often mentions how some of the people he gets to know on his rounds could be so much better served in terms of their medications if only the doctors who prescribe them understood their lives and lifestyles better."

"You mean if the doctors could take a more holistic approach?" It was a conversation I'd had with Gordy on a few occasions.

"Exactly." Ann's tone told me she was relieved I understood what she, and her husband, meant. "And Colin makes a good point; I see the doctors often enough at the emergency room – they're printing out a prescription before you can blink. People walk out with a bag full of pills and not a lot of oversight about what they do with them. If only there were more nurse practitioners – the ones who can prescribe medications, and other forms of treatment, like doctors do – that would take the strain off the doctors, and allow the nurses more time to be able to listen to the patients."

"And that was something Colin was suggesting?" It was something I'd heard Gordy say over and over again.

"Yes."

"Is Colin thinking of taking the exams to become a nurse practitioner?"

"Oh, I don't know…" Ann's voice broke, with exasperation, I judged. "Sometimes he wants to, then he says he hasn't got the time. Which he hasn't – because of church. And we're back to that again. As soon as he gets home tonight he'll be poring over his laptop working on some project or other. Thanksgiving is proving problematic at the moment; you'd think it would be all about being thankful, but in our church it's all about cliques – one saying Thanksgiving is too late for a harvest service, another insisting that's what Thanksgiving is for. I'd like to throttle the lot of them."

Having seen at first hand the absolute bloodbaths that could result from parochial church council meetings, when I attended them as a child with my father, I sympathized with Ann's point of view. I had a suspicion about what Gordy's two letters to the Evanses meant, but that was on the basis of a pretty focused rant on the part of just one of them. I was about to follow that line of thought, when I realized I really needed to try to find a path to working out if Ann Evans might be a potential poisoner.

"So you and Gordy didn't bond over gardening, or foraging? I know he and I spent a lot of time chatting about plants and so forth."

"Plants? Us? No. We've only got a patch of dead grass at the back of our townhouse and a basket full of weeds hanging at the front door. Why do you ask?" Ann sounded puzzled, but I wished I was looking her in the eye to be better able to assess her true reactions.

"Oh, nothing, really, I just wondered." *Quick, think of something!* "Gordy and Bud used to spend hours talking about plants. He was fascinating to listen to."

"I dare say he was." A harsh tone. "Now I have to go. I've got a list of things to get through before I go to work, one of which is cooking a meal to leave for Colin so he gets some proper food inside him. But it was nice to chat. You won't tell anyone what I've said about Gordy, will you? Especially not when you're talking to Colin. I don't like to speak ill of the dead. You just caught me at a weak moment. And I liked the way you spoke up when we were at the lawyers' office. I like a woman who knows how to take charge."

A surprised "thank you" slipped out before I said, "I really appreciate the time, and yes, if you could ask Colin to phone me later this evening that would be good. I won't say a word. Bye for now."

"Sure, and thanks. Goodbye."

I gave the conversation some thought, and absent-mindedly petted Marty.

Wherever I Lay My Hat

Bud was almost hopping when he lurched through the door. "Bathroom," he shouted as he skidded past me, kicking off his boots and frisbee-ing his hat toward the hat hooks, sending it hurtling against the wall. By the time he was settled on the sofa, I'd put a mug of tea on the table.

"No need to bribe me, I'll tell you everything I know." He grinned, slurped some tea, and grabbed a piece of cake.

"So?" I was agog.

"Nothing much until about an hour ago, then everyone got very excited. Someone found a finger. Skeletal. Human. Pretty close to where we chucked the soup pot – that's how they found it. Then someone else had a poke about and called a general halt to everything; had to get clearances to go any further. I managed a glimpse. Definitely a human skull. Didn't look ancient to me, but what do I know about that stuff. They'll have to check. So the big guns will be in – establish likely age of remains, then get on with examination and extraction. It could be a long job."

"Where exactly did they find the remains?"

"The finger was about thirty metres from the skull. Both within a couple of hundred metres of Gordy's house."

"Possible scattering due to predation?"

Bud nodded. "Likely."

We both sipped our tea in silence, then Bud puffed out his cheeks. "Not something either of us expected, eh?"

I shook my head slowly. "Nope." I looked across at my husband. "Nothing else?" He shook his head. "Nothing interesting before that? You were there a long time."

"Long story, short: I knew a couple of the guys and gals. They allowed me to hang about, out of their way. They even asked a few questions I could help with – about Gordy's habits, lifestyle and so forth. Showed them where the well was, the septic field, main outbuildings. We chatted. Caught up a bit. Guess what? Lyle Green got married, and now has twins. He's on paternity leave. Remember him?"

I smiled. "Leave it to Lyle…and he'll eat it. Good grief that man had an iron stomach. Remember when Richard Park brought in his grannie's kimchi and Lyle scoffed the lot? No idea how he survived that. Good luck to him with twins. Did he marry anyone we know?"

"Yeah, Richard Park."

I chuckled. "Lovely. As much kimchi as Lyle wants, forever. Maybe they'll make their own."

Bud and I reminisced a bit about our time together in the field. I was convinced, as he was, that what had happened up until the discovery of the finger had been a pretty routine – so, relatively boring – forensics examination of a contaminated crime scene. At least he was able to confirm that it *was* now a designated crime scene, which is how the scene of a suspicious death is treated around here. Then, of course, the finger changed everything, and the skull kicked everyone into high gear. I could imagine the rush of adrenaline those discoveries had probably given the team – finding something so remarkable would have had them all in a tizzy of professional delight.

"Does it sound weird if I say I absolutely understand how exciting this must be for them all?" I ventured.

Bud smiled. "Not to me."

"Good. But…all I feel, personally, is a bit sick. This is just far too close to home for me to feel easy about it. I'm struggling to come to terms with the fact that human remains have been found right next door. That's…that's not just me being weird in a different way, is it?"

"Most definitely not. In fact, I'd say that's pretty normal. For you, anyway."

He dodged my playful thump.

I'd settled down a bit, and was pouring more tea when my phone rang. I didn't recognize the local number, but decided I'd answer it anyway – I don't always. "Hello, Cait Morgan."

"What have the forensics people found at Gordy's place?"

The gravelly rasp was unmistakeable. "Hello Louise. How lovely to hear from you," I was determined to observe the niceties. "There's a forensic team at work on Gordy's property, yes. They've been there for some time. But as for what they might have discovered, I couldn't say."

"Word at the feedstore is they've found remains. My question is, what sort of remains?" Louise North's reputation for being nosey and blunt was well-earned.

I tried to sigh away my annoyance at the local rumor mill and replied, "There's been no official word on that, as yet." I wasn't lying – Bud's observations had been anything but official. "Maybe we could exchange information – I could keep you in the loop with what's going on next door, and you could share some stories about Gordy from years gone by I can include in his eulogy. Would you like me to phone you when we hear something?"

"No. But if you want to talk to me about Gordy, bring some buns. Anything with icing. I like iced buns."

I wasn't going to let the chance pass me by. "How about ten, tomorrow morning?"

"How about four this afternoon?"

I looked at the clock – it was gone one-thirty. "Where are you, exactly? Sorry, I don't have your address."

She barked out her street address as though I should have known it all along.

I was surprised that she also lived on Red Water Mountain Drive. "Oh, we're really neighbors – we live on the same street."

"Yes" – she used the sort of sing-song tone reserved for speaking to two-year-olds – "we do indeed. With a mountain between us, which is just fine by me. See you at four. Don't be late." And she was gone.

I looked at Bud. "I've been summoned. I have to make a sacrifice of iced buns to the goddess Louise North at four, sharp, today. If I'm not back by six, call the Mounties."

Bud snorted tea.

I was quite annoyed that the big forensic vans were arriving just as I was leaving; I had to allow enough time to drive to the bakery to get some buns, then to find Louise's house. I hadn't been aware that our street continued in that area at all, though it's far from unusual for streets and roads to have several parts around here, none of which join up due to rivers, streams, and the odd mountain.

Suitably supplied with buns I took the almost non-existent turning off the main road that was Red Water Mountain Drive, part two, and wound up our mountain, which was more precipitous on Louise's side than on ours. There wasn't a made road, just a track like a driveway, but I eventually arrived at what had to be Louise's house; there were no other homes on the track, and I'd reached the end. The structure wasn't set back very far and looked as though someone had begun to deconstruct it. The two-storey home was a drab green-grey, which might have been brighter when it was fresh, but was now anything but. The siding was in a pitiful state, and there was a deck with a partially collapsed wooden railing. The roof had a massive, shredded, blue tarp draped over it, and the brick chimney was only half-there. Surrounded by broken, rusted detritus, and some now-ragged fencing, it looked like the sort of place where no one lived, and about which no one cared. Incongruously, a massive satellite dish was attached at an acute angle on the far side of the house; I could see a bird's nest on top of it.

I didn't pull into the stubby, unkempt drive, because Louise's own vehicle – an algae-covered, ancient people carrier – was already all but filling it. She met me at the open front door before I could even knock, and almost smiled as she invited me in. Having managed to become accustomed to Gordy's home, I steeled myself for a similar type of set-up inside Louise's place, but I still wasn't prepared for what I encountered.

Gordy's house had been immaculate compared with Louise's, which reeked of decay. I tried to breathe through my mouth, which helped a little, then I got upstairs to her "sitting room", where the smell was worse. The "open concept area" was stuffed with large, ancient furnishings, and the kitchen counters were covered with pots, pans, and dishes, none of which – I suspected – had seen water or washing-up liquid for some time. I was horrified, and immediately wondered how I was going to be able to get away with declining any type of refreshment.

Louise had returned to being her usual unsmiling self by the time she urged me to sit on a sofa I suspected might have been the original source of penicillin. I couldn't imagine how a person could live the way she did, but I tried my best to not let my horror show. I sat, and felt a spring dig into my rear. I shuffled forward a little, and perched.

Louise opened the box of buns I'd just handed her, plucked one out, and proceeded to chomp into it. I was glad she didn't even seem to consider offering one to me; her gnarled fingers, and vein-knotted hands, made me think of monkey paws, and I couldn't help but notice her chipped, blackened fingernails.

"What was it, exactly, that they found at Gordy's? And where, exactly?" Louise talked through the mouthful of bun.

I knew I couldn't give away Bud's inside information. "They're trying to determine the exact nature of the remains. There were more team members, with special equipment, arriving when I left to come here." I did my best to not lie; Bud says I'm a dreadful liar. Which is good, under normal circumstances.

"It'll be human," sprayed from my host's lips.

"Why are you so certain?" I was genuinely curious.

Louise's eyes became mere slits. "No reason."

"Oh, come on – you know something. If the remains are human, who do you think it is? I think you know who it is."

Louise's mouth curled from its normal, sullen, resting place to a straight line. I guessed that was her version of a grin. "I don't."

"Really?"

"Really." She pulled another bun from the box and her eyes devoured it before she licked the icing with the tip of her tongue.

Everything about her body language told me she wasn't going to budge; I told myself to focus on my reason for visiting – to try to identify a potential poisoner – so I could get away as soon as possible. I cast my eyes around the room searching for something I could comment upon to break the ice, and noticed Louise shared Gordy's desire to own as many books as possible.

"You're a big reader," I said.

She didn't follow my gaze. "Gordy used to make fun of all my books – trashy, he called them. Don't think he'd ever cracked the spine of anything beyond a plant encyclopedia."

I chuckled inwardly as I thought of the thousands of spines Gordy must have cracked over the decades – then I shuddered a bit, because I hate the thought of a book-spine being cracked at all.

I spotted a black-and-white photograph in a rough-hewn cedar frame. I got up to take a look.

"Are you in this?" I couldn't see anyone who looked remotely like Louise.

"Mmm…" She nodded again, then gulped and added, "Second from the left."

I peered more closely. The person who was second from the left in the photo was a man. I pointed at the person and said, "This is you?"

"Other left," she spluttered. "Next to Gordy."

I looked again. The young woman who was second from the right was gorgeous: long, flowing hair; a petite, lithe figure encased in a revealing swimsuit; arms held aloft above a joyous smile; total devil-may-care body language. The man next to her was also lithe, but muscular too, and clean shaven. If she hadn't told me it was him, I'd never have recognized it as being Gordy – I'd only seen him up until his teen years in the photo album we'd found at his house…by the time this photo had been taken he'd filled out. He looked so different from the hunched, bearded, old man I had known. Age changes our bodies so much. I decided I needed to choose my words carefully.

"When was this taken?" I hoped it was a good way of avoiding suggesting she'd aged poorly.

"Fifty years ago. Roughly. That was the day we met. Me and Gordy. Big party up at Harrison Hot Springs. Summer. A golden day." Her voice rasped, but it was tinged with something else. Regret?

I studied the woman shoving a bun into her face, and could see the ghost of the girl she'd been. How had that vibrant, young thing become this husk? I know ageing's a natural process, and I'm all for allowing our experiences to show in our hair, skin, and wrinkles, but Louise seemed to have had all the joy sucked out of her, with anger and spite replacing it. How had that happened?

"You all seem to be having a fine time," I said, hoping it would lead to recollections of happier days.

"All stoned, of course," she said. I tried to take the surprising remark in my stride, but must have failed miserably because she cackled at me, mercilessly, through bun crumbs. "Kids these days think they invented 'BC bud'. We were smoking it long before most of their parents were even thought about, let alone born. Good that it's legal, now. It could mess with your life if you got caught with it back then."

I wasn't sure what to say; my interest was in Gordy, not her, nor the social history of marijuana, BC's largest export crop – legal or not. But I reckoned it was best to take the lead I'd been given, and follow it. "Did you and Gordy spend a lot of time together, after you'd met?" I wondered if she'd answer me.

Louise North's hooded eyes glinted as she studied me, her grimy fingers rolled a tiny ball of icing, which she popped onto the end of her tongue. It disappeared like an insect into a frog's mouth. She chewed, but said nothing. Then she tilted her head and asked, "What are you after? I guess you want to make a good job of Gordy's eulogy, fair enough. But that's not why you're here. What else did that letter of his ask you to do? Did it mention me at all?"

Again, I was uncertain about how to respond. Louise might be aged, she might be filthy, but her eyes, words, and manner, suggested an acute intelligence, and not a little suspicion. I decided to go with "guardedly open".

"Yes, I want to do a good job with the eulogy, but I'm genuinely interested in knowing more about Gordy's life, too."

"Haven't seen him to talk to in thirty years. What could I possibly tell you? I heard he got God, at one point. Guess he had to say sorry at last."

Odd. "But you did know him well, prior to that?" I pressed.

"You're a psychologist, right? A criminal psychologist?"

I nodded.

"I looked you up on your university's website." She waved toward a table in the middle of the room; it was a complete shambles, but I could just about see a corner of a laptop on it – I assumed the satellite dish still worked. "Quite the woman, aren't you? I like that you research the victims not the serial killers – they get all the attention. Time someone was bothered about the people they hurt."

I was tempted to explain that wasn't, in fact, what my research was about, but suspected I'd get sidetracked, so said, "Thanks. It's fascinating. But I'm more interested in hearing about you and Gordy." I considered mentioning Gordy's diaries, but decided against it.

Louise sucked her lips until it looked as though she had no teeth at all, then she let out a noise halfway between a bark and an oath. "He's gone. No one cares. Ask me whatever you want. I'll be gone soon enough, too, then there'll be no one left to remember anyway."

I felt like I'd found a treasure chest, but didn't have the key. I really didn't have any specific questions in mind, but thought it worth starting with something I did know a little about. "Gordy was from Saskatchewan – did he ever tell you about his time there, as a young man? Before he came to BC."

Louise shook her head. "Not a big talker. More a man of action, was Gordy. I met him just after I arrived in BC from the States. He was a grower and a businessman by then. Had that nursery thing going with Terry Dumas. Knew how to have fun, too. That's how we met – he'd given a few people a ride to Harrison in his truck. He loved his truck. I can remember how it gleamed in the sun that day."

Louise's eyes were either watering, or she was crying; they were so rheumy it was hard to tell which, and the rest of her face was a heavily wrinkled mask. I pressed on. "Were you close?"

Louise's hooded lids closed, and she licked her purple lips. "You could say."

"I don't want to say so if it's not true."

"We understood each other. I didn't know anyone when I got here, which was why I came. Guess I blew off a bit of steam at first. And Gordy knew lots of ways to do that. Got a job. Got a basement suite in Mission. Finally had my own money, and made my own choices."

"What job did you do?"

Louise's eyelids slid open. "Nursing. Canada wanted nurses back then." She didn't elaborate.

"You were one among many Americans moving to Canada in the early 1970s, I suppose. For various reasons."

Louise sat back in her armchair. I wondered if it was more comfortable than the one I'd had to return to perch upon – I doubted it could be. She chewed an invisible something as she thought; I could almost see the wheels turning.

"I came here because I didn't agree with what my country was doing. I'd already got into some trouble for saying so. If I'd stayed longer I'd have gotten into more trouble. Someone I felt a great deal for pointed that out to me, and she was right. I left for Canada soon after. In a hurry."

"Before you acquired a police record?"

"Uh huh."

"Have you ever been back?"

Louise's look was disdainful. "Why would I? This is my home. Canada took me in. I'm Canadian now. Worked, paid taxes, took up my citizenship. I ain't going nowhere. Came here, never left."

"You haven't been out of the country on vacation, ever?" I wondered what it would be like to not travel.

"Everything I want is here. Besides, travel costs money, and I've always been on a tight budget. Except when Gordy treated me. We went to Kelowna together, for a whole week, and stayed in a hotel overlooking the lake. Only time I've been anywhere but a motel. It was a good week." Her dark eyes glittered when she spoke, and I was left in little doubt that she and Gordy hadn't had separate rooms. I struggled with the idea, then set it aside.

So, there'd been a Rachel, and Louise in Gordy's life. I wondered if any of the naked women in Gordy's Polaroids had been Louise. "Is that generally known? Not that you spent a week at a hotel with Gordy, but that you two were an item?"

Louise's laugh cracked like lightning. "An item? Jeez, are you some sort of Oldey Timey matron? We met in the seventies. All hope for peace and love might have vanished in the jungles of Vietnam, but there was weed, and booze, and contraception, and as much sex as you wanted. As you can see in that photograph, I didn't always look like this, and I didn't always live like this, either. Before I broke my back, I could keep house, chop wood for the fire, look after myself. I was the one who worked and saved up to buy these five acres off Gordy, then I damned near built this place alone. You probably wouldn't believe how much I did, and all while I was nursing, too."

I hadn't imagined her pronounced stoop was as a result of an injury. As I realized I'd made some grossly inaccurate assumptions about Louise, I filed away the fact she'd also bought five acres off Gordy – which meant he must have bought twenty-five to begin with.

"How did you break your back? It must have been a difficult thing to recover from." I thought about my own challenging recuperation after the incident in Budapest, and wondered how I'd have coped if I'd not recovered as well as I had.

Louise sucked the end of a grubby thumb. "I was up a tree, fell out. One of my fellow nurses came looking for me the next day. Not a lot of people had cellphones, back then. They still don't work here, anyhow. I was fifty. In my prime. Ended up as a patient in my own hospital for months, which was odd, then I came back to this place, but I couldn't do much for myself after that. Things kind of slid past me."

I scanned the room. "No one could help out?"

"Didn't ask. Then…then it was too big a job to expect anyone to help, so I couldn't ask." Her voice had softened, and my heart went out to her.

"Bud and I could help. Even now. If you wanted, we could come in and fix up a few things for you; help you have a bit of a clear out."

She roared back at me, "I don't need no help. And I don't want any of my stuff cleared out. It's mine."

Bud's mentioned that, sometimes, I can be a bit too pushy when I'm trying to be helpful. I grappled with how to retrieve the situation. "I'm sorry, Louise, I didn't mean to offend you. Now – is there anything I can tell people about the Gordy you knew in his eulogy?"

Louise seemed to calm down a little. "He gave me my first dog. Other than being a nurse, the best thing you can do in life is be with dogs."

I looked around. "Do you have a dog now?" I hadn't seen any signs of one.

"Lily died three and a half months ago. She was the last to go. Born last of her litter, so I guess that's right."

"What was she? We have a black Lab, Marty." Maybe that would help.

"Golden retriever. Blonde, really, almost white – hence the name. Sweet character. Bred from champions." Louise's tone was almost warm.

"Was she your only dog?"

That cackle again. "Had four at one time. Worked up to four, then down to none. They come, you love them, they go. Like people. I can show you photos, if you like."

I nodded, wondering if I was doing the right thing. Louise pushed herself out of her seat and made her way, slowly, to a shelf unit sitting on the uneven floor, precariously balanced against an uneven wall. Heaps of books, magazines, directories, old bits of packaging, and any number of knick-knacks were strewn on every shelf but, even so, she turned with a cracked, and heavy-looking album in her hands almost instantly. I jumped up and took it from her – which she allowed me to do, retaking her seat. I stood beside her so she could turn the pages as I looked at the photos.

The next ten minutes or so was filled with a stream of uncharacteristically enthusiastic chatter by Louise about each of her four dogs, their entire pedigrees – both lines – and me having to "Oh" and "Ah" at a gazillion pictures of each creature from their heart-achingly cute-puppy stage, to the time when age was displayed in their gait and on their muzzles. Louise's passion for her dogs still burned; I wondered how lonely she must be without a canine companion after what appeared to be the better part of thirty years of having had at least one.

As Louise continued flapping pages, I caught sight of a photo sticking out behind yet another shot of Lily's happy puppy-face. It was almost sepia-toned, but in the way that photos from the 1970s lose their color. I could only see a head, but it was definitely Gordy, with his characteristic buzz-cut, and he was with another man with what could only be described as being "a good head of hair" – another giveaway that the photo was from the seventies.

"Who was that, in that photo with Gordy?"

Louise stuffed it further behind the picture of her dog. "Nothing more for you to see," she said. The miserable Louise returned the second she snapped the album closed.

I took a chance. "Was that Terry Dumas, by any chance?"

"Uh-huh. They were doing real well, then he wanted to change everything. Gordy said he didn't have the stomach for a fight. Moved on, he said."

I was intrigued. "Did Terry Dumas buy Gordy out of the K. Dumas business?"

Louise glared at me, and clutched the album to her concave chest. "I don't know what they agreed on, but Gordy was out of the business. I guess he must have gotten some money from the company, somehow, but I never knew the details."

I decided that – after dinner – I'd plough on through Gordy's diaries to see what else I could find out about how the business had developed.

"Am I right in thinking that – as long as I tell everyone that Gordy was a kind man – you'd be alright with me saying you have special memories of him, and will always be grateful that he introduced you to a love of dogs?"

Louise shrugged. "Kind? Wouldn't say that. Determined, yes. Knew how to live life, yes. Kind?" She shrugged again. "There was the dog."

"And how did the gift of a dog happen, exactly?"

"After they let me out of the hospital, he showed up here one day with a puppy he said he'd found at the side of the road. Asked if I could look after it. I protested a bit – because I was having a hard enough time looking after myself – but the little thing was so damned cute and fluffy, once I held it, I couldn't let it go. That was Prince. My Prince. Handsome Prince. You saw him in the photos. Good-looking boy. Lived to be sixteen, a very good age for a Lab-mix. Only non-pedigree dog I ever had, and the one who lived the longest. I guess that says something for a mix, eh? Certainly says something for the bit of Chow Chow that was in him, anyways. Strange thing, a blue tongue, right? What's yours? Pure or mix?"

"Marty? Pure, but not posh. I think two families with Labs put them together and he was part of the resulting litter. No papers, but we love him anyway. I could bring him for a visit if you like. Or you could come to us and give him a good old petting."

Louise almost smiled. "Not the same when they ain't your own." Her tone was hollow and echoed with loss. "But, yes, you can say that about Gordy and my Prince. Folks won't know that. They'll know about my dogs, but not why I got started with them. That all?"

I felt I was being dismissed, and I hadn't really got any further with delving into possible suspects for Gordy's poisoning. I couldn't see Louise as a candidate. I gave it one last shot.

"Did Gordy ever pass on his love of plants to you?"

Louise balanced the album on the arm of her chair and pushed herself to a standing position – yes, I was most definitely being dismissed.

She cackled again. "Other than showing me how to grow great weed no, he didn't. I wouldn't know one end of a geranium from another – as you can see if you look around outside. My land ain't the way it is because I can't work it any longer, it's the way it is because I don't care to. If it's green and it's growing, and it doesn't block the driveway, it's fine by me."

"But your tree-climbing accident…what were you doing up a tree if you weren't there to work on it somehow?"

"If you're gonna hang yourself, and you choose to do it from the branch of a tree, you have to climb the tree first. Just my luck I didn't even get the rope around my neck, instead I fell and broke my back. Now goodbye. Shut the door on your way out. I'm not gonna do those stairs again today."

I was rather glad I was leaving, because I had no idea how to respond to the fact that Louise North had just told me that she'd once tried to kill herself.

Dinner, But No Candlelight

After I'd driven the winding road up our side of the mountain – the hemlocks and red cedars flanking my route, rising black against the sunset-flamed sky – I passed Gordy's drive, and was not terribly pleased to see the place alight with arc lamps. It wasn't going to be a restful dinner time at home.

Marty greeted me as I kicked off my shoes inside the front door, and Bud called from the kitchen. "Welcome home, Wife."

I immediately felt safe, and much more relaxed. "That smells exotic – for you. What is it?" I could pick up the tang of garlic, and something spicy.

"Red Thai curry. Opened a jar of the stuff. With chicken and orzo, because – as we both know – I can't cook rice."

Bud was right; no matter how hard he tried he just couldn't cook rice without burning it, or producing a tasteless, sticky mass. Neither of us had any idea what he did wrong, it just didn't work out for him. Ever. On the other hand, he was really good at cooking orzo – so we'd agreed that orzo would be "his" rice.

My mouth was already watering as I lifted the lids on the pots to check on progress. I got my hand smacked twice – lovingly, of course – and I also got a pat on the bum to encourage me to get out of the kitchen. I didn't need much encouraging – I wanted to change my clothes and have a good wash after having been at Louise's place.

"How long until it's ready?" I asked, petting Marty who was being a very good boy.

"Ten minutes or so. I just put the orzo on to boil."

"Okay – I'm going to have a quick shower and I'll pull on some comfies. Back in ten!" Why only wash my hands and face when my entire body felt...greasy?

I presented myself at the table with a playful salute, and an offer to open a bottle of wine. Thus, we sat enjoying an excellent meal, accompanied by a delightful blended red from the Okanagan, with the entire room illuminated by the crime-scene lights filtering through the curtains – which had only ever been meant as decorative, rather than functional, since the window looked out onto, basically, nothing but our natural surroundings.

Oddly, it was a lovely meal. I shared the information I'd gleaned from Louise. Bud responded in all the right places with interest, surprise, and absolute disbelief. Then he told me about everything I'd missed – which wasn't much, because he'd been banned from being anywhere near the crime scene, and he'd been able to see very little, even when using the binoculars, or walking Marty around our property – which he'd done three times.

I congratulated him on having done the best he could, under the circumstances, but we both felt the sting of human remains having been discovered next door to us, and our not being able to find out anything about...well, anything.

"We're no closer to having any suspicions about even one person wanting to kill Gordy, are we?" Bud looked pretty miserable – I wasn't sure if that was because of a lack of suspects or because he'd just drained the bottle of wine.

"No. To be honest, everyone I've talked to so far was – in some way, shape, or form – saved by Gordy. He'd inspired them, encouraged them, connected them with people who could help them fulfill their dreams or, in Louise's case, he'd given her a reason to get up every day – a puppy. If he hadn't been around..." A penny dropped. "Oh, George Bailey...from the movie *It's a Wonderful Life*. Of course – that's why you mentioned him; he changed people's lives for the better. That's odd – I didn't even know I knew the name of Jimmy Stewart's character."

Bud chuckled. "Good job, Wife – knew you'd get it eventually. Now – onwards. So, the only questionable person might be Terry Dumas," he said, then sipped his remaining wine as sparingly as possible.

I agreed. "But he's dead."

"His wife's not. Might she want Gordy out of the way for some reason? She was the only one who asked a question about her letter at the lawyers' office. Might she be trying to hide something?"

I emptied my glass. "She's top of the list of people I want to talk to next. I thought I'd give her a ring tonight, to try to set up a coffee date for tomorrow."

Bud nodded, swirling his glass, staring into space. "Should you be spending some time at that new office of yours? I know they expect you to be doing research, rather than teaching, but – you know – don't they sort of think you'll do that *there*?"

"I can't – the internet access is terrible. They're working on it, but I *am* researching, here. I'm researching a person's life and trying to identify someone who might have poisoned him. I have to go where the research takes me – Gordy's probably a victim, after all. I might find a new wrinkle in my methodology that can be replicated somewhere down the line."

Bud tried to raise just one eyebrow. It never works. "You have the most amazing ability to justify doing whatever you want to do, rather than doing what you should. You know that, right?"

I adopted a heroic pose, with my hands on my hips. "It's my superpower."

Bud shook his head, looked down at Marty's upturned face and said, "What can we do with her, boy, eh?" Marty perked up at the attention and eyed the plates on the table. "Not for you, boy. Too spicy. Come on, I'll get you a proper treat."

Bud rose and headed for the cupboard, with Marty an inch behind him. I cleared the table, pushed everything into the dishwasher and said, "We could risk an Irish coffee after that wine, couldn't we? Dessert in a mug?"

Bud grinned as he petted Marty's head. "I'll put the kettle on. You get comfy and choose something to watch on TV. I know you want to."

I punched the air. "There's a new Scandi-Noir series – they dropped a whole season. I need to vegetate for a couple of hours."

"You and your grisly serial killers. You know they're digging up a body just the other side of that fence out there, right this minute? How can you want to watch that stuff? Isn't there something a bit lighter we could try?"

I gave it a moment's thought. "Cozy copper who loves country music in New Zealand? Woman who used to do PR now sleuthing in the Cotswolds?"

Bud sighed. "Okay, serial killers it is. I'll get the coffee sorted."

"And I'll line up the detective with the dysfunctional family, all of whom wear fifteen layers of woollies. I bet he'll have to drive miles across a frozen wasteland – which we'll see from a bird's-eye point of view – to talk to someone face to face for ten seconds when he could have texted instead." I was looking forward to it already, then remembered I'd planned to phone Janice Dumas. "Oh poo, I need to call the Dumas woman – I'll do it in my office and I'll be right back for that coffee."

"Don't be too long," called Bud as I fake-skated along the hallway's hardwood floor in my socks.

I found Janice Dumas's cell number quickly and dialled her from our house phone. A woman answered, but it wasn't Janice; the person at the other end didn't have any haughtiness in her voice.

"Hello, could I speak to Janice, please?" I asked.

"Who's calling?"

"Cait Morgan. I met Janice in relation to Gordy Krantz's death." It was true, but sounded odd.

"Oh, hello, Cait. It's Maddie speaking, Madelaine Dumas. You know…I deliver – sorry, delivered – Gordy's meals. Janice is my mom, but she's gone to bed early – bit of a headache."

I was speechless for a moment – which doesn't happen often. "Oh. Maddie. I didn't know you were related to Janice." I paused, gathering my thoughts. "I…I wanted to come to have a chat with your mother – was hoping to drop in tomorrow morning. Would that be okay, do you think?" There was no immediate response. "It would be lovely to chat about Gordy with you, too. I have to give his eulogy, you see, so I'm trying to gather stories about him." I forced myself to shut up; Bud's mentioned that, on occasion, I have been known to babble.

"Sure, I don't see why not. There's nothing on her calendar – her day at the spa was yesterday, so you might have a chance! But I should warn you, we're in a bit of a mess because they're filming a movie here. Not in the house, but out near the stables and paddock. They all park off site, but there are loads of vehicles coming and going. Bit of a gong show – but Mom calls it a 'good little earner'. I'll be here too – but I have to leave around eleven-thirty. Would ten work for you? Of course, I'm hoping Mom will feel better in the morning – she gets these headaches, but they pass. If she's not, I'll call you. When would you set out to get here?"

"Depends where 'here' is," I replied; cellphone numbers don't give away anything helpful.

Maddie rattled off the address, which I knew was on the Surrey/Langley border, out where the acreages allowed for horses to be kept, and the houses could either be stunning, or horrendous McMansions. I closed by telling Maddie I'd probably leave home around nine, and that I was looking forward to the meeting, and I was…because I'd never been inside one of the multi-million-dollar properties in that neck of the woods, and there are few things I like more than a good old snoop around a posh house.

When I'd plopped onto the sofa, snuggled up to Marty, and grabbed my coffee, I said to Bud, "So, it turns out that Maddie, who used to deliver Gordy's meals, is Maddie Dumas, Janice and Terry Dumas's daughter. Which gives me a couple of things to dwell on as food for thought: first, maybe they aren't a particularly close mother and daughter, because it was evident that Janice hadn't told Maddie about Gordy's death at any point between the meeting at the lawyers' office and Maddie arriving here to deliver Gordy's meals – which is odd, to say the least; and, secondly, now – at last – there's someone with a possible reason to have something to hide, and an opportunity to put a poisonous plant in Gordy's food…Maddie. I'm going there tomorrow, for coffee."

Bud stared. "Maddie Dumas, eh? Okay. Yes. Right. Well, just make sure you enjoy the coffee cake at a potential poisoner's house, Wife. Now take me to Iceland, or Finland, or wherever it is we're off to next, where no doubt horribly mutilated bodies are waiting to be discovered by a group of cops who'd be sent packing in real life, because they're simply too dumb to live."

"It's Iceland, and – if you recall – two of them didn't survive in that last Norwegian series we watched."

"Point proven." Bud clicked the remote, but I didn't get a chance to sink into something mindless, because the blessed phone rang.

As soon as I'd established it was Colin Evans, returning my call after his shift at the hospital, I told Bud I'd talk to the man in my office.

Once I'd settled at my desk I was able to focus on Colin.

"What can I do for you, Cait? Ann's note said you wondered if I had anything I could tell you for Gordy's eulogy, is that right?"

I knew it was as good a place as any to start. "That would be wonderful. Did you know him well?"

It was like the floodgates had opened; to say that Colin gushed about Gordy would be an understatement. After a few minutes I understood what Colin's wife had meant when she said she wondered who it was Colin worshipped more – God or the memories he had of Gordy being the best possible thing that ever happened to St. Peter's church. I let him rattle on about a great many specific interactions he'd had with Gordy when he was in his teens. Overall, I got the impression that Gordy had put his heart and soul into making the church as vibrant as possible, creating all sorts of channels for connectivity between the congregation and the local community. It turned out that the youth club Ann had been so dismissive of had begun as an outreach to the homeless; the Bible study group had also provided literacy-building sessions for local adults who needed them; the church hall had been all but rebuilt during Gordy's time there, and substantially extended. It was clear Gordy had completely shifted the role of the church in the community by spearheading new initiatives, all of which Colin was now trying to revive – singlehandedly, by his own account. It sounded as though he had his work cut out for him, but he was evidently loving every minute of it, and feeling vitalized because of it.

All the time he'd been speaking, Colin Evans had been telling me about a Gordy I felt I knew, and of how inspiring he'd been;

there were so many parts of what he was telling me I could use for a eulogy, that I knew at last I'd found someone who'd really liked Gordy.

When Colin drew breath I asked, "Do you have any photos of some of these events at the church that I could use at his memorial?"

Colin sounded delighted. "Sure. Of course, no one had a camera in their phone back then, but there was usually someone with a real camera at the big get-togethers. I'll dig out some snaps for you, for sure. Happy to do it. Anything else?"

I pondered how best to ask. "Your wife suggested Gordy had encouraged you to follow your dream to enter the nursing profession. Was that typical of him?"

"I bet she did – and I bet she told you I've been thinking about going back to school to get better qualifications, and that Gordy's recently been urging me to do that too, eh?"

"She might have mentioned it in passing." I hoped that was a neutral enough reply.

Colin sighed. "I've seen you several times, and I know you were the one who set it up for nurses to visit Gordy in his home, Cait, but I don't know you real well and I don't want all my personal business talked about at Gordy's memorial, so let's keep this focused on him, okay? He helped me when I was a kid, then again when I had to stand up to my father who wanted me to do what he did, not what I wanted to do. When I connected with Gordy again, about eight months ago, he was the one who suggested Ann and I should try counselling together, because we've just been growing further and further apart over the years. Our shifts and rotas mean we don't get much time together, and it's tough to keep your life zinging along when you're both tired all the time. But that's not something I want folks knowing. Gordy was a good man. Gordy was supportive whenever he could be. He understood the way a church can make a real difference in the community when it reaches out into it, and doesn't just end up being a building where people go to pray and bake cakes for each other. That's my vision, too. I hope one day Ann will share it. And I think I can be a better professional by gaining my nurse practitioner qualifications – I want to be the best I can be in all parts of my life, and I hope my wife wants that for me too. But not everyone needs to know that. Okay?"

Colin had worked himself up a bit, and I'd let him run with it. I hate interrupting people when they might tell me something interesting. I swirled a pen on the desk in front of me as I asked, "Do you happen to know why Gordy left the church?" I hoped he'd answer.

"I was young at the time, and blissfully unaware of all the politicking that goes on. As church warden myself, these days, I know only too well how overwhelming that aspect of church life can become. From my point of view, back then, he just simply stopped being there. No one said anything, there was no great blow-up mentioned, and when I asked where he was, I was told it was none of my business. So I can't say, sorry."

"Could you put a date on when he left? I'm trying to build a timeline of his life, you see."

"Ah, that I might be able to do, but I'd need to give it a bit of thought. I really have to eat my meal now, if you don't mind. Can I get an email address for you and I'll write when I work it out? Or how about I text you, on your cell, okay?"

"A text to this number would be great, thanks."

We disconnected, and I joined Bud and Marty – both of whom were asleep in front of the TV. They were battling over who could snore the loudest.

Home On The Range

Bud and I are more comfortably off than I'd ever expected us to be, since a professorship isn't a golden ticket to a high tax bracket. However, the Dumas family must have been rolling in it, if their home was anything to go by. Yes, I know a lot of people are "house rich, spending-money poor" but I got the impression Janice Dumas could afford to splurge on anything that took her fancy.

My GPS had delivered me to the Dumas property without any problems, and Maddie had been right in her assessment of there being a bit of a gong show atmosphere there – golf carts were shuttling along the wide, straight driveway as fast as they could go, and they all seemed to be carrying people who'd stepped out of the Wild West of the 1880s…which I guessed was the period of the movie they were filming at the Dumas's barn and stables. The magnificent red-and-white building made what I could only imagine would be a too-fancy backdrop for whatever was going on, but I could see certain areas had been "dressed" to look more decrepit than they really were, and a gaggle of people were busy throwing straw over all sorts of items that would be anachronistic in an historical movie.

I parked as directed by a young man with a headset and tablet, and rang the main house's doorbell – shaped like a horse's head – and waited. The house itself was large and imposing, but wasn't in any way an ugly monstrosity. Its all-white exterior and red roof were delightful, and I had high hopes for the interior.

A short, bald, emaciated man invited me inside, in French, then asked me to wait in the massive sitting room that led away from the entry hall to the right. I didn't sit, I didn't dare; I was afraid to disturb anything. The magazines on the side tables were stacked in perfect alignment, and each tasseled scatter cushion – of which there were many on the four, cream, overstuffed sofas – had one of those dents in the top that tells you that whoever placed it did so with a final flourish of a karate chop into the center of the top edge. Delicate orchids arched in perfect clusters in wide porcelain planters, voile at the windows softened the light so everything glowed, and even the air seemed to have been specially imported from some exotic locale, its light fragrance telling me everything was as luxuriously exclusive as it appeared. It was possibly the least horsey place I'd ever seen, until Maddie wandered in, decked out in quite grubby riding attire. She welcomed me with open arms.

"Mom's on her way down. I mustn't let her see me in here dressed like this – stinky horse-clothes are *interdit!*"

Having now been greeted in French, twice, the penny dropped that the Dumas family name had probably originated somewhere in French-speaking Canada, but thought I'd check.

"Nice to see you again," I replied. "Is the Dumas family from Quebec, originally?"

Maddie laughed. "Dad's father was, but Mom's from Manitoba – the fifth daughter of a Ukrainian immigrant family that also had four boys in it. On balance I prefer Dumas to Kowalchuk, because I think I'd get tired of always having to spell it."

"Ha! Small world. One of Gordy's nurses is named Kowalchuk. Oxana. I hate to do the 'Do you know Dave from British Columbia?' thing, but do you know her?"

Maddie rolled her eyes. "Aunt Oxana, you mean? Mom's sister. We used to laugh that between the two of us we were keeping Gordy alive, in more ways than one. Okay – excuse me – I'm just going to change, and I'll be right back. Edouard is getting some coffee sorted. He won't speak English to you, though he could if only he chose to. Lovely guy, nonetheless. Been with us forever. Used to be a jockey for Dad's horses. Okay – you hang on here for Mom, I'll be right back."

A wonderful aroma wafted from beyond the staircase, and my saliva glands kicked in. I turned away, trying to tell my mouth to stop watering, then heard a voice behind me.

"Ah, Cait, how delightful of you to take the time to visit." This sentiment was followed by a trilling laugh which immediately grated on me. I hoped Janice Dumas wasn't going to punctuate our chat with a constant stream of joyless pseudo-jocularity. I steeled myself.

"Hello, Janice. I hope your head's better this morning." I was being polite – I really didn't care.

Janice looked so confused that I knew her "headache" had been some sort of ruse – but I couldn't be sure if she'd been avoiding me, or had been lying to her daughter. Either way the cat wasn't just out of the bag, it was running around the room doing cartwheels.

Janice deflected and responded with a vague, "I'm just fine, thanks." She added, "I thought we'd take coffee in the kitchen – less formal for a tête-à-tête." Her fake laugh tinkled, her bracelets jangled, and I groaned inwardly.

Truth be told, I was quite relieved we wouldn't be drinking coffee in the sitting room, because it meant I wouldn't have to crush a perfectly puffed cushion, or be terrified I might spill something on the cream furnishings. However, when we'd crossed half an acre of hardwood flooring and entered the gargantuan kitchen my heart sank again. A row of dizzyingly high stools were set against a marble-topped island – which was the size of an *actual* island, where an *actual* community could live – and I'm not good on barstools…which isn't for the lack of years of practice at quite a number of bars. What those years have taught me is that there's no elegant, or safe, way for me to hoist myself up onto one, I'm just not built for it.

I hoped we'd be heading for either the table with eight chairs surrounding it – each sporting a perilously balanced scatter cushion – or the sofas arranged in front of the log fire roaring in the fireplace replete with their own cushions; I surmised the cushion budget alone for the Dumas household would represent a small fortune. I was pleased when Janice made a beeline for the sofas, where coffee and pastries had been set up on the expansive – and probably expensive – coffee table…which might well have been large enough to hide an entire coffee plantation beneath it.

I sat on the sofa timidly, then realized I was still sinking; the upholstery might have looked plump and firm, but it yielded beneath my backside quite significantly. It was an interesting feeling; not unpleasant, just unexpected.

The crockery was exquisite, and the pastries looked as though they'd been snatched from a Parisian patisserie's countertop. And the smell? Heaven. I immediately spotted a *pain au chocolate* that I could swear was winking at me with its nuggets of deliciousness. I was determined to enjoy the refreshments even if the company left a lot to be desired.

"Please, allow me." Janice served me with coffee from the *cafetière*, poured a cup for herself, then settled back, waving at the pastries with a: "Please, help yourself". She looked exhausted – no doubt from all her hostess duties.

I watched her watching me as I took the pastry that had my name written all over it; she was weighing me up, in a rather obvious manner. I dare say my clothes didn't impress her, nor

– probably – my overall appearance. She was in great shape for someone around seventy, and presented herself immaculately. No expense had been spared on her hair, skin, nails, face or clothing. If it could be buffed, curled, dyed, straightened, squeezed, plumped or sculpted, she'd had it done. No surgery that I could spot, but they say you can't if it's the really good type. She was wearing a Ribkoff pant suit teamed with John Hardy jewelry, whereas I'd picked out horizontal stripes for my trip to the Dumas home – I love it when people think they make a person look fat, because then they must imagine I'm thinner than I am. *Touché*, fashion police.

I knew I had to break the ice so opened with: "I'm writing Gordy's eulogy, as you know, and wondered if you'd had a chance to think about any stories, or remembrances of him, I could use? It would be most helpful. You and your husband must have known Gordy so much better than Bud and I did."

Janice placed her cup on the table and settled back into the sofa. She managed to look so unutterably elegant when she did it that I reckoned she'd practiced. "But of course. Gordy was terribly good with rhododendrons, did you know that?" I nodded as I made the most of my opportunity to eat my pastry. "Hydrangeas were another of his favourite plants – he got faster results with those, he always said, and he was very good with maples too. The *acer palmatum* were his favorite, though he'd had great success with many *acer japonicum* too."

I wondered if she planned to list all the pants Gordy had ever grown, so thought I'd better nip that approach in the bud – even my internal monologue enjoys puns, it seems. "I was hoping for something a little more personal, to be honest, Janice." I thought that gave her enough of a hint.

"Personal? I didn't really know Gordy very well. Terry did, of course, but…they had a bit of a falling out about their business practices quite early in our marriage."

"Yes, I'd heard about that. Do you know what happened to break up the business?" I hoped she did.

Janice picked up her cup. "Maddie was born thirty-six years ago next week, and that was about the time Gordy left the business – so I don't really know exactly what happened. I know Terry was terribly upset by the whole thing, but he didn't give me all the gory details because he didn't want to worry me when I was pregnant, and then caring for an infant. And we were building this place at the time, too, while we were living in Thornhill, not too far from Gordy's cabin, so Terry was back and forth here when he wasn't at one of the nurseries. I didn't see much of Gordy after our wedding." Janice kept fiddling with her coffee and her eyes kept darting toward the fireplace.

"Did Gordy attend your wedding?"

Janice visibly stiffened. "Gordy was Terry's best man." She put down her coffee; her hand trembled a little as she did so. "He even wore a suit for the occasion."

It didn't seem Janice was going to elaborate.

"That should entertain people," I said, "the sight of Gordy in a suit. Could I maybe borrow some of your wedding photos, to use at the memorial?"

Janice picked up her coffee again and gulped it; I didn't think that was how she usually drank coffee. "I'm not at all sure I know where they are, though I dare say I could track them down."

Odd. "Thanks, that would be most helpful."   I did my best to sound eager, and expected Janice to rise at that moment, but she didn't – she remained seated and stared into her empty coffee cup.

Rather surprisingly she said, "I had a difficult time with Maddie. A very weepy baby. Demanding. I was overwhelmed, and alone with her more often than not. Terry found it difficult to share our small home with a baby. Some…bonding issues. I don't have many memories of that time at all."

I judged she did, and that none of them were particularly happy ones. "So you didn't see much of Gordy after he severed his business ties with your husband?"

Janice snapped her attention back to me. "No, I never saw him at all. It wasn't as though our social circles overlapped. I know Terry bumped into him at a few horticultural events over the years, because he always told me when they'd seen each other, but that was it. They usually kept their distance."

She'd drifted off to another time and place again, her eyes glassy in the firelight, then she said, "Gordy's letter told me to find the documents relating to the 'disposition of the company' so I could realize how generous Terry had been. That was what he wrote, but I have no idea what that means. And I also haven't a clue where the paperwork might be."

I was surprised. "But surely something that important would be lodged with a lawyer, or an accountant? If the company was a legal entity, there'd have to be official records."

Janice nibbled her lip. "Well, that's the problem, you see. Andrew, who was one of the sales managers, and is now CEO of K. Dumas, and a wonderful, wonderful man – we're due to cruise to Australia, via the Hawaiian Islands quite soon, you know…"

I nodded. "Yes, you mentioned that at the lawyers' office."

"Ah, right…well he says the company was incorporated as K. Dumas on Maddie's first birthday, thirty-five years ago. But that can't be, because I know it was a company before that. Terry was always so proud of the fact. I'm sure I'm not mistaken. But there are absolutely no papers of any kind anywhere that suggest Gordy was ever a part of K. Dumas, or that it existed before Maddie's first birthday. It's very strange.

Everyone knows he and Terry set it up together, and yet there's no record of it."

I was delighted – at last something really puzzling…besides a poisoning, a buried corpse, and the disappearing *trousseau*.

I was thinking about the oddities that had arisen as I'd been delving into Gordy's past when Maddie loped into the room, reminding me of the way Gordy had walked before the shuffling gait associated with his Parkinson's disease had reduced his mobility.

Maddie's damp hair suggested she'd showered after horse riding, and she was dressed in an autumnal palette – a casual sweater above narrow-cord pants – which suited her natural coloring. In direct contrast to her mother's carefully applied make-up, her skin glowed with health, and her manner was easy, while her mother's was anything but. The overall effect was of a force of nature blowing into a carefully staged simulation of reality. I wondered how she felt, living in such sterile, contrived surroundings. Her body language told me she was used to it.

She curled herself onto the sofa nearest the fireplace and twirled her hair into a knot on top of her head; I had no idea how she made it stay that way. She looked instantly younger than her years. "How's it going? Have I missed anything?" She smiled broadly as she spoke.

"I was talking about hunting out our wedding album," said Janice, although she hadn't been. There was a reserve in her tone I hadn't heard earlier; no warmth at all. "Cait said she'd like to see Gordy Krantz in a suit."

Maddie scrunched her face. "Oh yes, that's a good idea. I saw those photos, gosh…it must have been years ago. I don't know where Gordy got the suit, but it was high fashion for the period – if you can call what people wore in the seventies 'fashion'. I can't imagine anyone looking good in it, let alone Gordy. Like grooming a wolf and entering it in one of those primpy dog shows. Yes, you should get that – no one would believe it's him."

Janice didn't move. "I believe the album might be in your father's office. I dare say I'll have to wait some time before they'll let me in."

I was confused, and Maddie answered my frown with: "Dad's old offices are all in the top of the barn, above the stables. The movie lot are there, and we're not supposed to bug them. I'm allowed over there, though, Mom – they know the horses need their exercise. I could have a hunt about later on, if you like. I'm just as likely to be able to find it as you are."

Janice smiled wanly at me. "I think I mentioned at the lawyers' that Terry left a lot of paperwork behind him. That's where it all is. Nice and dry over there."

I thought it strange that a widow wouldn't have wanted to look back on her wedding photos after her husband's death, to reminisce. However, I know folks all grieve in their own way, so wondered if it had been too painful for Janice to see those images again.

"I'm surprised you haven't dug them out to show to Andrew," said Maddie. She didn't look at her mother as she spoke. "Did Mom tell you that she and Andrew are off to Australia together? Andrew is Mom's…what is it you call him, Mom? Oh yes, he's Mom's 'good friend and *confidant*'. Right?" As she spoke, she reached for a pastry; her fingers grabbed it a little too tightly.

Janice smiled brightly. "Exactly. We share confidences."

"And the rest." Maddie winked at me. It wasn't a playful wink.

"Well, if you're hunting things out in your father's office, maybe you could also try to find some papers your mother's trying to track down." I felt the devil in me and added,

"Gordy's last letter to her asked her to find the papers relating to how K. Dumas was split up when Gordy left it."

I knew in my heart that I possibly shouldn't have gone that far – because the letter to Janice had been a private matter, after all – but I suspected she was trying to put off doing what Gordy had asked, and I was intensely curious about what she might be trying to hide. Would telling Maddie annoy her?

It did. Janice sat upright, and began to pour herself another coffee.

Maddie looked puzzled. "You're having more coffee, when it's almost eleven? Not like you, Mom." Maddie looked at me and added, "Mom's pretty strict about her caffeine intake, aren't you, Mom? Says it's ageing."

"Dehydration is the enemy of a woman's skin," said Janice earnestly, as she poured what must surely have been cold coffee into her cup.

"And we can't have you looking your age, can we, Mom?" I guessed the edge in Maddie's voice was something with which her mother was familiar; these two women weren't shy about giving each other the needle.

I adore observing family dynamics, and I was starting to get the hang of the Janice/Maddie relationship. But I wanted to know more, so pressed. "It might be something worth finding – that paperwork. Gordy said he wanted your mom to find out how generous your father had been. There could be information about – oh, I don't know – a hidden bank account, or something." I'd thrown out the idea as a silly example, but as I spoke the anger in Janice's eyes made me wonder if I'd touched a nerve.

Maddie laughed. "That would be great. Imagine, Mom, a bank account with money in it. I haven't known what that feels like for a long time, have I?" She turned to me and added, "I run the charitable side of things – retired racehorses and the meal service. I run the rest of the stables as a business. We also make some money from renting out the property for movies, as you've gathered. But that's not a predictable income, more of a windfall. And Mom's good with windfalls, aren't you, Mom? This one's taking her and Andrew off on a luxury cruise halfway around the world. I'm sure it'll be idyllic. Meanwhile I'll be here holding the fort at the stables, being the main point of contact for a company whose chief executive and owner have swanned off together for a month – incommunicado, by the way – and I'll be trying to continue with my volunteer work at the meal service."

Janice rose, almost elegantly. "Your choices, Maddie. I know the retired racehorses were your father's idea, but you could have chosen to move on. And you choose to work with that unstable chef person, driving all over the place with him when he'd be better off in some sort of psychiatric facility. Your choices, daughter, dear. Your father indulged you, I have to live with that. When he put all those stupid conditions in his last will and testament I dare say he thought he knew what he was doing, but he had no idea of the consequences. He never did."

Janice was hovering beside the kitchen island, tapping her manicured nails on an ice floe of white marble. "My headache's returned. You'll have to excuse me, Cait. Maddie will see you out."

She headed off in a huff.

Maddie sighed heavily, sounding like one of her horses. "Mom's headaches are legendary, and convenient. I'm sorry you had to see that, Cait. We're both a bit on edge with each other at the moment. She can't wait to sail off into the sunset with Andrew, and I'm absolutely raging that she's doing it. But I dare say you worked that out, right?"

I shrugged and looked as sweetly innocent as possible. "Mothers and daughters – it's never easy." I tried to sound sage.

"Too damn right in this family. She's always been…aloof isn't the right word, but I could tell when I saw schoolfriends with their moms that mine was different. I saw a warmth in their relationships that I'd never known at home; not from Mom, and not always from Dad. The joke around here was that he'd wanted a son, which I guess led to me growing up as something of a tomboy. But not even that pleased him, and it annoyed the heck out of Mom. She'd wanted a princess, but I don't think I got that gene."

I couldn't help but smile. "Me neither, though it wasn't expected of me; as long as I studied well, my parents were happy."

Maddie nestled into the arm of the sofa. "Ah, now that's where I was fortunate; neither Mom nor Dad had an academic background, and there wasn't the slightest pressure for me to do well at school. Dad poo-pooed the entire education system and would tell anyone who'd listen how he'd left school at sixteen and had done very well for himself, because he reckoned a person could learn everything they needed from a book. Which meant that if I got poor grades, he didn't have a leg to stand on. To be fair, Mom's right about Dad never really thinking through the consequences of his actions. But at least he did act. Mom? Totally reactive, her whole life. It's like life happens to her, rather than her playing any part in making her life what she wants it to be. I guess she was lucky Dad did as well as he did, because I've never known her to be anything but happy to live in the lap of luxury and use whatever money he had to make her look better, or feel more comfortable."

As she spoke, Maddie got redder and redder – I didn't know if that was because she was so close to the fire, or if she colored up when she was angry. By way of an answer to my unasked question, Maddie pushed herself out of the sofa, and looked at her watch. "Come on, I can put off leaving here until about noon. Want to come to the stables with me, to help me look for the album and those papers you were talking about? Mom clearly didn't want me to know anything about all this, so now I really want to find them."

I was delighted, and agreed immediately.

Shutting the Stable Doors

The Dumas property was buzzing with people. No wonder movies cost so much to make – there were dozens of people on the property, most of whom seemed to be hanging about doing nothing. Maddie negotiated the various bits of equipment, wires, and rigs with ease – I trotted behind her like a puppy, afraid I might knock into something that cost thousands of dollars. I was relieved when we reached a door in the side of the barn, which opened onto a sturdy set of internal stairs.

As we climbed, the air changed; it became warmer, sweeter, and there was a definite undertone of animal presence. It wasn't exactly unpleasant, but it wasn't as fresh as I'd hoped. The stairs led to a landing where Maddie opened a locked door, and we entered a massive area that accounted for about a third of the roof space of the building. It was nothing fancy; all the structural elements of the building were visible, and they weren't at all quaint or pretty. Light streamed in through dormer windows on three sides, but Maddie threw a switch to turn on buzzing fluorescent strip lights in any case. She marched across the bare, wooden boards, her boots clattering as she walked.

"This was Dad's world," she said, waving an arm. "If he wasn't out at one of the nurseries or at the office where the admin people for the entire company worked, he was here. The house? All Mom. This? All Dad."

The two worlds couldn't have differed more; one for show and comfort, one absolutely utilitarian. Despite the horsey smell, I knew which I preferred; I was beginning to be sorry I'd never met Terry Dumas. However, while the man might have been good at business, he certainly hadn't been good at organization. One wall was completely shelved, another had rows of old, metal filing cabinets, some pretty badly dented, many rusting. There were box files stacked on the shelves, and on the floor in front of the shelves, and piles of papers – many yellow with age – on top of the four desks, only one of which had a chair beside it.

"It's hard to know where to start, isn't it?" Maddie sounded surprisingly cheerful. "But if I recall correctly, Dad kept the more personal stuff in the filing cabinets, some of which he locked. He used to let me come here to play when he was working, and Mom was out doing whatever it was she did that required fancy frocks and someone to drive her home. I liked those days. But there were never enough of them. He left us too soon."

I wondered if that comment was something I'd have time to dissect later on, but was aware Maddie had a deadline, so didn't want to take her focus off our search. "How about you tackle the more personal area, and maybe find those wedding photos, while I try to work out if there's any sort of system being used for these box files? We might both find what we're after a lot quicker that way."

Maddie agreed and I headed off to read the notes on the spines of the boxes. A few minutes later I'd pretty much got the hang of Terry Dumas's idea of filing: each box was labelled with what was in it, but there was no order to the boxes. So it was easy to tell what would be inside, but no way to track down a subject easily. I reckoned there were at least a couple of hundred boxes, so feared a long job ahead if I wanted to find something pertaining to the pre-incorporation days of the current iteration of K. Dumas.

I'd thought I was sighing internally, but I must have done it out loud because Maddie said, "Daunting, isn't it?"

I agreed, but forced myself to look cheerful. I wasn't. Luckily for me Terry's block printing was a heck of a lot easier to read than Gordy's diaries had been, and I was able to speed-read along shelves without too much bother. Terry had filed at the granular level, with boxes dedicated to topics like "Spring 1973 grafting results" and "New astilbe 1982". I had a suspicion that the boxes had been his way of not really making decisions about what was important and what was irrelevant. I quickly noticed that quite a number of boxes said they held photographs, so I pulled one down and opened it. Sure enough, a collection of Polaroid prints was inside, each of which showed a rhododendron in bloom. On the characteristic white border of each photo were written the species plants that had been crossed to create the hybrid in the photo, the date the cross had happened, and the date the photo had been taken.

"Quite beautiful," I said.

Maddie wandered over, took a look at a few of the prints, and raised her eyebrows. "Yes, they're pretty, aren't they?"

"They are, despite being faded." I put the box file back in position, and pulled out another that claimed to contain photos, to see if the contents were similar. It was, but this time the handwriting on the pictures was most definitely Gordy's. I checked the dates on the photos and the spine. 1982. Years after Gordy had, apparently, severed his ties with K. Dumas, however that might have happened. I mulled pointing this out to Maddie, and decided I should.

I showed her, and explained the conundrum. "Well, that's a puzzle," she said.

"Did Gordy become a supplier to K. Dumas when it was solely your father's business, perhaps?" I suggested. It was the only explanation I could think of.

"No idea. I was too young to even really understand what Dad did, other than to know it involved a lot of plants and flowers, and I never met Gordy until I began to deliver meals to him. He wasn't someone who was ever spoken of in the family, so I had no real awareness of him until Max and I met him on our route. And even then it was Max who explained to each of us who the other person was. I remember Gordy being shaken by that – he got rid of us pretty quickly that first day, though he was fine at all our future visits, and was happy to chat for some time. Most of our recipients do, you know, because sometimes we're the only people they see for days at a time."

I digested that information as I replied absently, "I'm sure you are. Good for you for doing it."

"It was a stipulation of Dad's will that a certain amount of money be put to use to help people who couldn't help themselves. I know there were lots of things I could have done with it, but getting healthy food to our elders fitted well with what Max was wanting to achieve."

I gave my focus to what she was saying. "Do you mean that the meal delivery program is somehow funded by your father's estate?"

"Yes, but it's not generally known. He left a chunk of money with a specific condition attached, and I'm responsible for using the interest – and I can use some of the capital if I want, annually – to help the community. I had to give a lot of thought to how I could do most good with what was available, and I was having a drink with Max one night when he told me about this idea he had. I thought it was brilliant – it would allow him to get himself back on an even keel after his breakdown, use his expertise, and allow elders to benefit. We bought the truck out of the capital, and we've used the interest since then to keep the scheme going. It's very successful; we're only sorry there's so much more demand than we can meet. Indeed, we've been having some discussions about how we might be able to use the capital to grow the service beyond that which we're able to manage at the moment, but scaling the whole thing up isn't as easy as you might think. It's not just about supplies, and food safety, it's about finding the right people to help."

It seemed that Terry Dumas and Gordy Krantz had shared another trait: a desire to control the actions of those they knew even after they'd died. I wondered if there was a book entitled "Will Writing For Control Freaks", and realized that, if there was, I might enjoy reading it.

This consideration apart, I dwelled on Maddie's words as I scanned more box files. Finally I saw one that had promise: "Gordy". That was all it said, so I plucked it down and took it to one of the desks; unlike the two containing photos, this one was heavy, and I didn't want its contents to scatter when I opened it.

I shifted a pile of papers to give myself some space, and popped the little closure device. The top flew open, and I was glad the box was lying flat because my expectation that it was full was correct. I let out a little, "Oh," which drew Maddie's attention.

When she peered at my find her eyes opened wide. "That'll take some sorting." She looked at her watch, then at me. "Would you like to take that home with you? I have to go and – well, I hate to make you feel unwelcome, but I'm not really comfortable leaving you here alone. I don't want to offend you. It's not that I don't trust you…"

I saved her from embarrassment by saying, "I understand. No offence taken. But I'll accept your offer to take this with me, thanks. I don't suppose you found the wedding photos, did you?"

Maddie waved her arm toward the filing cabinets. "Nope. Six down, about thirty-two hundred more to go!"

We shared a smile. "I'll take this and get out of your hair. Thanks, Maddie, this is most kind of you. I really want to do the best I can for Gordy, whenever his memorial might happen."

"You're welcome." We headed for the door, with Maddie casting her eyes around and switching off the lights before we left. She locked the door behind us. As we descended she asked, "Any idea when the memorial might be?"

"No word yet." I definitely wasn't going to mention anything about poison hemlock and the police being at Gordy's property. "I dare say the lawyers will give us enough notice for me to be able to pull his eulogy together for the day."

As Maddie stood holding the handle to the outside door, and I waited on a stair above her, she looked up at me with a wistful glance. "I'm glad I met Gordy when I did. I didn't get to know him well, but his relationship with my father meant I felt close to him through Gordy, for a while, anyway. He's been gone such a long time. I miss him."

I realized I didn't know when Terry Dumas had died, so I asked.

Maddie's brow furrowed. "Who knows? The official date was set as being almost twenty-seven years ago, but I dare say we'll never be certain."

I was puzzled. "I don't understand."

"Oh course, not everyone knows, though it was a pretty famous case at the time: Dad didn't 'die', he disappeared. He went to work one morning, left one of the nurseries that evening to come home, but never did. They never found his vehicle, nor his body. He just simply disappeared. However, he'd taken $100,000 out of the bank the day before, which is why it took Mom over five years to get him declared legally dead – everyone thought he'd simply done a runner. Luckily the business was doing well enough to weather the loss. When they finally acknowledged his 'death', his 'date of death' was legally agreed as the day he went missing: October 3rd, 1994. But, like I said, who really knows?"

My mind whirred as Maddie opened the door, where we were met by a mass of activity; it seemed that everyone who'd been hanging around doing nothing when we'd entered the barn had been commanded to run about like a headless chicken a millisecond before our exit, and we were caught in the maelstrom. Which provided good cover for my surprise.

Country Roads

I phoned Bud, hands-free, as I headed for home. The box file sat on the back seat inside one of our reusable grocery bags, because it would have slithered about and spilled its contents all over the place otherwise. I was looking forward to getting home and being able to settle down with Gordy's diaries and the box file – both of which needed my attention. But I also wanted to know what was happening about the human remains they'd found, and I knew if anyone would have information, it would be Bud.

But I wasn't ready for what he told me. "They brought in the dogs. Cadaver dogs. And now they've erected a second full-sized tent, which I believe means a second locale...a second find. Down near the old cabin. Marty and I went for a drive because we were a bit bored, and I saw it from the road. Not far from those towering brambles we navigated the other day." He sounded excited. I shared his emotion – gruesome though that might have sounded to anyone but we two.

"Why do you think it's a second discovery, rather than more parts of the same one? We both assessed predation might have led to distribution of the original remains; it could have been spread as far as the cabin."

"Resource management, Cait. There's a massive amount of activity over there. Too many people for one body."

I bowed to Bud's superior knowledge of norms for the circumstances. "No inside scoop other than that?" I was hoping for something more tangible – a part of the solution, not an increased size of problem.

"Not a sausage, as you like to say. I've sent a few texts but haven't had any responses. This is looking serious, Cait. What do you make of it?"

I suspected we were both thinking the same. "Husband, it looks like our gentleman neighbor might have been burying bodies on his acreage…but neither of us believes Gordy Krantz capable of that, do we?"

"Exactly." Bud sounded resigned.

"However, if he *had* been the sort of person who could have done so, that might give us some fresh leads about who might have wanted him dead, because I still don't have any."

"Agreed." Bud still sounded glum, with good reason. "What news from your end of things?" Was that desperation in his voice?

"I have successfully escaped from Stepford. Well, Little Stepford, anyway."

"What?'

"You know, the movie about the women who live in Stepford, *The Stepford Wives*, all in their perfect outfits and perfect homes. The horror film about the men who replace their wives with automatons?"

"Oh, right. Yes. It was all a bit weird, was it?"

"It was perfection. On steroids. I'll tell you all about it when I get home. But, in the meantime, you can think on this: Terry Dumas disappeared, and was declared dead after five years. His body was never found."

Bud's "Oh" echoed like a death knell. "Do you think…next door…one of the bodies?"

"Well, it makes you wonder, doesn't it?"

Silence.

I said, "Okay, I'll hang up and get there as soon as I can."

Silence.

"Are you still there?" I asked.

"There's someone coming through the gate in our fence. Gotta go." And he went.

I pressed the accelerator, and focused on the winding road ahead of me, trying not to think about corpses being exhumed just yards from our house.

Finally home, I fought off Marty's joyous welcome, petted him a great deal, then I enjoyed an extended hug with Bud; I was feeling a bit frayed around the edges. I rallied in moments.

"I need a full update, Husband. Who was it who came through the gate while we were on the phone? And what did you learn from them?"

Bud scratched his head. Never a good sign. "Ah, yes. Well, the first thing you need to know is that we are both completely and totally *persona non grata* on Gordy's property. Any part of it, for any reason." I opened my mouth to speak, but Bud held up his hand and continued in his calming voice. "Second thing – and we do not know this officially – there *has* been a second set of remains discovered. Human remains. Which means—"

"We're suspects?" I mugged a terrifying face.

Bud tilted his head and gave me one of his most loving looks. "I received a courtesy call from Jacques Pelletier, who's now heading this up. We go back. In fact, he worked the investigation into Jan's death. He's good people. Hence the visit. He took the time, personally, to walk over to tell me what's going on there – and with everything he's juggling at the moment, that was kind."

Bud reached out to hug me again, and I hugged back until he couldn't breathe, so I let go.

"He questioned me – informally, of course," he said with a grin. "Not specifically about the discoveries, but about Gordy. I told him about you being asked to write Gordy's eulogy, mentioned a few things we've been doing to allow you to do that. He didn't say the words, but you might find we're going to have to hand over those diaries pretty soon. Which is why, if you want to work on anything, I suggest that's where you focus. Cait, I know you're fast, I know you're good, and I think now's the time to be both."

I agreed, headed to my office, and shut the door to keep Marty out. Bud promised him a treat and a walk, and I got on with the mammoth task at hand.

Bud brought me a sandwich for lunch, and filled me in on how his parents – Ebba and Leo – were doing; he'd enjoyed a long chat with his mother. It turned out they were even busier than usual, because Ebba had agreed to share baking duties for a large Thanksgiving celebration being held at the Scandinavian Center in Burnaby she and Bud's father frequented. The hip replacement she'd received about a year ago had turned out just fine, and it seemed she was determined to make the most of the fact she was able to "get about like a girl again", as she liked to put it. We agreed we were quite relieved they'd be busy with a group for the Thanksgiving holiday, because that meant we'd be able to have our own celebration in a way that suited us…and have an entire turkey to ourselves. We both like turkey enormously.

I declined a cooked dinner, so got another sandwich and some fresh coffee around that time, and I pressed on. Luckily, both of us are familiar with the way the other works, which meant Bud allowed me the time I needed, and didn't bug me.

I fell into bed at something past one, fought Marty for an almost-fair share of the duvet, and must have been asleep within a few moments because the next thing I was aware of was a bit of a kerfuffle outside the unusually closed bedroom door – it's always open so Marty can go wandering in the night if he wants. Now he was protesting about something outside it – loudly.

I was groggy, but pulled on my dressing gown and popped my head into the hall. Bud was hanging onto Marty as a couple of uniformed officers were carrying evidence bags – full of Gordy's diaries – toward the front door. Bud had been correct – we hadn't had long for me to get through them all, but I winked at him to let him know I'd finished my task. Bud managed a quick thumbs-up. I closed the bedroom door, then shut myself in the master bathroom; the contents of the box file I'd brought from the Dumas house was still inside its reusable grocery bag and sitting in the linen closet, safe from prying eyes, and the grasp of anyone wearing a uniform.

I showered, dressed, and presented myself for breakfast. Bud kissed me and said, "They asked for everything we'd brought from Gordy's place. I told them they didn't need to get a warrant. They're happy, we're happy, right, Wife?"

I kissed him back. "Right, Husband." Breakfast was delicious – an everything bagel with spicy whipped cheese…a complete indulgence, which I felt I deserved.

"Now they've gone, I'm taking Marty out with me to the grocery store – he'll enjoy being in the truck, and it's a cool, cloudy day. We only need a couple of things – and I'll beat the Sunday morning rush," called Bud from the side door. "I'm going to lock you in. I've got my keys. I suggest we keep everything secure for the foreseeable future – until this is all cleared up, anyway. Okay?"

I called, "Okay," and the pair of them bounded out. Well, Bud didn't so much bound as get dragged, but they were both going to be gone for a couple of hours, of that much I was certain, because the shops are over half an hour away.

I sipped my coffee and contemplated the situation. I'd never sat in this house, alone and locked in, before. My flat in London? Yes, always locked. My flat in Cambridge? Always locked after I'd kicked Angus out, initially because of him stalking me and my wanting to feel secure, and then – after he'd been found dead on my floor – because I was constantly being hounded by the press. My little house on Burnaby Mountain near the University of Vancouver? That had felt secure, but I'd always lived there alone and was still in 'personal secure-zone mode', so I'd always locked everything there, too. It wasn't until we'd moved to this house, the place Bud and I had made our home together, that I'd begun to lose track of what was locked or unlocked; we live – quite literally – in the middle of nowhere, and are blessed with a noisily crunchy drive, and a dog who's always keen to "greet" visitors. I had felt utterly safe.

Now I'd been robbed of my sense of security; that's a terrible thing to take from a person. It's the effect that crimes of many sorts have on the lives of countless thousands of people every day. They might not have been victims of crime, but they are, nonetheless, the victims of criminality. I mulled that thought, and a kernel of an idea came to me: the focus of the research I'd begun the previous year could be shifted a bit and taken in a different direction...what if I expanded the notion of "victims" to include those peripherally impacted by crime?

When my phone rang it frightened me out of my wits, and I managed to spill coffee all over the table. I grabbed the phone and answered as I pulled a tea towel off the cooker to mop up the coffee which seemed determined to run off the edge of the table and all over the upholstery on the chair.

The number told me it was Dayton Woodward, the lumberjack. "Hi, Dayton."

I was surprised when Dayton replied with an abrupt, "I'm sorry I shouted. Please let's put it behind us."

I was confused. I tried again. "Hello, Dayton? Are you okay?"

A gasp. "Who's that?"

"Cait Morgan. Red Water Mountain Drive. Gordy's neighbor. You just phoned me."

There was a pause, and I could tell Dayton was driving, with a window open. "Sorry, Cait. I must have misdialled."

"Ah," was all I could muster. "So you didn't want to talk to me? That's a shame, because I could do with a quick chat about Gordy, if you don't mind."

Another pause. "Now's not a good time. Can I drop by in an hour?"

I was delighted. "Absolutely. I'll put the kettle on and we'll share a pot of tea when you get here." Dayton had guzzled as much tea as I could give him when he'd come to our place to semi-decapitate a cedar, so I hoped the temptation would work.

"I'll bring cake," he replied. "Lemon poppyseed, right?"

He remembered. "Lovely. See you later. Bye."

"See you." He was gone.

I wondered who he'd thought I was – who did he want to apologize to? And why?

Knowing Dayton was coming to visit, I took a few minutes to clear around a bit. I'm not terribly houseproud, but there's a level of messiness that even I think is too much to inflict upon a guest. Marty provides an excellent excuse for the place never being truly clean – he sheds for all but two months of the year and produces tumbleweeds of fur which seem to appear from nowhere just after I've put the vacuum away. And I swear he brings dust into the house by the pound. My party trick is to swoosh around with one of those fluffy-headed things that are supposed to trap the dirt just before anyone visits, and hope whatever dust I don't put away in the cupboard attached to said magic mop doesn't settle until after visitors have left, so surfaces look relatively clean when they're here.

Dayton phoned from the bottom of the mountain to ask if it was okay to come to the house early; when I said it was, I flicked on the kettle and pulled my trusty pot from its parking spot on the counter – there's never any point putting it in a cupboard because it's in such frequent use.

When Dayton arrived, I observed the pleasantries as I fussed over the tea, and he plopped a cardboard box on the counter. We exchanged a few comments about how healthy the cedar he'd topped for us was looking, then I dared ask, "So you'd been having a fight on the phone when you called me?"

Dayton shrugged. "I've been having a running argument with my aunt, and I'd lost my temper with her a bit, so I meant to call her back to apologize, but got you instead. Sorry."

I slid the box of cake toward Dayton; he poked in his hand, took out a slice and more or less stuffed it all into his mouth, then chomped down on it. Bits fell all over the place, and I thought of Marty. I waited as he ate, and my sipped my tea.

"If you want to talk about it…" I allowed my offer to remain open-ended.

Once he could speak, Dayton replied, "It's all Gordy's fault. His letter asked me to get in touch with my uncle. We haven't spoken for years. My aunt is livid that I've phoned, and she wants to keep telling me how awful she thinks I am."

I decided on my path. "What happened to your relationship in the first place? Was it something your aunt finds it difficult to deal with?" So many strange reasons create fissures in families that I didn't want to guess.

Dayton nodded and eyed a second piece of cake. "My dad was a lumberjack. Died on the job. It was terrible. Mom found it tough to cope, so I ended up living with Uncle Albert and Aunt May. They were delighted when I decided to become an electrician. They saw it as a trade that could take me across Canada and even anywhere in the world I wanted to go. You see, when I was little, I told them I dreamed of seeing the world. Becoming an electrician would have allowed me to do that, they believed."

I must have looked puzzled, because Dayton paused, then said, "You didn't know? Of course not. Before I became a lumberjack, I was an apprentice electrician – studying at college and working with a small electrical contractor out this way."

"What led to the career change?" I asked.

"To be honest, I didn't like the idea of becoming an electrician at all – that was my uncle's idea. Uncle Albert can be quite forceful, and always believes he knows what's best for everyone. Anyway, the big problem was that the reason I took the job with that particular company was because my Uncle Albert knew the guy, Aunt May knew him too, and I think she'd been a bit sweet on him, once upon a time. It came a big shock to them when I quit. They said I was throwing my life away. That a trade was the best I could do with my life – and a lot safer than wielding a chainsaw a hundred feet in the air, as they put it. Anyway, we came to Gordy's place, to do an electrical job for him, and he and I got chatting. We hit it off, and I offered to come back to his property to give him a hand with some emergency limbing. He saw how happy I was working with trees. He was the one who put me in touch with the guy I then apprenticed with as a lumberjack, I took all my arborists' exams, topped it off with some classes online at the college where I'd been doing my electrician's stuff, and I set up my own company three years later."

I was impressed, and told Dayton so.

Dayton munched some cake and looked sad. "I should be real proud, I know, but I haven't really spoken to my aunt and uncle since then. They couldn't understand why I wanted to do something that had killed my father, and caused so much distress to my mother. They thought I was being reckless. And all I could say was that I preferred working with trees than with a bunch of wires and stuff."

Dayton looked pretty dejected, and cakey.

"So why did Gordy ask you to get in touch with your uncle again?" I was curious; this seemed to be the second example of Gordy intervening in what would normally be considered family matters.

"His letter said that family is too important to not fight for it, so I should get in touch and try to heal the wounds."

More sipping of tea.

"Do you think you'll be able to build bridges with your aunt and uncle?" I was curious.

"They're coming to visit me in Mission over Thanksgiving, from their home on the Sunshine Coast. So that's a good sign. We're going to Tom White's new place for an early Thanksgiving dinner on Saturday – the only day we could get a table. But Aunt May and I were talking earlier, and I get the impression that while Uncle Albert might be ready to come around, she's the one who's really angry. Dad was her brother. Being a lumberjack is what took him from her. We ended up snapping at each other, which is why I was calling her back – to apologize. If I want this to work, I have to be prepared to do quite a lot of that, I think. And Gordy was right, it's worth it for family."

"Good luck." I gave him a thumbs up, and a big grin.

"But now I really must be going. Invoicing to do today. Not my favorite thing, but I want the decks clear before Aunt May and Uncle Albert arrive – then I can give them one hundred percent of my attention."

"As you should. Good luck, Dayton. And thanks for telling me about how Gordy impacted your life. I'm glad he gave you a helping hand to find a career you love, and are really good at."

Dayton threw me a giant grin as he slung his backpack into his truck, hoisted himself in, and crunched along the drive. It was nippy outside, and the smell of woodsmoke was wafting up from the valley on a more than gentle breeze.

As I was heading for the bathroom – all that tea has to go somewhere – my phone rang in my pocket.

"I need to see you. Now."

It was Louise North. I rolled my eyes heavenward. "It's not a very good time for me. Could this wait?"

"No, I cannot wait. I need you to come here, now. There's something I have to tell you."

I swore, silently. "Can I call you back?"

"Don't call, come." She hung up.

I swore again, aloud this time, and rushed to the bathroom.

Coming Round the Mountain

The drive to Louise's house seemed shorter than it had felt on my first visit, and I parked where I'd parked before. I was surprised Louise wasn't at her door to greet me. It was wide open, so I stepped inside and called her name. The stench of the place hit me as soon as my nose crossed the threshold, but there was no reply. I called again. Nothing. I had an uncomfortable feeling. Louise's vehicle was parked in front of her house, with her little motorized scooter inside it. I had no idea where she might be, if not indoors; there wasn't an obvious path through, or into, the thick brush surrounding the place. I steeled myself and went inside. I checked every room, every area. No sign of her at all. I was relieved to not have found her in some sort of state of collapse, or worse, but was equally delighted to be able to leave the house, shut the door, and get a breath of fresh air.

I went back to my car and yelled Louise's name as loudly as I could, several times. All I managed to do was frighted the birds out of the bushes. I pulled out my phone and speed-dialled Bud. No signal. I wandered about, holding my phone up in the air but there was still nothing – it never helps. I turned on my vehicle's ignition, waited for the GPS to kick in, and noticed I wasn't even registering as existing, so I drove down the mountain toward the main road. It wasn't until I was just about to turn onto it that I regained cell reception and my call to Bud went through. I waited where I was until he answered, and told him what was happening.

"I just got home and found your note. I'll see to Marty. Stay where you are, I'll be there as fast as I can," he said. I agreed that was the best course of action.

It took about twenty minutes, but, finally, Bud's truck came into sight at the base of the mountain. I'd already turned my vehicle around, so headed up the hill in front of him. When we'd both parked outside Louise's house, we repeated the process I'd been through, together. Still no sign of the woman.

"She specifically asked me – no, she *told* me – to come, Bud. Her people carrier is here, and her scooter. She can't have walked off the property, she's too bowed and frail to do that – you saw the state of the track up to this pace. And we'd see a break in this brush if she'd headed off through that."

Bud agreed. "Time we called this in," he said gravely. "I'll drive down to the main road to do it. I haven't got any reception here either. Do you want to wait here?"

"Yep, I'll stay. Just in case." Bud left, and I sat in my SUV, trying to work out what could have happened to Louise. It made no sense. How could a woman in her eighties just vanish from her home?

Bud returned. He'd explained the connection between Gordy and Louise to the cops to make sure that an appropriate amount of attention was paid to her disappearance, however brief it might have been so far.

We both waited in Bud's truck, which sits a good deal higher than my SUV, and that's when I saw it – a reflection of sunlight off an old, corrugated tin roof, deep in the brush. It would have been impossible to spot it from ground height, even now it was only a sliver.

Bud wrote a note, stuck it under his wiper-blade, opened the compass app on his phone, and we both pulled on the thick jackets we always have in the back of our vehicles "just in case". They'd languished there for a couple of years waiting for this moment, when we had to push through biting brambles in search of an elderly woman. Even so, it wasn't pleasant; the further we went the less likely I could imagine it was that Louise had done this herself. Besides, why would she?

We finally reached our goal, which turned out to be a few upright remnants of what had once been some sort of open-sided shed.

"Possibly a wood-store," Bud suggested.

"Way past being useful," I replied.

Bud called Louise's name. We both listened. Nothing. The dilapidated structure was in a relatively clear area. There was even a sort of path leading away behind it. Bud and I exchanged a glance within which we tacitly agreed to go wherever it took us. He led. There were more brambles, but there was a definite track through this lot. For some reason, I felt it was critical to remain silent. Instinct? Terror? No idea. At one point Bud turned to me and put his finger to his lips. He felt it too.

The noise of a bird fluttering about somewhere in the thicket gave us both a start, and it made me shake my head. What were we playing at? What on earth did we expect to find?

Then the brambles gave way to another relatively clear area and we each gasped aloud. In the center of the clearing were two cedars of absolutely massive proportions – they had to be three-hundred-feet tall – and beneath them was a bundle of rags. A moving bundle of rags.

"It's Louise!" I was off, with Bud at my heel. It seemed impossible, but, sure enough, Louise North was curled in a ball at the foot of a cedar, a gash on her forehead, blood drying on her face. She was pale and shaking – but at least she was conscious.

"She needs medical attention," I said to Bud.

"Duh! There's no cell signal here either, besides, how are we going to get them to this spot? How did *she* get here? Cait, try to find out what happened."

I swept the hair out of Louise's eyes, and she reached her arms toward me. I knew I shouldn't move her, but she'd already moved herself, so I responded. Between us, Bud and I propped Louise against the base of the closest tree.

"What happened, Louise?" I spoke as gently as I could.

"Deer," was all she said.

"A deer?" I couldn't imagine what she meant. "How did you get here, Louise?"

"Followed the deer."

Bud and I exchanged a glance. Bud whispered, "Possible concussion? Might be confused."

I leaned closer to the elderly woman's ear. "Louise, we're on your property, beside a couple of very big cedars. Bud and I are here. I'm Cait. Bud and Cait are here. There's help on the way – but we need to get them to you. It would help if you could tell us how you got here from your house."

Louise's eyes focused on me and she cackled, weakly, "I know who's here, and I know where I am. There was a deer out back of my house. The deer came here. I followed it because it looked lame – wondered if I could do anything to help it. I startled it. It bucked. Kicked me. My own stupid fault."

"But we're such a long way from your house," I said. "Bud and I have walked for some time through lots of brambles. You haven't got a scratch on you. How did you get here?"

Louise's cackle became a coughing fit. Once she stopped, she gave me an almost toothless grin. "You musta been going round in a circle. House is just over there." She waved an arm, and Bud set off.

He was back about three minutes later looking cross. "She's right. Narrow path back there, takes you to the rear of a shed filled with old propane tanks. Walk through that, you're at the rear of the house. That compass app is useless."

We helped Louise back to her home, slowly. By the time we got there a cop car had arrived, and they put out a radio call for an ambulance, which Louise was not at all happy about, but – frankly – she had no choice in the matter. Her head wound needed stitches, and that was that.

Bud took Louise in his truck to the base of the mountain, where the cop waited with them until the ambulance arrived; we'd all agreed there was little point forcing the paramedics to negotiate the track to Louise's house. The irony of the fact that Louise was about to be treated at the hospital where she'd worked decades earlier wasn't lost on her, and Bud told me later – when I too descended the mountainside – that Louise had diagnosed herself, and suggested suitable treatments to the paramedics as they'd been strapping her into a chair in the rear of their vehicle. I suspected the first things they'd wish they could do with her was gag her, then bathe her. At least we knew she was safe, about to be well-cared for, and we'd told her we'd meet her at the emergency department a little later.

"I wonder what it was she wanted to tell you," said Bud when we got back to our house to let Marty out and drop off one of our vehicles.

"It wasn't really the time to ask," I replied. "Maybe she'll tell us when we collect her from the hospital."

"We'd better check if she's safe to be left alone. Do you think we should invite her to stay here until we're sure her head is okay?"

I stared at Bud; he was speaking from his heart, but I was horrified by the prospect of having Louise North anywhere near our place. "Of course we should invite her," I replied, knowing very well that Louise would decline any such offer – she was a classic case of the headstrong, independent sort of person who just won't be helped.

However, it turned out I was completely wrong about that, because when we met her, and Bud offered, Louise jumped at the chance. We were having a house guest. Our first ever. Oh joy.

The first thing that happened when we brought Louise home was that Marty went absolutely nuts. On the rare occasions we have guests to dinner, he takes a little time to settle to other humans being in his kingdom, but he does, eventually, allow them their space. With Louise, he didn't leave her for a moment. He even followed her to the guest room, and plodded behind her as she cast her eyes around the attached bathroom. I hastily pulled towels from the linen closet and showed her how the plumbing worked – I swear it's the most complicated shower/tub ensemble I've ever seen.

While she was in the bathroom, I plumped the pillows and made sure the bedclothes still smelled fresh – I'd put them on a few weeks earlier, and had used those perfumed laundry beads that last for months, because I always like to have a spare room made up, "just in case".

It seemed that Louise North was a person who made all the "just in case" things in life necessary.

Bud and I hustled around the kitchen. We'd only defrosted two pork chops, so alternative dinner plans were needed. Luckily, I'm good with pantry cooking, and I got a big pan of pasta on the go, with some hearty tomato, caper, and black olive sauce. Bud grated Parmesan as though his life depended on it, which eventually tempted Marty away from sitting in the hallway outside the guest room.

When Louise emerged she looked like a different person. I'd given her a choice of a long-sleeved, velvety kaftan thing, or a sweatsuit, and she'd plumped for the kaftan; the burgundy color which always made me look as though I was at death's door gave her a healthy glow. I couldn't work out how she'd managed to wash and dry her hair without getting the giant bandage on her forehead wet, but she'd done it somehow, and had what could only be described as surprisingly lustrous grey locks, longer than I'd imagined, with a natural wave. Despite her deeply wrinkled face she looked as though she'd stepped out of a pre-Raphaelite painting – in which the delicate young subject had aged considerably.

The surprise must have shown on my face, because she cackled and said, "Brush up good, don't I?"

"Indeed you do," said Bud, and pulled out a chair for her at the dining table with a flourish. He then went on to act like a *maitre'd* by telling her about the meal we had prepared, and offering wine, all of which she accepted with the air of a gracious patron. As I plated the food, Louise endeared herself to me by having an entire conversation with Marty as though he were a person which – to us – he is. Every tilt of his head, and snuffle of his snout suggested to me he adored her, and he settled himself at her feet, which gave me just the slightest twinge of jealousy.

We ate, and we drank; Louise's appetite amazed me, as did her ability to knock back the wine. The atmosphere was bizarrely convivial, as though she hadn't been through what she had. The chatter was about the hospital, the care she'd received, and about how she was feeling. Her gratitude for us inviting her to stay was unmistakeable, but I began to get a bit frustrated because there were so many topics we were all avoiding.

The time came when I just couldn't hold back any longer. As Louise declined more pasta and Bud cleared the dishes, I asked,

"What was it that you needed to tell me so urgently earlier today, Louise?"

Louise wiped her purple lips with the corner of her napkin, and settled back into her seat, as far as her bowed back would allow. "That was an excellent meal, thank you. But, as for why I wanted to talk to you on my property, well, I'm not so sure about that anymore."

I was close to being cross, and Bud must have sensed it because he said, "I think what Cait means is that – well, whatever the reason, we're glad we were able to help out today, but it would be nice to know what you know. Because we're curious – as anyone would be. Right, Cait?"

I nodded and smiled. "Yes, very curious."

Louise's hooded eyes glittered in the subdued lighting. "I saw something I shouldn't have seen. Years back. I heard word they found a body next door, on Gordy's acreage, and I thought I might know who it is."

Bud and I were agog, as was Marty, it seemed.

"Go on," I urged.

Louise shook her head.

I couldn't stand it anymore. "Do you think Gordy killed Terry Dumas and buried his body next door?"

Louise's lined mouth made a little "O". Her eyes narrowed. She emptied her wine glass. "How did you know?"

"You first," said Bud.

"I don't know if you realize it, but my place used to have a clear view down to Gordy's cabin, that's what I wanted you to see. Trees have all grown up now, of course, but he and I always pretty much knew what the other was up to, on account of us being able to see each other's homes. It was early one evening – still light. I saw them fight. Knock-down, get-up and start-again brawl, it was. Then it got too dark for me to see. Next day Terry's truck had gone, and I never saw Terry again after that. That's all I'm saying." She clamped her lips together as if to prove the point.

I pressed on regardless. "When was this, Louise? When did you see them fight? Can you remember?"

"Twenty-seven years ago, this month."

"That's very precise," observed Bud dryly.

"It was six years after we got divorced," said Louise, looking oddly satisfied with herself.

"When who got divorced?" I almost shouted. Marty shot me a look of what I took to be disdain.

"Gordy and me. Divorced thirty-two years ago this month." Louise eyed her empty glass.

"You and Gordy were married?" Bud sounded as surprised as I felt.

"You gotta be married to get a divorce," replied Louise coolly. "That night? I wasn't supposed to be at home that night, supposed to be on duty. But sometimes things used to overwhelm me a bit – they did that night. It was the anniversary of our divorce, like I said, and it was about the baby, too. Losing a baby's something you think you're over, then you aren't. I needed to talk to someone. Gordy was the only one I could talk to. I started to walk down the mountain to his cabin, but I saw them fighting. I left them to it and walked home. They were still at it when I got back to my place. Then it got dark, like I said."

Bud and I exchanged a glance. "What baby, Louise?" I asked.

Louise ran her finger around the rim of the empty glass. "I was forty-eight. We didn't think I'd get pregnant. Too old, we thought. I didn't even know I was pregnant, at first. Imagine that, a nurse not knowing. When I realized what was happening to me I told Gordy I'd have an abortion, unless he married me. I had to be sure a kid would be well supported, you know? He put up a bit of a fight, but he was very much against abortion, so in the end we did it. Got married. But then it didn't matter, because I miscarried. No one else had even spotted I was pregnant, so only we two knew, and then it was gone. I was too old for it to all work out, I guess. Anyway, it was for the best, we both agreed."

I knew I was staring at the woman, but I couldn't help myself. "What happened to the…baby…the foetus?"

Louise looked directly at me. "Foetus. Not quite three months along. I buried the bloody sheets and towels in the bush. I was down at Gordy's cabin when it happened, but he couldn't help because he had a broken arm at the time – he'd taken a tumble off the edge of an escarpment when he was going back to his cabin from my place one night a couple of weeks earlier. Had to go to the emergency room to get it fixed up – I drove him in when I went to work. When the rumors started about human 'remains' I wondered if someone had dug up the sheets and so forth – there would have been human 'matter' on them, I guess. Then people started to say it was an actual body they'd found. That's when I started to wonder about the fight."

"I've got a call to make," said Bud, pushing back his chair.

"You're gonna tell people what I've just said, aren't you?" Louise sounded a thousand years old.

"Yes," replied Bud, and he walked along the hallway toward his office to pass on the information we'd just been given.

"Why didn't you tell anyone about this fight when Terry Dumas was originally reported as missing, Louise?" I asked.

"Gordy Krantz married me. Course, he set things in motion for the divorce not long after the miscarriage, and he never wanted to speak to me again. Divorce is okay with the Catholics, it seems, but abortion isn't. Weird people. I tried to understand it, but it got me down. When I climbed that tree, with the rope, I couldn't see my way through it. Then, I broke my stupid back. Only time we ever exchanged a word after that was when he brought me the puppy. Maybe he thought it could be like a kid to me, and in a way that's what my dogs became…they sure as hell got me out of bed every day – I had no other reason to do that. Gordy Krantz wasn't kind. He wasn't gentle. But he'd told me how him and Terry had butted heads over the business often enough that I didn't feel kindly toward the Dumas family. And all I really knew was that Gordy and Terry had fought. Used to be like brothers; brothers fight. Sometimes they fight too hard. It wasn't until that lot started digging around" – she nodded toward next door – "that I thought something of it. So I'm speaking up. Besides, Gordy's dead now, so what does it matter?"

"But Terry's family were hoping every day he'd come back. Surely it would have been kinder to say something."

Louise's lips squeezed into a thin line. "Like I said, I never thought Gordy had killed him. That only came to mind these past couple of days."

I tried to process everything Louise had revealed.

"Thanks for telling us this. That must have taken some doing," I said.

Louise wiped tears from the folds of skin beneath her eyes with her napkin. "They won't charge me, will they? It was a miscarriage. A lot of women have them."

"I can't imagine why they would. I think they'll be more interested in a few other points."

Louise sniffed. I wasn't sure why she was crying – had the memories been painful, or was she relieved someone else knew her story?

Coffee House

As requested by the officer in charge, we drove Louise to the police station to be interviewed the next morning. She'd accepted the sweatsuit I'd offered, and even accompanied Bud and Marty on their morning constitutional. I thought she was walking a little better than I'd seen her manage before, and wondered what sort of state the bed at her home was in – maybe all she needed was a bit more comfort in her life to be in better physical condition. In fact, she was holding her back almost straight, and her head almost high, as she walked into the police station alone, which was at her insistence. She said she'd make sure the cops drove her home.

Both Bud and I had wanted to stay and wait with her, or at least for her, but it became obvious Louise wouldn't stand for that. So we did what we rarely do, we drove to a lovely coffee place overlooking the river; there's something about watching a river flow – especially one as wide as the Fraser – that gives a wonderful sense of perspective. Tugs were busy pulling booms full of massive logs downriver, aided by the tide, and raptors were fishing, no doubt enjoying the salmon run; life continuing in its circle.

"We need a timeline of everything we've found out so far," started Bud, once we were settled at a table beside the window. "All this information about things Gordy did that we couldn't even have imagined…it's coming in from so many people that I'm having trouble keeping it all straight. That said, I still haven't heard anything that suggests a single person might have wanted him dead."

"I read all his diaries, so I can easily write up a timeline for you later on when we're back at home, from memory, so let's talk about our potential candidates for being suspects first," I replied. "That's where we need to compare notes. Do you want to start?"

Bud rolled his eyes. "Let's consider Louise first. She's front and center in my mind right now, but I can't come up with a single reason why she'd want Gordy dead. She had a failed marriage and a miscarriage with him, but as for her killing Gordy? I know we only have her word for it that she hasn't seen him for the past thirty years or so, and it's pretty obvious that the end of her relationship with him was so traumatic that she tried to take her own life. Maybe she'd have hated him enough to have wanted to kill him back then, but now? Why wait? No, she's not on my list of people with a reason to want him dead."

I agreed. "We now know she saw something years ago that might suggest Gordy killed Terry, but what about someone else suspecting that had happened, and wanting revenge? Maybe someone else saw that fight. Terry's wife for example: Janice is like a cat, she just wants to be comfortable, and pampered, but she also struck me as the sort of person who might lash out to protect anything she felt should rightfully be hers. Yes, I believe she'd do it if she thought she was going to lose what she holds most dear: her money and possessions."

Bud sipped his coffee. "I've only met her once, at the lawyers' office, so I'll have to agree with your assessment. But in what way was Gordy a threat to her? Or to anything she owned or held dear? And how could she have poisoned Gordy anyway?"

"She could have given something to her daughter to give to Gordy."

"Maybe," conceded Bud, "but that's pretty unlikely, I'd say. But what about the daughter? I've seen her many times, and have chatted with her on a few occasions, though I didn't know who she was back then. I'd always thought of her as an intense, earnest person. I guess I formed my opinion of her based on the fact she was delivering good food, for next to nothing, to someone we cared about – as a volunteer doing good for the community. It's difficult for me to reassess her as Terry Dumas's daughter without having the chance to interview her further."

I gave Bud a shove with my foot. "Don't start thinking like a cop again." Bud's eyebrows shot up. "Sorry, Husband, you'll always think like a cop because you'll never actually stop being one – in your head – but you can knock off the lingo, okay? You won't be 'interviewing' anyone."

Bud shrugged. "You know what I mean; it's over to you regarding the daughter, then."

"The mother's a right old snob, but Maddie's lovely. Not overly horsey, considering she runs a very horsey business, and she seems to be truly interested in community outreach. I think there might be more to the relationship between her and Max Muller than meets the eye; even though she says they aren't a couple I think there's something there. Maybe she just wants to take care of him; some relationships have been successfully built on less, I suppose. But as for her standing in the potential suspects' league? I can't see her wanting to harm Gordy. Now, it's true she'd have had the opportunity to poison him – he'd have trusted her, and she could have given him anything to eat or drink and he'd have done so…but why would she want to? Might she have suspected that Gordy killed her father? If so, might she have wanted revenge? I know we've met some incredibly duplicitous people in our time, Bud, but I couldn't read anything in her at all that suggested she's a vengeful person. Quite the opposite – I suspect she might be one of the few people I've ever met who really *would* turn the other cheek.

She's certainly a vocal, and practical, supporter of second chances – retired racehorses, and a chef who's been through a breakdown and started over, for example."

Bud cleared the crumbs of muffin off his front – you can't buy just coffee in a coffee shop, ever, so muffins had been purchased. "Okay then, what about Max, the chef-turned-community-supporter?"

Bud still had a crumb on his cheek, which I reached over to brush off. I considered his question. "Gordy inspired him. Talk about second chances – Gordy was the one who convinced him to give his career in the kitchen another try. Max's reaction when he found out about Gordy's death was – I believe – genuine; he'd lost someone he admired. Again – opportunity, and possibly means, but motive? I can't think of one."

"Do you think both the daughter and the chef might have known enough about the sources of the poison on Gordy's property, to have picked it, and somehow introduced it into something Gordy would have consumed?" Bud asked.

He'd made a good point. "Yes, I think they could have found out enough about it to use it. Even an internet search will show you what poison hemlock looks like. And I still believe that even if they – or anyone else for that matter – couldn't tell the difference between it and its equally deadly cousin, water hemlock, it really wouldn't have mattered which one they used or gave him. I'm sure the exact choice of poison is irrelevant – beyond the ability to access it easily – as each would have proved equally deadly in its own way." I paused for a moment and added, "Which is quite worrying, when you think about it – there are so many things growing all over the place that are absolutely deadly."

"Always have been, Wife. But it's the will of a person to use them to kill that matters, right?"

I nodded. "No real suspects so far, then…what about Colin Evans and his wife Ann? Fancy either of those two?"

Bud scooped the foam from the bottom of his mug with his spoon. "He seems to owe his career to Gordy's influence, though she hardly knew Gordy," said Bud.

I gave the couple a little thought. "There's a friction in that marriage, which Gordy urged them to address by attending counselling. With those sessions behind them, and the friction still causing distress, might they have seen Gordy as the source of that friction – or of the fuel lending it heat? Get rid of Gordy, get rid of the friction?"

"Gordy would have trusted Colin enough to consume something he was offered by him, and Ann might have prepared something to be offered to Gordy by Colin, without her husband knowing. Means and opportunity for both, with a possible, but weak, motive." Bud pushed his empty coffee cup away from him.

"And I haven't spent enough time with either of them to give a definitive yay or nay about whether they might be psychologically capable. Even if I believed they weren't, we both know we've encountered people before who've been able to fool me, so there's that. And let's not forget the other nurse."

Bud nodded. "Of course. Oxana. Oxana Kowalchuk. I'd never known her family name, and I have to admit to being annoyed by yet another coincidence – her turning out to be Janice Dumas's sister. Could she have been driven by a suspicion that Gordy killed Terry many years ago, leading to his 'abandonment' of her sister and niece? Seems like a bit of a stretch to me – and she's been away for the past couple of weeks on vacation, so not on the spot to administer any poison."

I nodded my agreement. "What about Dayton Woodward?"

"Our lumberjack? What's he got to do with any of this, anyway?" Bud sounded truly puzzled, and I realized I hadn't got around to telling him about Dayton having dropped in for tea the previous day. In my defence everything had been a bit busy since then, so I filled him in.

"Nothing there, Cait. Essentially, he's yet another person Gordy helped out, saving him from an unhappy career, and now his posthumous letter is urging Dayton to reconnect with family," said Bud when I finished. "There can't be a motive for him to want Gordy dead, though he'd certainly be able to find and administer the poison. And there we are again – it seems that, given what we thought of as his relatively hermit-like lifestyle, a surprising number of people *could* have poisoned Gordy, but no one wanted to."

I agreed we'd almost come to the end of our list of possible suspects without even one of them leaping out at us as a highly likely candidate. "What about Tom or Colleen White?"

Bud's fists clenched. "I know you're just being thorough, Cait, and possibly even playing devil's advocate, but Tom? Really? I think not. I feel I have the measure of Tom, and he's not a killer. Yes, he, too, could have done it, but why would he? Gordy was someone he saw as a mentor. And – though I only really know Colleen as Jack's sister, I can't see her wanting Gordy dead, can you? I mean, why would she?"

I admitted I was at a loss on that count, too.

After a few moments watching the river current racing seaward, I said, "It could be that the culprit is out and out lying to us, or just not telling us something. That's what guilty people do, after all. Look at what we found out from Louise last night: a secret marriage, an unexpected pregnancy, and a miscarriage. I wouldn't have imagined any of that as possible having known Gordy, would you?"

Bud shook his head, looking quite dejected. "No. But there's also the fight between Gordy and Terry that she witnessed. To be honest, that's what I find most disconcerting, and I guess it's what Pelletier and his team will latch onto. If there's now a witness to two men fighting back then, and one of them has never been seen since, I know where my mind would go."

I nodded. "Me too. But Gordy? Really? Do you think that's why his letters to us said we'd find out things about him that might lead us to reassess his character? It could explain why his diaries stop around that time; I had thought maybe there were more of them at his house, or somewhere else in the cabin – though goodness knows there really wasn't anywhere else in that cabin they could have been – but maybe he just stopped writing them. Guilt. Survivor's guilt – he even mentioned that in his letter to you. If he'd killed Terry, and buried him on his acreage, he'd have been living with that knowledge, and that guilt, for decades. That's caustic."

Bud started to fiddle with his spoon. "When Colleen White talked about Gordy being a church warden, that would have been after the fight Louise saw, correct?"

"Yes. Ann Evans said Gordy hadn't been at the church in the past twenty years, but Louise said he never went to church – so his time as a church warden must have been within that window."

"I hate to say it, but that might suggest Gordy was – what? – seeking redemption for something bad he'd done?"

"Like killing Terry Dumas and burying his body?"

We sat in silence for a few moments; I, for one, wasn't enjoying my thoughts.

Eventually I asked, "How long do you think it'll be before they know if the remains they found belong to Terry?"

Bud shrugged. "Without any leads as to the identity of the remains, they'd have begun general analysis. With what Louise is telling them, right now, they'll be checking Terry's dental records immediately, I'd say. That's what I'd be doing, anyhow. I can't imagine that would take long. All based on the assumption they have enough to go on with the remains they found, of course."

I dwelled on that point for a moment. "If it *is* Terry they've found, I wonder how Janice and Maddie will take the news."

Bud scratched his head for a moment. "I've dealt with missing persons cases, of course, and I'd say there's a definite desire to know what's happened to a loved one, even if that's the worst news possible. The not knowing can gnaw away at people in the most terrible way. I can recall a couple of times when I had to inform families that we'd found the deceased remains of a missing person, and they were understandably devastated, but there was an element of relief, too. Maybe it'll be that way for Janice and Maddie. It's been a long time – they must have grieved for Terry by now. Did you get the impression either of them really imagine he's still alive? Out there, somewhere, living his life, without them."

I picked up the last few crumbs of my muffin with my finger. "I've been thinking about that since Maddie told me how angry her mother was after he'd disappeared. Taking all that cash with him suggested he'd planned it. And that's an odd fact right there; if Terry Dumas *wasn't* planning a disappearing act, why withdraw all that cash from the bank? Might that have somehow been related to the fight Louise saw at Gordy's place?"

Bud's eyebrows popped up. "A fight over money, you mean? Well, we know Gordy didn't have any, so I think it unlikely. Why would Terry hand over what I reckon would have been a fair-sized bagful of cash to Gordy. And if he did, or if Gordy somehow got his hands on it after he'd killed Terry, what did he do with it all?"

"We're both starting to accept the idea that Gordy killed Terry, aren't we?" I'd heard it in Bud's voice.

Bud reached for my hand. "I know, because I've seen it too often, that sometimes a death occurs because of one swipe of the arm, or two seconds of lashing out. That's why we have first degree murder, second degree murder, and manslaughter charges. Homicide is homicide, but so few homicides are planned. Most often it occurs as the result of someone committing a once-in-a-lifetime violent act which results not only in the death of another human being, but also the devastation of the lives of all those who loved and knew the person whose life has been taken, *and* in the life of the one who committed the crime being altered forever. In the case of Gordy and Terry fighting, who knows, it might even have been deemed self-defence."

"Had Gordy not buried Terry's body, and kept it a secret."

"Exactly. Those actions suggest guilt on Gordy's part, as do several changes in his lifestyle after the event."

"And let's not forget that this is the second body found on Gordy's property. If one of them is Terry Dumas, who on earth is the other one? Oh, Bud, we were living next door to a killer for years, and we had no idea. We're pretty useless, aren't we?"

"He hid it well."

"Too true. I really liked him."

"Me too."

We sat in dismal silence for a few moments, then Bud shoved my arm. "We should head home."

I agreed, and we drove slowly from the river to the highway. As we were waiting for the lights to change a police cruiser passed us, and there was Louise North sitting in the back seat looking like the queen, head up, smiling.

"Seems her plan to make them drive her home worked," said Bud.

"Did you doubt for one moment she'd manage to bully them into it?"

"Not really. How do you feel about her going back to her place? Think her head wound allows it to be safe for her to be left alone?" Bud sounded dubious.

"The hospital cleared her to go home – we swooped in and offered her a place to get cleaned up, enjoy a decent meal, have a bed for the night, plus some fresh clothes. Maybe we've done enough?" I didn't want to sound mean, but I really wanted to get back to the box file I'd brought with me from Terry Dumas's office. I said as much.

Bud turned onto the highway. "You're right. Let's get back, and you dive in. Wouldn't mind helping out. I always seem to miss the juicy discoveries."

"Shall we tackle it in your office, or mine?" I asked playfully, as Bud negotiated a corner.

"Yours, by all means," he said, smiling. "If it's a box full of smelly old things you've got more floor space in yours to spread out."

"And my door closes properly so we can stop Marty from walking all over it."

"Critical. I'll take him for a walk to distract him while you get started, okay?"

"Good thinking, Batman."

"You're welcome, Dobbin."

Bud likes his little jokes.

Box Room

By the time Bud got back from walking Marty I'd already covered about half the floor space in my office. I'd been pretty good at simply placing items where they could be seen properly, and reached, rather than taking time to examine them. I learned during my time working with Bud that it was dangerous to fixate on one, or a few, items when trying to get a sense of a victim's lifestyle; by taking as broad a view as possible I developed a more useful overview, and I could drill down from there.

But it's so tempting to stop, look, read, and consider – it's a bit like the problem I face if I'm ever trying to sort out things to keep, dump, or donate…it's such a battle to keep moving and not get sidetracked. But, having learned that lesson on the job, I applied it in this case too. And at least it was just one box file to deal with.

Even so, Bud's eyes bulged when he saw what we were faced with. "All that was in one box?" I nodded. "And this was one of how many Terry Dumas had in his office?"

"Must have been a couple of hundred. Though some that I saw contained only a few photographs."

"Even so…" Bud scanned the room. "Where shall we start? Where would *you* like to start? It's your thing."

"First, what I can immediately tell is that everything here relates to Gordy in some way, at least in Terry's mind. I suggest we make piles of things that are similar to each other, or have something in common. Surveying this lot I'd say some obvious groupings would be: photographs – excluding plants; business papers; anything to do with plants – including photographs; papers that look to be more personal than related to business. Okay with that?"

Bud nodded, and we dug in. About half an hour later we had four piles, one in each corner, and a scattering of items that didn't fit any of the four categories.

"Let's call that mound 'sundries' and start our proper sorting with it," I suggested. "One item at a time – if it looks like it fits the other categories, add it, if not, make any smaller piles that seem reasonable. Go!"

When we'd finished I announced, "I have a couple of small piles here, if any of yours match, add them: motor vehicle stuff; a lot of newspaper clippings about uranium. Any matches?"

"Yes, weirdly, uranium stuff" – he added it to my pile – "and a few bits about truck servicing." He passed them over.

"Right, what are we left with? Some receipts that don't say what they're for, a few fancy dinner menus with no event noted, a pressed rose, three Christmas cards from Gordy to Terry. Can I read those, please?"

Bud passed them to me. "All cheap, all traditional, all simply signed: 'To Terry from G'."

"Thanks," I said, "not enlightening. Pop them on my desk, please." Bud did. "Now I want to start with the business papers. Let's take half each. We're looking for something – anything – that tells us about the joint business arrangements relating to K. Dumas, okay?" Bud nodded, and we set to.

The papers were old, yellowing, and – in many cases – the typing or handwriting on them was faded. It took time to work out what some of them were; many were incomplete, or records of sales or purchases on behalf of K. Dumas. My suspicion that Gordy had continued to supply K. Dumas with hybrid rhododendrons after the business rift in 1974 was proven; at least we discovered that much, but it was slow going.

"Got something," said Bud triumphantly. "Look, dated 1963, Gordy agreeing to lease land to Terry Dumas. It seems to be describing Gordy's lower meadow."

The two sheets were inexpertly typed, with many errors, handwritten notes, and amendments. One such handwritten note was signed by both men. "Look, this is it. It says D. Krantz will be incorporated. *D. Krantz*, not K. Dumas. Oh Bud, I've made a terrible mistake – when I was reading Gordy's diaries he only mentioned that he and Terry had set up a company – he didn't name it. I took that entry to mean the company was K. Dumas – because everyone had said that was the company Gordy and Terry founded. But this looks like they originally incorporated as D. Krantz. We need to find any papers relating to the winding up of D. Krantz, if there are any. If there's nothing here, at least now we know what we're asking the lawyers to try to find out more about."

"Yes, this has put us on the right path. We can make something of this. Let's keep going."

"Good job, Husband." Bud had scored first, I was determined to even the match.

I rustled, and read, and rummaged. "Got something – it's from 1975. It's a letter from Terry to Gordy. Oh my word – look…Terry promised to put twenty percent of profits from the company K. Dumas he had just incorporated into the accounts of the company D. Krantz on an annual basis for fifty years, or until the death of Terry Dumas, whichever was earlier. Which means two things…"

"Gordy had a source of income we knew nothing about, and…"

"Gordy had a very good reason to *not* want Terry dead."

"Correct." Bud sat back on his heels. "So, if Gordy fought with Terry, and killed him, next door, in 1994, he was losing out on another thirty years of income. Which I think at least suggests that if Gordy did kill Terry – and I'm hanging onto 'if' by my fingernails – this would be yet another reason to suggest it was unintentional."

"Fair point. But, come on, we can't stop now, we need to get through all of this. Let's finish this pile first – there might still be something we need. But I'll tell you one thing – when Gordy's letter to Janice asked her to find the papers referring to the disposition of the company he and Terry set up I bet it's D. Krantz he was talking about, not K. Dumas…and I think he wanted Janice to know how much money Terry had promised to funnel to him. I wonder how Terry managed to cover up transferring such a large portion of the profits for two decades. Come to that – and knowing how Gordy lived – I wonder what Gordy did with it all."

"Don't forget, Cait, that income would have dried up back in 1994, and who knows how 'profitable' K. Dumas even was to that point. Maybe Terry Dumas worked the books to make it look like there was next to no profit, so Gordy got very little. Businesses do it for tax reasons, why not do it so he didn't have to give it away to Gordy?"

"You're right, Husband. But, hang on, let's not get caught on this one point – we have to plough on. Literally." So we did, but nothing matched the success of those finds.

The pile about plants was very plant-orientated; the pile that was personal was not at all illuminating. The pile of photographs was mainly of plants, and there were some informal groups of people – none of whom looked familiar – and there were a few of dressy events as opposed to casual groups, but nothing that made either of us go "Oh" or "Ah".

Eventually we helped each other up, and called it a day. Back in the kitchen, I made us a pot of tea and a cheese and Branston Pickle sandwich each; I'd introduced Bud to Branston, and now he's as addicted as me.

Bud said, "I'll email the lawyers about the D. Krantz thing. They must be able to find out about it more easily than us – and they're responsible for Gordy's estate, after all."

"Do you think we should tell Janice what we've discovered?" I called as he headed for his office.

"I'll ask the lawyers. They can bill Gordy's estate for giving me advice."

"Hey, don't be so cavalier with Gordy's money – you know he promised us a 'gift' for delivering his eulogy and all that."

Bud stopped and turned. "I reckon the 'gift' will be something like us being allowed to choose from all his books and plants, before everything...I don't know...gets bulldozed over by whoever buys his land."

"Don't talk about that," I called back, "I can't cope with the idea of something awful happening next door to us. It's quite terrifying. Possibly even more terrifying than them finding bodies there. Thank heavens every home here has to have at least a five-acre parcel, because of the water and septic situation, otherwise it would be ripe for developers."

"Emailing the lawyers," called Bud.

Come Into My Garden

Marty got lots of attention during lunch – he loves cheese, so was drooling and on full alert while we ate our sandwiches, then was rewarded with some small nibbles and a proper dog treat. Bud and I managed to talk about things other than Gordy Krantz, though the presence of the forensic vehicles in the driveway next door meant we had to make a real effort for that to be the case.

"I'm going to write up that timeline of Gordy's life you wanted this afternoon, and I'll incorporate all the key dates and information I got from the diaries when I do it. Okay?"

Bud nodded. "I'm due a call from Ms. Singh, and then we'll make a plan if we're supposed to tell the Dumas family what we've learned. Will you be in your office?"

I nodded, and I got a kiss to send me on my way. I shut the office door, tiptoed over the piles on the floor and sat at my desk. I wondered how best to create the timeline; I'm not a spreadsheet sort of person, but I knew typing it was the way to go. However, first I needed to recollect everything I'd read in the diaries, and fit that together with all the additional facts we'd gathered so far. My favourite way to use my eidetic memory is to sit with my eyes closed just to the point where everything goes fuzzy, then to hum – it helps enormously. But I can't type that way, so I knew I'd have to do it a bit at a time, which would be a challenge.

I love doing focused recollection – it's like reaching out into the ether of my memory and pulling together strands of everything relevant that's out there, then weaving them together to make sense of a topic. It's incredibly satisfying when it goes well, but can be dreadfully frustrating if there are too many gaps in my knowledge to allow for a close-to-complete vision to form. On this occasion I was well equipped with facts, data, and timings – all I had to do was put it all in order.

I sat, squinted, and hummed…and pictured Gordy being born near Bear River, Saskatchewan in 1928, then immediately realized I knew nothing about him until 1954 when his diaries began – other than he'd bought some sort of property, and presumably sold it again to allow him to move to Hope, BC with enough money to then buy twenty-five acres on Red Water Mountain. So, a frustrating start – but I persisted. He'd arrived in Hope in 1954, had bought and cleared the land in 1955, and built his cabin too, then removed stumps and so forth while he worked at the cedar mill over a few years.

In the 1960s he met Rachel, she left; he met Terry, and they started a business called D. Krantz. They worked hard together, grew the business, and greenhouses were built on the part of his acreage where our two houses now sat. He got a new truck.

The 1970s saw him becoming annoyed with Terry's future business plans; he got to know Louise North, was into growing marijuana and living a pretty free and easy lifestyle. He was best man when Terry married Janice, but soon after severed ties of both a business and personal nature with the Dumases – except for the income he received from then on from Terry's new company, K. Dumas.

In the 1980s he secretly married Louise, lost a baby, and divorced Louise. Terry and Gordy were still in touch at this time, with Gordy still supplying Dumas with plants.

The 1990s kicked off with Gordy giving Louise a puppy, then not much (except for lots of diary entries about his work on rhododendrons) until Louise sees him fighting with Terry in 1994. He stops writing diaries (as far as we know). He's a member of the congregation, and becomes church warden, at St. Peter's somewhere between 1994 and 2000 (NOTE: ask Colleen White about exact dates) when he inspires Colin Evans to give his personal life to the church.

During the 2000s he convinces Colin Evans to go into nursing, though Gordy's no longer going to church.

In the 2010s-2020s he meets Max Muller, inspires him to try being a chef again; gets to know Tom White and teaches him about foraging to help his new restaurant; persuades Dayton Woodward to give up a trade and become a lumberjack; he advises Colin and Ann Evans to attend counselling to save their marriage. Otherwise he's known for not mixing. Bud and I arrive. Parkinson's diagnosis. We get meals delivered to him, nurses tending to him, he writes highly convoluted last will and testament. He dies, from ingesting poison hemlock, somehow.

I sat back, and pressed SAVE.

I was tired, and time had not only passed for Gordy in terms of my having summarized most of his life, but it had flown for me too; it was gone six. I checked my work. Had I left anything out? I didn't think so. There were gaps, but I knew now that Colleen White might help me get a better idea if Gordy could have made any enemies during his church-going years – which sounded odd as I thought it, but I justified my reasoning by filling in the blanks from having been brought up within a church-going family in Wales; congregations can be incredibly fertile breeding grounds for all sorts of rivalries.

I headed to the kitchen to make a plan for dinner, and was pleased that I'd taken some salmon out of the freezer that morning. There are very few things in this world that are faster to prepare, or taste better when simply cooked, than wild Pacific sockeye salmon. I knew Bud and I would enjoy it, and we did. Luckily it was a light enough meal that it didn't make me want to immediately flop onto the sofa and lose myself in something on TV, so, by eight o'clock I was ready to phone Colleen White.

I'd hoped that phoning Colleen meant I'd get off lightly; I wasn't sure I could cope with her torrent of word-salad face to face. But I should have known better; when she answered the phone she was clearly distracted by something, which she explained – at great length – was the world's largest house spider, ever. She left me in no doubt that she hated and feared spiders, so I steeled myself to have an entire conversation with a woman who was absolutely convinced that a monster was hiding from her until it had worked out how best to attack. It wasn't going to be easy, but the mere fact I'd called her meant she wasn't going to let me not tell her why. So I did.

"I really just wanted to check a few dates with you, for Gordy Krantz's eulogy, Colleen."

"Of course, you'd want to get things right. Sheila told me that's how you operate."

I didn't take that to be a flattering description of me, but knew I was still working at warming up my friendship with Sheila after our time in Jamaica a few months earlier, so I let it pass. "Thanks, yes, I do," was my guarded reply.

"Now just give me a moment to think…oh no, I can see its leg, it's behind the curtain." Colleen sounded terrified.

"I suggest you stay away from the curtain." It was the best advice I could come up with, and sound, I thought.

"But it can climb the curtain." Colleen now sounded petrified.

I couldn't see how that put her at any greater risk, so repeated, "So just stay away from the curtain. When do you think Gordy joined your congregation?" I was determined to plough on.

"Ah, yes, I think that would have been the winter of 1994. We'd had a broken bell for years, and Gordy got involved with bringing it down to get it mended. Of course, it turned out we couldn't afford that, but we decided we could afford a bell machine, which is like a recording of a bell. That was 1994. I know that because we had to get it all sorted out for Christmas, and it was a terrible rush. And we've just had a meeting about what we'll do to celebrate thirty years of the new bell in 2024. So I know it was 1994. We kept the old one, of course, because of its historical relationship with the church. Cast in 1927 it was. Amazing, when you think of it, right? We have some photos of it on our website, if you'd like to see it."

I couldn't wrap my head around the need to celebrate the use of a recording of a bell, let alone planning so far in advance to do so. "Thanks, I'll take a look when I have a minute," I replied. I hoped that was the end of the bell conversation. "And what about when he left?"

"Who? The Reverend Hopkins? He wasn't even there when the bell was replaced."

I sighed, and resisted the temptation to say I had no idea who the Reverend Hopkins was. "When did Gordy stop attending church?" *Focus, woman!*

"Oh, right. Oh no – it's disappeared altogether now. Where's it gone?"

I bit my tongue. Literally, because I knew exactly where I wanted the blessed spider to go. "Probably gone outside, somehow. They do that. They prefer being outside." I was lying, but what the heck.

"Really? I thought they liked the warmth, inside. Well, I'll just open the slider, maybe that will tempt it out. It's been such a lovely day, hasn't it?"

It had, but I wasn't going to bite. "So, when would you say Gordy left the church?"

"2000, I'm certain of that because of the bishop."

I weighed my response. Yes, I needed to know what Colleen meant. "How did Gordy leaving have a connection to the bishop?"

"Gordy was there when the bishop visited, and he did that to celebrate the millennium. Visited every church in the diocese in the first three months of 2000. Marvellous man. An absolute inspiration. But when we sent the letter thanking him for coming, Gordy had left. He was church warden at the time, so should have been one of the signatories, but he'd just disappeared, so we had to set up a committee to decide who should replace him, because it wasn't the right time to do it. Special votes and all that. And we had to decide who should sign the letter of thanks if we didn't have a sitting church warden. We ended up having a pot-luck night to talk that one through."

I could picture it all: committees to decide about setting up committees, and every get-together having to be catered in some way. My childhood recollections of the conversations my parents used to have about the details of church machinations came flooding back, bitter-sweet.

At least I had a couple of useful dates for Gordy's timeline. But I wondered why he'd left so abruptly, and – again – weighed the desire to know against the desire to get off the phone.

"Any idea why Gordy did that – left the church, or 'disappeared' as you said?" I had to know.

"Arrgh, it's back. It's behind the TV." I heard clattering, and suspected Colleen had dropped the phone. The muffled squeals and shouts of: "Get away from me," and "No you don't" continued for a few moments. Then Colleen's voice boomed, "I got him, with my slipper. Absolutely flattened him, his body's out in the garden, thank heavens."

I wanted to say so many things, most involving the meaning of the words of the hymn "All things bright and beautiful", but decided against it. What was the point?

"Oh good," was my pathetic attempt to remain neutral on the subject. "Now, about Gordy leaving the church?"

"It was probably something to do with that Colin Evans, when he was a boy. His parents weren't the most forgiving people, and they thought their boy was spending altogether too much time at church, so they banned him from attending most of the activities beyond the Sunday Eucharist."

I recalled what Ann Evans had said about her husband, and Gordy's role in the church at the time. "You mean Colin had to stop going to youth club, bible study, that sort of thing?"

"Yes. It set a lot of tongues wagging. Why wouldn't they let their boy join in activities with Gordy any longer? What did they know, that they weren't saying? That sort of thing. I didn't think for one minute there was anything questionable about Gordy getting so involved in all the church groups, but people do talk when there's a man involved who's never been married."

Married and divorced, if only you knew, was what I thought. "In what way did tongues wag, exactly?" was what I asked.

Colleen made a sort of spluttering sound. "You know how these things are. No one says anything outright, there's just a certain way they say nothing. A look here, an eyeroll there. The phrase 'No smoke without fire' being bandied about. You know."

Indeed I did, it was exactly the sort of treatment I'd received back in Cambridge after Angus had been found dead in my flat – all amplified by the tabloids who were only too happy to put into print that which no one actually dared say to my face. I hate gossip, with a deep-seated loathing that makes me almost instantly angry. Even as Colleen was describing the situation at the local church – which one would have hoped would be home to a segment of society rather more inclined to be forgiving than the general population – I could feel myself getting hot around the back of my neck, a sure sign I'm getting cross…or starting to have a hot flash. One can lead to the other, so I told myself to calm down, but my internal monologue never seems to capture the calming tones Bud has managed to master over the years.

"You're saying Gordy was hounded out of the church by gossips, with absolutely no evidence to suggest there was anything amiss?" I sounded angry in my head, and was certain that's how I'd come over.

Colleen's tone suggested she'd been personally slighted in some way. "I guess you could put it like that."

Typical! was what I thought. "How terribly sad for Gordy," was what I said.

"He could have spoken up for himself," was Colleen's wounded reply.

And be told he was protesting so much he must be guilty of something, was what I thought. "I suppose so," was what I said. "And he never returned to the congregation after that?" I thought I'd better check, though I knew I wouldn't have gone within rock-throwing distance of the place after being subjected to such a campaign.

"No, he didn't even turn up to support our Christmas bazaar that year." Colleen made it sound as though he'd dipped a small child in aspic and eaten it whole…in the middle of the church hall. "He'd organized that for years, so we all had to come up with a new way of doing it, and share the work," she added, which made my neck even hotter.

"Other than his potential as a pedophile, is there anything else you can tell me about Gordy Krantz?" I was beginning to lose the will to live, so didn't even bother to try to make my voice sound sympathetic.

"Oh, please don't misunderstand me, no one ever said anything like that about Gordy," snapped Colleen.

They didn't need to say it aloud, was what I thought. "Good," was what I said.

"He was such a rock at the church before all that started," continued Colleen as though I hadn't said anything at all. "We all realized when he stopped coming how much he'd done. The reverend was quite overwhelmed when he had to temporarily take over organizing all the groups Gordy had set up, and then there was the church-cleaning rota, the maintenance of the vestments, the managing of the supplies, counting the collection and doing all the banking…oh, the list went on and on. We all do a little bit each nowadays, which seems to work well."

I didn't think I was going to get anything else useful from Colleen, but dared one more question. "What did you think of him, personally? Did you know him well, beyond his church role?"

Silence. I wondered if the spider had revealed itself to not be quite as dead as Colleen had believed.

Eventually she said, "I don't suppose you'd call it 'dating', really, but we did share a few meals over the years."

This was more like it. I laid on the charm as thick as I dared. "That must have been nice for you both. Did you come to Gordy's house, here on Red Water Mountain Drive?"

Colleen giggled. Like a schoolgirl. "Oh heavens, no. We met in public places. Restaurants, coffee shops. It was all quite proper."

I couldn't believe I was talking to a woman in the twenty-first century. So many questions were whirring around my head – not one of them was even remotely appropriate. I counted to five, then asked, "If you had to characterize Gordy, would you have said he was a helpful person, or an interfering one?"

Colleen didn't hesitate. "Oh, most helpful. And not just while he was at church – we kept in touch, on some matters. Gordy knew people across our local community who could do a good job. A few years back he put me in touch with a wonderful young man who's now my lumberjack, he's yours too, I think. Dayton – he was there the other day with us all. It's so tough to find a reliable lumberjack. And Gordy pointed me in the right direction when I had to get the house rewired. It always surprised me that he knew so many people, considering he had a reputation for being a bit of a hermit."

I had to agree with Colleen's last point. "Thanks for that, it all helps. For the eulogy, I mean."

"No news on needing the church hall for his memorial? Our rates are very reasonable, you know." Colleen sounded smiley.

"No idea when that might be, yet." I was determined to not let any cats out of bags, at all.

"When do you think those police people will have finished on his property? It's been days now."

Of course Colleen knew about the forensic investigation at Gordy's place – everyone knew. There really is no such thing as a secret in a rural area – not even when it's a complete untruth, I suspected.

"Oh, I dare say they'll be gone soon," I lied. "And I must go now. Thanks Colleen, you've been most helpful. Goodnight," I said, and disconnected.

I added the relevant information to the entry about Gordy in the 1990s, then handed the printed pages to Bud for him to read before bed.

Home Alone

Bud and I were relieved to see some additional activity by the forensic team at Gordy's the next morning; as we shared a pot of coffee we counted two more vehicles than had been present to date.

"Extra people coming in to dismantle the tents and so forth, I guess," said Bud, staring out of the window, blowing on his coffee. "Should only take a couple of hours, then Gordy's place will look like Gordy's place again. It'll be good to not have people coming and going, up and down his driveway all the time, setting Marty off on a totally justified territorial barking frenzy."

I agreed, and got on with breakfast. There's something unique about Marmite that means that when you want it, there's no other flavour that will satisfy your tastebuds. I'd woken up wanting Marmite on toast, and was luxuriating in the first oozing mouthful when Bud swore, and almost spilled his coffee.

"What?" I asked, with my mouth full.

"You're not going to believe this. They're putting up another tent. That'll be their third. What on earth is going on over there? Look, it's way over there, beyond the house – but you can just see it."

It takes a great deal to make me walk away from Marmite on toast, but it appeared this was enough to get me out of my chair and over to the window. Bud was right, of course. My tummy clenched, and it was nothing to do with the great big dollops of brown malty, salty goodness and about half a pound of butter I'd just stuffed down my throat. No, it was totally driven by the fact that it was beginning to look like there really was yet another body buried next door – because neither Bud nor I could think of any good reason for yet more of what would undoubtedly be an overstretched forensics budget being thrown at an acreage halfway up a little mountain.

"I'm gonna call Pelletier. He might tell me what's going on. This is driving me crazy. It's all happening right there" – Bud waved his arm – "and I cannot do a thing about it."

Bud's got his calming voice off pat, but I've never been very good at it; must be something to do with the way we Welsh have that sing-songy thing going on with our inflection. But I gave it my best. "Husband, we *are* doing something – in fact, we're doing a great deal. We're both actively investigating Gordy's life. You had a chance to read through the timeline I did for him, didn't you? And we've sussed out, questioned, and analyzed potential poisoners. We're being as pro-active as we've ever been for all our non-professional investigations, aren't we?"

Bud looked down at me, his shoulders sagging. "I guess. But I wish…I want to do more. I want to know what's going on. They're right there, Cait – people I worked with for years have been doing their jobs within yards of my home, for ages now. They don't even wave when I walk by with Marty anymore."

"Hang on, it's Tuesday morning, Bud. It was only last Thursday that they got an indication from the coroner that Gordy's death wasn't from natural causes, and they only discovered the first lot of buried remains on Friday. They didn't even get them off the property until first thing Saturday. We both know this is still very early days in their inquiries. Their forensic effort is likely to be focused on Gordy, first and foremost, because his is the most recent death. Whatever they can do with the other remains found there will take time. We both know how stretched those people are. The labs will be backed up, and I bet you Pelletier is pulling his hair out. Like you used to. Remember?"

Bud nodded, still looking dejected.

I risked adding, "And if you will insist upon walking Marty along the fence line four times a day, no wonder they've stopped waving. It was probably a novelty at first; now they must feel like you're stalking them, or at least spying on them."

Bud tutted. Loudly. I stood and hugged him, tight. "I love you, Husband. I hate seeing you like this. Look, yes, why don't you try to get hold of Pelletier, and see if he can tell you anything at all, and I'll get onto the lawyers and grill them about Gordy's early life. I don't know how long they've been his lawyers – Rylan Oishi looks ancient, he could have been dealing with Gordy's affairs for many years. Fingers crossed, eh?"

Bud shook himself, like Marty does when he leaps out of our pond. "You're right, of course," he said, sounding quite Bud-like again. "I'll get hold of Pelletier and find out whatever I can. I'll take Marty out first, then settle myself in my office until I'm done. Best to be businesslike about it."

I love it when Bud's Bud. I kissed him. "And I'll clear up here and put in a call to Rylan Oishi. I shall be my most charming self, and winkle out of him whatever I can. Go team!"

Bud rolled his eyes at me, then patted his thigh – the sign that tells Marty they're off on an adventure. Marty was immediately excited, as was I at the prospect of having direction, and a goal. I'm good when I have goals. And lists. And plans.

Showered, dressed, and with a list in front of me, I phoned Rylan Oishi. The youthful receptionist said he was between meetings; she made it sound as though he only rarely stuck his head up, like a meerkat, between meetings. Lucky me.

I waited, and eventually the lawyer's thin voice said, "Professor Morgan, what can I do for you?"

Straight to business – good. "Thanks for taking my call, Mr. Oishi. As you know I'm working on Gordy's eulogy and I have some questions about the time before he arrived in British Columbia. I wondered how long you'd represented him, and what you might be able to tell me about that part of his life."

Silence.

More silence.

I wondered if we'd been disconnected from each other. "Hello? Mr. Oishi?"

"I was thinking," he said sounding vague.

My spirits sank a little; I suspected this was going to be like pulling teeth – slow and painful. I decided to make his task easier. "Maybe we can start with how long you've been his lawyer."

"Yes, I can tell you that. Mr. Krantz first appointed this practice to represent him in 1963. I was just starting my career, under Ms. Singh's father at that time."

I hadn't realized Mahera Singh was following in her father's footsteps. "Can you tell me anything about the nature of the work you undertook for him back then?" After just one second of silence I added, "It might help me better understand what Gordy was doing at the time, for the eulogy." Neither Oishi nor Singh knew I'd read almost forty years' worth of Gordy's diaries, and I didn't feel the need to tell them that.

"I believe I'm able to do so without breaking any confidences, as the issues would all be a matter for the public record. My colleagues and I witnessed and notarized various documents pertaining to his business, on his behalf." The lawyer's dry tone matched the aridity of his prose.

"Would that be the company D. Krantz?" I thought it best to be direct.

"Indeed. We incorporated the company for him, and then worked on some realignments in the early 1970s."

He obviously didn't imagine there to be anything fishy about the company, or he wouldn't have sounded so unperturbed.

"You never undertook any work for him to dissolve that company?"

"Why no. The company is still incorporated and doing extremely well. Mr. Krantz took our advice, held onto the business, and has used its income to benefit so many. Surprisingly – to me, at least – he became a real pillar of the community, in many ways."

I was lost. "I'm sorry, I don't understand. Are you saying Gordy has...or had...a successful business which is still operating?"

"Indeed he does. *Did.* My apologies. The company you yourself mentioned moments ago, D. Krantz incorporated. We assisted Mr. Krantz – in tandem with his accounting firm – to fold his original company, Charity Holdings Inc., into D. Krantz Inc. back in 1975. Both businesses have been run under the D. Krantz name since then."

"What type of business is it?"

"The main income derives, of course, from the uranium mine. A smaller, but still substantial, amount comes from the plant licences."

I was gobsmacked. "Gordy Krantz owned a uranium mine?"

"Indeed. The Charity Mine, in Saskatchewan. He purchased the land in 1948, uranium was discovered in 1949, and production grew steadily, though it was one of the smaller outputs amongst the uranium mines in that province at the time. I understand the mine became more or less dormant during the 1960s, but, once the need for uranium for nuclear power began in the 1970s, the Charity Mine returned to full production, as it continues to this day. Mr Krantz had a highly proficient management team in place there; he was, essentially, a hands-off owner."

I was agog. "And how much money does it make? Do you know?"

Rylan Oishi cleared his throat. "Since the information is publicly available, I can tell you that Mr. Krantz has benefitted to the tune of many millions of dollars over the years. When he set up the trust to build and maintain Krantz Hall at the University of Vancouver, he arranged it so that most of the money went directly to that fund, and it will continue to do so, per his wishes."

My mind was swirling. The Krantz of Krantz Hall was our Gordy Krantz, after all. I hadn't seen that coming. And I just couldn't fathom Gordy – the man who loved nature, and lived like a hermit in a hovel – was a millionaire many times over because of uranium, even if he'd chosen to give all the profits away.

"You mentioned plant licenses?" I needed the full picture.

"Mr. Krantz was a talented plantsman. He created many new hybrids of plant, and signed deals for them to be cultivated around the world. That part of the business fluctuates, however, it alone produces a considerable income flow each year."

Gordy creating and licensing new breeds of plants made much more sense to me than his owning a uranium mine; I'd witnessed his diligence, and even his obsession with them, in many of his diaries.

"Did Gordy give you the instructions for this incredibly complicated will of his during the past nine months or so?"

The lawyer cleared his throat again; a good way to give himself thinking time. "Mr. Krantz met with Ms. Singh on two occasions within the past nine months. Other than that, we dealt with him on the telephone. I know only too well how the challenges of age can make one less mobile; Mr. Krantz is one of very few clients for whom I perform any services these days, having been away from the office for some time due to personal health matters. He was happy to work with Ms. Singh on a more regular basis, as I have not – prior to his passing – been at the office very often. I have, however, been here every day since his unfortunate demise. Once his affairs are satisfactorily wound up, I shall fully retire from the firm."

I could hear in his voice that he wanted that to be soon.

"You didn't want Ms. Singh to give us the letter Gordy wrote in case of his death being ruled unnatural. Why is that, Mr. Oishi?"

Silence. More silence. "I cannot, to my own satisfaction, rule out the possibility that Mr. Krantz chose to take his life, rather than having had it taken from him. I did not believe he meant that letter to be opened unless the 'unnatural causes' were established as more than 'suspicious'. I am closer to Mr. Krantz's age than is Ms. Singh. I believe that the prospect offered by the diagnosis of a painful, debilitating disease might be viewed differently by a person in their nineties than in their forties. I would not discount the taking of one's life as being beyond the bounds of reason for a man like Mr. Krantz."

I let his words sink in. "And what sort of a man would you say Mr. Krantz was, Mr. Oishi? It sounds as though you've had fairly regular dealings with him over the years – you must have formed an opinion."

A dry laugh. "Much of our business took place in short bursts of activity. It's the way with our role in most people's lives. A connection in the early 1960s, more work in the mid-1970s, then again in the 1990s, with the work surrounding the University of Vancouver during the early 2000s. His final wishes were put into place earlier this year. Personally, I haven't sat in the same room as Mr. Krantz since... oh, the early 1990s, I'd say. Various colleagues have had meetings with him since then, but I…let's just say I didn't feel the need to meet with him face to face after our earliest encounters."

Now the lawyer wasn't being professionally reticent, he was verging on the cagey. I decided to push. "I realize your responsibility is to act in your client's best interests, but – on a personal level – I get the impression you didn't like Gordy Krantz."

"Mr. Krantz was a singularly driven man, Professor Morgan. I shall, as you say, represent his interests to the best of my ability, but I, for one, am glad I shall never have to meet him again. Now, is there anything else?"

I jumped in. "Just briefly – did Gordy ever give you any insights into his life in Saskatchewan, or did he tell you why he came to BC in the first place?" I crossed my fingers, figuratively and in fact.

Another throat-clearing was required. Then a huge sigh. At last – the dam was about to burst!

Ryan Oishi sounded different – his voice had a metallic edge. "I shall speak to you in confidence, Professor Morgan, knowing you have signed an agreement which binds you in this matter. In decades past it was the norm to offer clients alcoholic beverages during meetings, or over lunches, and so forth. Mr. Krantz always availed himself of copious amounts of liquor on such occasions. He thereafter tended to lose any inhibitions he might have had, and spoke freely on all manner of topics. On one occasion he used highly inappropriate language in the company of young ladies during a meeting. I sent our two female members of staff home early that day, traumatized. I cannot recall all of his musings and meanderings from those occasions, but – to answer your specific points – I remember he mentioned attending a Catholic school in his younger years…I believe his parents were Roman Catholics. And he made quite a performance of telling those of us present that he'd come to BC hoping the girls were prettier and wore fewer clothes than in Saskatchewan, because it didn't get as cold in the winter. Other than that, I have no more insights into the man's formative years, though the wild streak evident in all my dealings with him suggested to me that his Catholic education didn't produce the desired outcome. Now, I really must get back to this paperwork, if you don't mind, Professor Morgan. I have a meeting in ten minutes."

I was processing information, so finished up with a polite: "Thank you, Mr. Oishi," and disconnected.

I sat for a moment, trying to take everything in. Krantz Hall? Uranium? Millions of dollars? Global plant licenses? Gordy drunk, and being obnoxious? *Our* Gordy?

I almost jumped out my skin when Bud knocked at my door and stuck his head in. He was aglow. "You'll never believe what I've just found out. Go on, guess?"

I chuckled. "I give in. Just tell me."

Bud was looking a little smug, "You know we've been thinking maybe Gordy had killed and buried Terry Dumas next door?" I nodded. "The first body they found, the one they discovered near where we dumped the soup, is female, not male. Been in the ground for over fifty years, they reckon."

I sighed as though I'd sprung a leak. "So, not Terry Dumas. Do they know who she is? Might Gordy have killed *her*?"

"Don't know. Hang on, there's more. Second set of remains found, down near Gordy's old cabin, is skeletal remains only, long bones and pelvis say male. Long bones say it might be about Terry Dumas's build, but no skull, so – until they can get DNA tests done – no ID on that body either, because dental ID's not in play. They're assessing waiting for DNA versus digging up a lot more acreage to try to find the skull."

"Any news on why the new tent they've erected this morning?"

Bud looked a little deflated. "More remains, definitely human, definitely female."

"I see. Two females, near the house, one male – maybe Terry – near the cabin. Three bodies buried next door, all the time we've lived here. Good grief."

"Yes." Bud looked grim.

"Want my news now?"

"Hang on, there's more." Bud's eyes looked even more blue than usual as he grinned and announced, "Poison hemlock found in the dregs of a broken mug of tea discovered beneath Gordy's body. So, we still don't know if it was self-administered or not, but we do know how it got into his body, which is…something."

"I'm glad it wasn't the soup," I said, feeling pleased that at least we hadn't messed up that aspect.

"Nope, not the soup. The soup was totally innocent." Bud had clearly enjoyed his fix of cop-ly interaction. "I bet you can't top that lot, can you?"

I hated to burst his bubble.

Home Delivery

"There you are – cold salmon with arugula, in a wrap, with a slathering of Maggi mayonnaise. Okay?" I held the plate towards Bud as a sort of peace offering. Not that he was angry, it was just that my news about Gordy's questionable past had rather taken the shine off his discoveries.

"Sounds great. I love leftovers. And when you put Maggi sauce in mayo? Yum!"

I settled beside him at the table.

Bud bit into his wrap with great enthusiasm and enjoyed chasing the mayo as it ran down his chin. He was just fine, really, but a bit stunned about the characterization of Gordy I'd been given by Rylan Oishi, and was still – like me – struggling to come to terms with the news about the uranium mine…and the millions of dollars.

After we'd both finished, Bud said, "Do you think you should phone poor old Frank McGregor up at your university and tell him it was our next-door neighbor who'd been funneling millions into Krantz Hall after all?"

I chuckled. "I might – though quite how the news that the environmental research jewel of Western Canada has been funded by uranium money will be received, I cannot guess. Maybe I could give him a heads-up…by letting the chancellor get ahead of the game he'd score a lot of brownie points, and Frank's all in favor of those."

Bud chewed his lip for a moment. "Not to advocate playing politics, Cait, but could you do with some of that currency being in your favor with the chancellor? The higher up the food chain the goodwill lies, the more it's likely to benefit you."

I put the almost crumb-free plates on the kitchen floor for Marty as I replied, "Not to play politics, Bud, but I happen to know the chancellor's thinking of moving on. Frank won't – he'll die in harness. Thus, I think if there are any brownie points up for grabs, I'd like it to be Frank who's indebted to me, not the chancellor."

Bud was puzzled. "How on earth do you know that about the chancellor? You haven't even been at the place for a year."

"He attended that lunch I went to at the beginning of September, to congratulate the profs who'd made last year's Roll of Honor. We exchanged pleasantries over non-alcoholic drinks and nondescript nibbles, which is when he said he hoped to see my name on next year's roll. I told him about my then mythical plan to take a semester to work on research – which would put me out of the running – and he said it might be someone other than him doing the hand-shaking in the future. Then he thanked me for the way my research has drawn attention to the university. His body language and micro-expressions were a veritable symphony of tells – he's looking to move."

Bud shook his head, and smiled. "When you say you'd be no good at undercover intelligence gathering you're doing yourself a disservice, Cait."

I wasn't having that. "Husband, you know I've told your old mate John Silver I don't want to work for him not because I don't think I could do it, but because there's no way I'd want to be away from you – nor do I think undercover work would be right for me. You're always telling me I'm a terrible liar."

"True, but if you're living a lie, the best way to get through everything you have to do and face, is to believe the lie yourself."

"Careful now – you can't risk revealing a state secret." I like to tease Bud about the fact he can't tell me every detail of every operation he's ever worked on; it helps me believe it doesn't matter to me as much as it does. "Still, the psychological strain it must put on a person to live a false life must be tremendous. Not for everyone."

Bud's eyes crinkled. "That's why there's such a lot of research, assessment, and training done before officers are assigned to undercover work, but, even then, things can go badly wrong. I don't mean that their cover is blown – though, sadly, that does happen – what I mean is…well, the effects at the time, and later on. A colleague of mine was in deep cover for almost three years. It was a hugely effective operation, and the results had an impact on the lives of thousands of people in this area. Post-operation he had to completely amend his way of life, both professionally and personally. You see, there's not just the risk of being found out when you're actually undercover, there's also the long-term risk associated with being found out later on. Sadly, he'd had to do some terrible things just to be accepted within his undercover role, which he struggled to leave behind him; that sort of problem is sadly not unusual."

"The psychologist in me is suggesting your colleague realized he fitted in rather too well – that he came out believing there was something in his psyche that allowed that to be the case. He couldn't shake off the adopted identity in some way. Maybe every time he looked in a mirror, he didn't like what he saw, because that other persona was peeping through."

Bud nodded. He nibbled his lip. "Counselling didn't help. None of us knew it was as bad for him as it was." He reached out and held me. "Poor guy couldn't see a way past it. Took his own life. Tragic."

"Sorry, Bud." I hugged him tight.

Marty nuzzled at our legs, afraid he wasn't getting a look-in, and we broke apart. I was so happy we were at home, safe and together, that I tried to wish away everything that was happening almost literally on our doorstep.

"Do you remember when we first saw this house?" I asked.

Bud nodded. "Couldn't believe our luck, could we?"

"I know, but I was thinking about what you said at the time."

Bud chuckled. "Well, I have no idea what that was, but I guess you can tell me word for word. So – what was it I said?"

I twinkled before I spoke, to make sure he knew how much I loved him. "You said this would be a great neck of the woods for someone to hide out in. We talked about how remote Red Water Mountain felt, though, to be fair, we're only half an hour away from all the civilization we'll ever really need. But I've been thinking…and what you said is true. Max Muller now lives in this area because he was looking for a quiet place where he could recover from his breakdown; Tom White was psychologically traumatized in Vegas, and he came here to 'lick his wounds' as he put it; Dayton Woodward lives and works here, having been cut off from his family; Louise North left the USA and settled on the other side of the mountain; Gordy had pretty much turned has back on the world, for whatever reason…and even we were both happy to not exactly hide from the world, but to be able to choose when we participate in what bits of it we need. This area is a magnet for people who have wanted to escape, in some way or other. We're all wounded. We're all trying to heal."

Bud's brow furrowed. "True. We're all very fortunate, because it's such a beautiful place. What do the Japanese do? Is it tree bathing? And we can dive right in."

"It's *shinrin-yoku*, or forest bathing. And you're right, we can, and I do. I recognize I'm not one of the world's naturally meditative people, but even I can feel my shoulders unhunching when I'm out there, surrounded by only the sounds of nature, the colors of nature, and the smells of nature. It's incredibly soothing."

The phone rang, calling me back to reality. It was Maddie Dumas, sounding like the breath of fresh air she always was.

"Hi Cait, I've found a few more bits and pieces about Gordy, and I finally dug out the wedding photos. Would you like me to pop by with them? We'll be finished soon, and our last call today is Louise, so I could drop them off after that, okay?"

I agreed, hung up the phone, and shouted to Bud, "Maddie and Max will be here soon. Want to see them? Divide and conquer? You grill him for anything he knows, I'll stick with Maddie. I'm eager to have another chance to weigh up her potential as a poisoner. Now that we know the hemlock was in Gordy's tea, it's even more clear that whoever gave it to him was someone he trusted. Maddie, or Max, could have given him anything in powder form for him to drink whenever he wanted – we have to consider that as a possibility."

"Sure," was shouted along the hall – Bud was already in his office, "but I've got to send an email to Pelletier first, about everything the lawyer told you…even if it's not relevant to his investigations at the moment. I only got what I did out of him by promising open lines of communication. Gotta deliver."

I did my thing with the fluffy duster again – that was twice in one week; a record! – and put the kettle on. There wasn't anything in the house to offer to nibble, so I raided my chocolate stash and put a mound of mini-bars in a fancy dish; it would have to do, even if I was hosting an ex-captain of the Canadian chef team – whatever that was. Maybe Bud could find out.

I also took the chance to phone Frank at the university, who reacted to my news about the proceeds from a uranium mine funding Krantz Hall as though I'd branded him with a flaming iron; he actually squealed. Various phrases rushed out of him, all along the lines of how the scandal of uranium money being accepted by the university could be the downfall of many a person – I suspected he meant the chancellor – and how "steps" would need to be taken. Once he'd calmed down, he was gushingly grateful, and I hoped his gratitude would weigh in my favour at some point in the future.

When our guests arrived, Marty did his usual thing of creating a fuss, and dutifully sniffed all of Maddie and Max's most embarrassing places before we settled for tea. Max presented me with a plastic zipper-bag full of oatmeal cookies, which looked as though they'd be terribly good for me, but turned out to taste almost entirely of butter, which was a delight.

There were the usual remarks about the weather and the price of gas at the pumps – which I'd learned quite soon after my arrival in the Lower Mainland were the inevitable first two topics of conversation when any group of people gathered. They were able to give us a report on Louise's health; "rude" and "good" were two of the terms used, which was excellent news, then Maddie produced the wedding photo album. I took this as my cue to allow Bud some time alone with Max, so I offered Maddie the chance to see what we'd found in the box file I'd brought home from her place. I was glad to leave the two men alone; Max's knees hadn't stopped bouncing up and down under the table since he'd sat down, and I find that sort of kinetic energy to be most distracting.

Bud kept Marty with him, but I shut the door to my office once we were inside in any case. Maddie looked surprised when she saw the piles on the floor, but I explained my methods, hoping she'd understand I had good reason for the place looking as though the box file had simply exploded in the middle of the room.

I cleared a space on my desk, and she sat on my spare chair as I looked through the album. Most of the photographs were Polaroids, though a few had been taken with a traditional camera.

"Who took the photos?" I asked; it's always useful to know who's behind a camera, because the person whose face you're seeing is looking at them, and might, therefore, be showing emotions related to the photographer, not just the occasion.

"I asked Mom that, when I found the album. She said her father took some of them, but Gordy took the most. He was the one with the Polaroid, apparently. Used it to take photos of all his precious things, she said, which – given the box files we saw the other day – must mean his rhododendrons."

My mind flew to the other Polaroids we'd found at Gordy's house, but I didn't mention them.

I flicked the pages; it had been a small, simple wedding, but Janice had looked like a princess – no surprise there, then. "Where was it held?" I asked.

"On the land where we live now. Mom will tell you – given half a chance – that it might appear idyllic, because of the position of the photographer, but she was looking at a building site at the time, because they'd just broken ground to lay the foundations for the house. I think she'd have preferred something classier, but all their money was tied up in the business, or being used on the house, so they kept it simple."

"Your father was a good-looking man," I said. He had been – the groom was tall, well built, with thick, wavy, dark hair; this being the 1970s, he had lots of it. There was a straightness to his back that spoke of more than good deportment; I suspected Terry had been a proud man. Maybe that was because it was his wedding day. "Do these photos show you your father as you knew him? A younger version of him, of course."

Maddie beamed. "Oh yes. He was always like that – so strong, upright, dependable. But not quite as much hair." She laughed.

I noted the deep cleft in Terry's chin; it suited him, and gave him a distinctive air. Maddie hadn't inherited it. "Your father has a unique chin," I said.

"I loved his dimple…he used to let me stick my pinkie finger in it when I was young. When I was very small, I believed it might bite off the end of my finger."

"It must have been terribly difficult for you – his disappearance."

Maddie looked out of the window, her glassy gaze not focussing on the trees outside. "I was nine. He was truly delighted that I had a genuine interest in horses. The home for retired racehorses was all him. That was Dad – he gave everyone another chance. Tried to, anyway. I guess he felt he'd given Mom and me enough chances, and that's why he left. We'll never know, now."

I couldn't mention the discoveries next door, but also couldn't help but wonder if Maddie and Janice would be pleased to know that Terry hadn't deserted them.

Maddie stood, and stretched. "It's funny to think I'll never see Gordy again. He was lovely. Which isn't what I'd expected. Mom rarely spoke of him, and even though I was only young, I recall Dad infrequently referring to him as 'that man', or 'him', like he was some sort of monster. Which was why I was surprised that Gordy was so nice. The first time we visited, Max told him who I was, and told me who he was. Maybe I mentioned it – Gordy acted really weirdly when he found out I was Terry Dumas's daughter."

I nodded. "Yes, you did."

Maddie picked at the side of a fingernail. "It was a notable reaction. He seemed fine with it by the next time we visited.

He asked me about Dad a few times after that...got me to tell him all about the times Dad and I would ride together, or just spend hours grooming the horses. And he peppered me with questions about what I'd done with my life – which is mainly about horses too, really."

I returned my attention to the album, and took a few moments to look at the one photograph that had been made up as an enlargement of the entire wedding group. Terry and Janice were in the center, a couple I assumed were the parents of the bride stood beside Janice, and there was another couple who had to be the parents of the groom. Then there was Gordy – who looked about as un-Gordy-like as I could have imagined. Yes, he was wearing a suit – as promised – but there wasn't a part of his body that it fitted; it was brown with a wide pinstripe, the lapels looked like wings, and it had clearly been intended for a shorter, wider person, with considerably longer arms than him. I grappled with the body shape that would result in. He looked as miserable as if he were about to be shot. His hair was cut as we'd always known it – a number three buzz cut – which he'd always been proud to boast to us was something done by his own hand with an ancient set of clippers. But we'd always known Gordy with a full beard, and the few photographs I'd seen of him clean-shaven in his own album, and at Louise's house, hadn't been sharp enough for me to spot his quite pronounced chin. The entire shape of his head seemed different than I'd known, and I could understand why he'd grown a beard, because it had given his overall appearance a better balance. Adding to the effect, the tie around his neck was almost as wide as it was long, and the knot was so big it appeared to be throttling him, which might have accounted for the more-than-usual level of floridity in his complexion. He looked – poor thing – desperately unhappy, yet ridiculous. If that had been Gordy's only encounter with a suit, I wasn't surprised he'd never worn one again. The additional layer of cognitive dissonance I was experiencing came from the knowledge I was looking at a man who owned a uranium mine that had earned him millions – even if it hadn't achieved that for him by the time the photo was taken.

"Fashion's a funny thing, right?" Maddie was musing, and smiling. "I think part of the reason Mom's never wanted to look at that again is because she thinks she looks fat in her wedding dress. Of course, it didn't help that I recall asking her when I was little why she was wearing a lace doily on her chest, which is what I thought that yoke above the band under her boobs looked like. She didn't think it was funny at all."

"Maybe it's just too painful for her to remember her wedding day, with your father having gone the way he did." I was trying to be kind.

"Maybe." Maddie didn't sound convinced. "But she at least looks happy in most of the snaps."

I gave more attention to the post-wedding Polaroids Maddie was referring to, and she was right, Janice looked radiant in most of them. Many of them were of her alone, or with figures just on the edge of the frame; maybe Gordy had been better at taking photos of flowers than people.

"May I take a copy of this formal photo? I might be able to use it for Gordy's memorial, in some way. It's one of only a few he's in."

"Sure."

As I sorted out the copier, and tried not to think of how a photo of Gordy being best man to the person he'd probably killed might prove useful, Maddie stood and peered at the piles of items from the box file on the floor. She bent down to pick something up, then let out a shriek.

"Where did you get that?"

She was pale, trembling. Her arm was outstretched, and she was waving at the old bag I'd found at Gordy's that I'd used to carry the bits and pieces we'd brought from his house. It might as well have been the monster that had been living under her bed when she was a child.

"That bag?"

She nodded, eyes wide.

"Why? Do you recognize it?"

"It's the bag my dad took when he left us. Mom went through the whole house – that was the only thing missing, That bag. His CP Air bag. It was his pride and joy. He'd been given it by a pilot on a flight to Montreal." Maddie was panting. "Where did you get it?"

"I found it at Gordy's," was out of my mouth before I had a chance to swallow the words.

"What was it doing there?" Maddie was screaming, and crying, and shaking. "Why did Gordy have it? I'm certain that's Dad's bag!"

Bud was through my office door a moment later. "Everything alright?"

He took in the scene, assessed there was no immediate danger to me or Maddie, but was concerned enough by Maddie's appearance to shoot me a look that demanded a response.

"I've just told Maddie I found that bag at Gordy's house. She's pretty positive it's the bag her father took with him when he walked out on her and her mother."

Bud's eyes told me he was processing the situation; both of us knew there was so much we couldn't tell Maddie, but now we were in a real pickle about how best to handle an all but hysterical woman, who wasn't supposed to be told anything – about anything – and might even be a murder suspect.

A Long Way from Home

Between us, Bud, Max, and I managed to calm Maddie, who was determined to "do something" about the discovery of the airline bag – though she was unclear about what that should be. Max was the one who was best able to help her stop wailing and sobbing, his still-strong German-Swiss accent making the words "No" and "Calm" sound like a song.

The pair hugged enough for me to realize their relationship wasn't merely professional or platonic, as Maddie had said, but there was a reserve in Maddie's reactions to Max's touch that made me wonder about the exact nature of their feelings toward each other. He adored her, that much was plain. But Maddie? Even in her despair she was trying to tough things out. I suspected a decades-old response mechanism, possibly resulting from her belief that her father had abandoned her; he was only in her life until she was nine, a delicate age, and emotional trauma can lead to coping behaviors we never quite shrug off in later life. One of the most frequently observed is a person refusing to allow themselves to admit they care for others, their damaged psyche telling them this means they cannot be as badly hurt if they aren't cared for in return; something I'd used as my own coping mechanism after Angus's death, until Bud and I had begun to date.

I offered to make another pot of tea, and called Bud over to "help" me, leaving Maddie and Max alone at the table. "How long can we keep this up? Believing her father's body might have been dug up next door, and yet saying nothing?" I hissed at Bud.

"Ssh! Not only have I promised we won't tell anyone that we know what we do, it would be irresponsible of us to mention it until there's a positive ID – and I'm guessing Maddie and her mother will be the first people to be advised of that. Not a word, right?"

I nodded, then took the pot to the table and poured everyone a nice cup of hot, sweet tea.

It was a stressful moment all round, and my heart went out to Maddie; she seemed less like the determined, hard-working, and successful businesswoman I'd met, and more like a confused teenager. Max was also looking a little overwhelmed; his knees were bouncing almost uncontrollably beneath that table, and his eyes betrayed a glint of desperation.

I felt I had to do something. "I tell you what, Bud's going to pass on this news about the bag to the team looking after the forensic examination of Gordy's place." Bud tried to hide his horror at my words, and he might have managed it as far as Maddie and Max were concerned, but I knew him too well for it to get past me.

"I've been thinking," said Maddie, "the talk among all our clients is that human remains have been found on Gordy's property. They've been saying terrible things about Gordy. Max and I have put that down to the power of the rumor mill among the older inhabitants, who can't wait to have something to gossip about on the phone – but, if it's true, could it be…might they have found…what if Dad…?"

All her unspoken fears, and maybe hopes, swirled above the teapot in the middle of the table, but no one addressed them – Max didn't know how to, and Bud and I didn't dare.

"I'm gonna make a call," said Bud moving away from the table toward his office, but before he'd gone two steps his phone warbled in his pocket. He pulled it out, looked at the screen and stubbed a finger at it. I heard, "Bud Anderson speaking..." before he disappeared.

I sat quietly, a rarity for me, and tried desperately to think of a way forward that didn't involve talking about Gordy or Terry – the complete opposite of what I'd been equally desperately trying to do for days. My mind was a blank, then Max sort-of rescued the situation.

"I don't like what people have been saying about Gordy – it is unfair to speak of him this way. None of it can be true. I wouldn't be here if it wasn't for Gordy. I was telling Bud, when you two were in the other room, it was Gordy who helped me find the courage to try something new. He encouraged me to set up my charity, and I knew my prayers had been answered when Maddie came along to support it. He let me see a way to create a new life for myself – and it was through him that I met you...you are so like him in many ways, Maddie; you, too, want people to have a second chance, and I have made the best of mine. But he also put me in touch with Tom White, and it did me good to mentor a young chef – I missed teaching and developing young people, which I did with the Canadian chef team...that was what it was all about, really, giving young people a chance to have a goal, that could put them on the world stage and get them a flying start to their careers. Gordy understood that – he'd done a lot of work with young people, getting them to work with those in need in the community, at one time. He said he wasn't up to it anymore, but that I could carry on the good work for him. It kept me going, trying to do a bit better each day...or at least as well as the day before. And here I am now, years later, with all this. Thanks to Gordy. I don't think he'd have done anything bad, Maddie. He wasn't the type."

I knew exactly what Max meant, but I also knew much more than he did about what type of person can commit murder –

and that's any type at all. Every known killer has had people in their life who thought they were a good person, or who trusted them, or who just wasn't able to believe they'd done such a terrible thing. Every single one. "He seemed very nice," is something that's been said of pretty much every serial killer ever unmasked; you really never know who's capable of killing, given a certain set of circumstances. I knew that; Max didn't. At that moment I envied him his ignorance. Researching and striving to understand human nature can create a great weight to bear – not least because the more you find out about why we humans do what we do, the more you realize we're only scratching the surface of the vastness of the unknown, and the possibly unknowable.

I was saved from having to say anything pithy by Bud almost bounding along the hall. "I have news," he announced.

I was on the edge of my seat.

"I've just spoke to…an ex-colleague. And I have been given the all-clear to give you some news, as long as you commit to not sharing it with anyone outside this room. Are you good with that?"

Maddie and Max looked confused, but both nodded dumbly. I did too, just for show.

"I can tell you that human remains have, indeed, been found on Gordy Krantz's property. The remains are of a male, but they are *not* those of your father, Maddie. That is a certainty; dental records held on file as a result of your father's missing person's case have been compared with those of the remains, and there's no match. I know this doesn't bring us any closer to understanding why Gordy had a bag at his house that's at least similar to one taken by your father when he disappeared, but at least you know something."

I had so many questions running though my head, and suspected Bud could see metaphorical steam coming out of my ears – of frustration – but I focused my attention on Maddie, as was appropriate.

Once again she dissolved into tears, but this outburst was more brief. "I'm so glad it's not Dad," she managed to blub between sobs, "but I don't know why…it means he might still be out there, somewhere, not knowing who he is, or who we are. Just lost…thinking he's someone else altogether."

At last I'd glimpsed a valuable insight into how Maddie had been trying to excuse her father for the past almost-thirty years – the old "complete loss of memory" theory. I wanted to tell her how extremely rare it is for someone to experience total and long-term amnesia, but judged there'd be a better time than this. Besides, I rather wanted her and Max to leave, so I could grill Bud.

"I do have one question, that I've been requested to ask you, Maddie." Bud was using his soothing voice. "Is it okay if I ask you now?"

Maddie actually smiled. "Of course, ask away."

"You mentioned your father was given the flight bag on a trip to Montreal. Did Gordy Krantz take that trip with your father?"

Maddie gave the matter some thought. "I don't know, sorry. What I can tell you is that Dad traveled a fair bit, but the bag was special…he took it with him on every flight, I remember. I can't recall a time when he didn't have it, so maybe Mom could tell you about the trip he took when he got it. I don't think Dad and Gordy would have ever made a trip like that together, they didn't work together by then, after all."

I realized I had to say something that might at least allow Maddie a chance of sleep that night. "Maddie, your mother said your father had run into Gordy at several horticultural events over the years; Gordy might have flown to any of those, so he could also have acquired a bag similar to the one your father owned. It might be that this bag has nothing to do with your father, and it's just a bag, with an airline logo on it, that people of a certain age used when they flew, back in the day...before the age of those hellish wheely-bags."

I could tell by Maddie's shifting expression that this idea was something she could cling to, to allow her construct of her father living a happy life somewhere, oblivious of her existence, to continue. I felt I'd done a good deed, and now I wanted my reward – I wanted them to leave, but I had to handle their ejection with the utmost care and civility.

At last Bud and I were alone, and I could make him sit down and bring me up to speed.

"Spill your guts," I said, dramatically threatening him with a teaspoon.

"You've got what I got. The only bit I left out was the fact they were able to locate the skull of the male some distance from the rest of the body – predation most likely – and immediately checked Terry Dumas's dental records. Not a match, as I said. So they have one unidentified male, two unidentified females. That's it. Honest. All I've got."

"Really?"

"Really."

I knew he wasn't lying. "So where does that leave our theory about Gordy killing Terry? Maybe it wasn't Terry that Louise saw, after all. She said his truck was there, then gone the next day...but trucks look very similar, especially from a distance. Maybe it was someone else altogether – and who's to say that was the exact day Terry disappeared anyway – we've only got Louise's recollection of an event nearly three decades ago to work with, and it's really difficult to remember specifics, as we both know from experience."

"She seemed so certain," said Bud.

"You've met eyewitnesses who were absolutely, one hundred percent certain of something until it was proved to them they must have been wrong, haven't you?"

Bud nodded. "It's the ones who are certain of something who are usually most likely to be wrong – depending on the exact circumstances. A special occasion, a particular note being made of the time or the date…that can happen. But this? Maybe she was mistaken about the identity, or the timeframe, you're right. We've hung our theory on that, and now it's all been proven wrong."

"What shall we do about it, Bud? Where do we go from here? I swear I don't feel we're any closer to working out who might have poisoned Gordy, or why. And as for the three poor souls who ended up interred beside our home…I feel we've taken three steps back, having only taken half a false step forward. This isn't a riddle, wrapped in a mystery, inside an enigma, as Churchill spoke of Russia; this is a maze of brick walls, all ten feet tall, with no apparent way out. There's no *reason* for any of it. I'm a psychologist – I know there's always a *reason*."

Bud held me tight. "Hey, maybe we need to get a good night's sleep, and start fresh tomorrow. But no grisly crimes on TV before bed – I suggest some soothing music, a big cuddle with Marty, and maybe a glass of wine, okay?"

"Satie, sandwiches – because I can't face cooking – and Shiraz. Perfect."

Home Alone?

I woke around three in the morning, and felt dreadful. Marty was allowing me about ten inches of bed to sleep on, and all my muscles were tense from hanging onto the edge of the mattress. I sat up, stubbed my feet into my slippers, and wrapped my robe around me as I crept out of the bedroom. Neither Marty nor Bud stirred.

I allowed my eyes to adjust to the darkness, and didn't turn on any lights. The moon was bright, the sky clear, and parts of the property looked as though they were bathed in white sunshine. I enjoy nighttime, alone. I could hear the owls outside, and felt cocooned in silvery security. The dread I'd felt a few days earlier had evaporated, and the relief of believing myself to be safe in my own home had returned. I was deeply grateful.

Me being me, I immediately asked myself why that was. What had changed?

We still didn't know who'd killed Gordy, or who'd tried to break into his house, or who had stolen the *trousseau* from the cabin. There were now three corpses in search of an identity. Nothing was different except one thing: we now knew the male corpse wasn't that of Terry Dumas.

Why had that piece of knowledge allowed me to feel safe in my own home again?

I couldn't fathom it.

I'd subscribed to the idea that the circumstantial evidence was stacking up against Gordy as being the likely killer of the "disappeared" Terry. If the body they'd found next-door wasn't Terry after all, did that make it less likely that Gordy had been a killer?

Yes, because I'd always imagined Terry's death to have been as the result of an uncharacteristic outburst on Gordy's part. So now I could rest easy that the man I'd liked and admired hadn't been a killer, after all.

Okay – but what about the two female corpses? Had some random killer dumped them on Gordy's property in the dead of night? I realized that would certainly be possible – for all I knew someone could be burying a body on the other side of our acreage at that exact moment and I'd be none the wiser. So, it was a possibility. But was it a realistic one? I couldn't imagine Jacques Pelletier and his team saw it as such. No, they'd be looking for something more tethered to reality. And I should be too. But what?

I decided I'd try my wakeful dreaming technique. By allowing myself to drift through my memories without trying to organize them, or impose my preconceptions upon them, the kaleidoscope sometimes shifts into a position where nonsense makes sense. It's a way of not thinking about something, thereby allowing it to present itself to me in a form that grants me the ability to see it more clearly, and understand it in a more abstract, yet meaningful way. It can take some time, but it wasn't as though I was doing anything else, and the velvety darkness, and security, of my home meant I'd probably be able to find the state of nothingness that is critical to allow it to work. I padded over to Bud's recliner, sat down, pressed the button to raise my feet and lower my head a little, and sought oblivion.

I'm sitting on the roof of our home peering toward Gordy's house. It's raining blood and the land is starting to flood around my home-island of safety. A skein of Canada geese pluck me up and carry me to Gordy's cabin, which is bobbing about in a ruby lake, with Louise screaming out of the window that someone must save her child. Her long red hair is blowing in the wind, which carries within it the sound of church bells and the heady aroma of incense. I sense Gordy behind me, and I turn; he's a young man, bronzed and muscular…and he's the one carrying an incense burner in one hand, and a mournful bell in the other. A bushy red beard springs from Gordy's impossibly long chin, he reaches up and wipes it away, but another grows in its place…and this one continues to get bigger and bushier no matter how often he wipes at his face.

He dissolves and becomes a priest, wailing that he's beyond redemption. Then he begins to glow from within, the light pulsing until his entire body becomes a green orb that lifts from the ruby lake and hovers above me, rumbling and crackling with lightning. As the orb rotates ever faster it spews out trees, rhododendrons, hemlock plants, hydrangeas, and puppies…then it explodes creating a nuclear mushroom, which becomes a meadow of mushrooms as tall as trees. Tom is running through the forest of mushrooms, and he's being chased by Max, wielding a cleaver. They are both in chef whites, and now they are swans running, almost flying, their wings beating to help them gain loft. Tom perches on top of a mushroom where "DAWN" is written in block capitals on the cap. I hear more wings above me and expect more birds, but diaries are flapping their pages to keep them aloft in the gales coming out of the mushroom forest. They are followed by a flock of letters, all white, like doves. Tom the swan swoops low over my head, with the DAWN mushroom cap in his orange bill, then he flings it into the rushing waters of the Fraser River. The river is overflowing its banks, gobbling up the ground.

I am awash, and terrified, my hair is floating on the water in front of me. It is long and copper colored, with lilies entwined within it. I reach out to try to save myself and my hand grasps that of another drowning woman. She has no face, but has locks like mine. Then she's gone, dragged into the waters by I know not what sort of monster, but I am aware I must find dry land...my life depends upon it. My foot touches something which rises beneath me. It's a massive teacup which lifts me up out of the waters and twirls and twirls and twirls as it rises, making me feel sick. My legs are numb, I cannot move my arms, I know I must get out of the cup, so I wriggle my way to its lip and throw myself out. But I do not plummet, I am lifted even higher by a faceless woman dressed in white, who's singing a mournful tune that sounds like the wail of a baby and the howl of a dog. Then she isn't a woman any longer, but a sleek horse galloping through the sky with abandon, carrying me toward a bleak landscape of flat, barren lands where I can see farmers struggling to grow crops in a terrible drought, all begging for rain, which comes, but it's blood, not water, and it burns the skin of everyone it touches.

I have no reins to control the horse, which is set on its path through the sky, taking me beyond the awful place I have seen until we get to my mountain, which isn't my mountain at all – it's much bigger than my mountain, but I know I am coming home.

I want the horse to stop, to rest, to let me rest, but it continues galloping and wailing, and I am now being pelted by papers that fly at me like a swarm, slicing into my skin. Every page is covered in tiny flowing script, and I know that if I can just read what the papers say I will possess all the knowledge in the universe, but they fly past me too fast, and keep cutting into me when I try to grab them.

Then the horse is gone, the papers are gone, and I am in a garden, sitting on a grassy bank overlooking a babbling stream. Bud is beside me, but he's not Bud, he's Terry Dumas, who's wearing a pilot's uniform and laughing to show me his horses' teeth. Maddie appears, but she's half wolf; she snaps at her father's cap, grabbing it and slinking off into the wilderness with it between her huge teeth. Then Gordy appears, and he's also half wolf. He grabs Terry's flight bag and follows Maddie into the wild. Terry is crying, and I notice that his head is lolling. I catch his head before it falls off. I have to hold it on, which he thinks is hilarious. He tickles me and I scream and run away, holding his laughing head in my hands.

Then I see Gordy, sitting in the giant teacup, pushing himself away from the riverbank into the swollen river. He's waving. He's happy. Terry is hanging onto the handle of the teacup. He's laughing with his horse-teeth. People are cheering them as they float past – there's Colin and Ann waving flags which have Gordy's young, clean-shaven face on them; Dayton is waving a chainsaw; Tom and Max are carrying a massive cake alight with sparklers; Colleen is ringing several handbells, and weeping; Maddie and Janice are wailing and screaming, begging Terry to come back to them; Louise is bounding along the riverbank beside the floating teacup, surrounded by barking dogs.

It's chaos, but happy chaos. There is no sense of menace. Then the teacup disappears and both Gordy and Terry are sucked into the river, which is glowing green and running red...and I see the pack of dogs accompanying Louise run toward me...

I fought off Marty's licks as I pushed the button to sit myself upright.

"How long have you been out here?" Bud sounded anxious.

"I got up around three, what time is it now?"

"Six. You okay? Did you get any sleep?"

I gathered my thoughts. "No. I did some wakeful dreaming instead."

Bud smiled. "Any help?"

I took stock. "That depends on the answers to a few key questions. How early do you think you could reasonably phone Pelletier?"

Bud smiled; he looked tired, pale. "I'll put some coffee on, we can drink that, get showered and dressed, and I'll speak nicely to him when I call in an hour – how about that?"

I hugged him. "Excellent – I have some emails to send, and we'll be going out later on. To the lawyers' offices, if everyone agrees to my plan."

I could hear Bud muttering under his breath as I headed to the bathroom.

Home Run

It wasn't until two in the afternoon that I was able to walk into the reception of Messrs. Oishi and Singh, knowing I was about to break some hearts, lay some old ghosts to rest, and answer some deeply puzzling questions. I was convinced it was only because Jacques Pelletier respected Bud so much that he'd agreed to undertake what must have seemed to him to be an extraordinary list of requests, though Bud wouldn't accept my praise – which was endearingly Bud-like. I'd also had to recruit the efforts of Mr. Oishi, and his long-standing influence in local legal circles, to access the final part of the route-map I was about to invite a motley band of individuals to walk, with me as their guide.

The meeting room at the lawyer's office was fuller than it had been the first time I'd seen it; in addition to the same group of people who'd been in attendance on that occasion, Maddie Dumas, Max Muller, Jacques Pelletier, and a lawyer by the name of Vince Chan had joined us. The extra chairs required made for a snug seating arrangement around the large table, and many curious faces turned as Bud and I entered the room. Pelletier greeted us; he was standing to attention. I did my best to keep my expression neutral, despite the fact I was feeling excited, though somewhat exhausted.

As agreed, Rylan Oishi formally greeted everyone, and invited all those present to introduce themselves, which some did with professionalism, others with a sulky, or puzzled tone. I noted it was Louise North who looked most full of gleeful expectation – though I suspected that delight would soon be erased.

Finally, it was my turn to speak. All eyes were on me; I chose to remain seated, as the arrangement in the room meant everyone could see me, and I could see everyone – oval tables are wonderful for allowing that to happen.

"Thanks to everyone for being here," I began. "I know all of you have given your time today because you want to find out what happened to Gordy, and probably you'd all like the full details of what's been going on at his property since his death. Jacques Pelletier" – that was how he'd asked me to refer to him – "has been heading up the investigation, and he's offered to give you a summary of findings. Jacques."

The detective was standing at the opposite end of the table to my seat, so everyone turned to face him.

"Thanks, Cait. As you say, a summary. Before I begin, I shall tell you I am now going to share information which we would prefer remain confidential. I hope I can rely upon the discretion of all present." It didn't sound like a question.

Nodding of heads all round – *good*.

"Excellent, then I shall begin. Eleven days ago, Mr. Gordon Krantz of Red Water Mountain Drive was discovered in his home, deceased. An investigation into his demise was carried out by the coroner, observing the norms for a person who was under the care of a physician, but who did not die in a medical facility. Initial examination suggested some further tests should be conducted, and it was eventually established that Mr. Krantz had died as a result of *conium* poisoning – the chemical signature of poison hemlock, a plant which grows in great profusion not just in this geographic area, but also on Mr. Krantz's own property."

A ripple of shock and horror ran around most of the room; the information about Gordy's cause of death had not been known to anyone but Bud and myself, the lawyers, the cops…and – I was certain – one other person.

"Gordy was poisoned?" Colleen White clutched at her breast with one hand, and grabbed her nephew's white-knuckled fist with her other. Tom wrestled his hand free, and rested it on his thigh, bouncing beneath the table.

He didn't make eye contact with anyone, but pulled at one end of his moustache with his free hand. "How long have you known this?" He spoke quietly. He seemed to be addressing the tabletop.

Pelletier replied, "The test results were made available to us five days after Mr. Krantz's death, so six days ago. It was agreed we'd follow normal procedures and keep the information confidential as we carried out a more detailed forensic examination of Mr. Krantz's property."

Tom glared at me and snapped, "Did you know – then?" I shrugged. "I wish you'd said something," he added.

I bet you do, I thought. I didn't speak.

Tom stopped pulling at his facial hair and I could see him picking at the edges of his fingernails as his hands lay in his lap.

"That's terrible news," said Colin Evans, looking distraught. "Who on earth would want to poison Gordy?" At that precise moment his wife Ann's expression told me she could well have been the first to volunteer.

Pelletier waited for the surprise in the room to subside to a pulsating anxiety, then continued. "As a result of our investigations on Mr. Krantz's property, a number of – shall we say 'unexpected' – discoveries came to light. We managed to establish that Mr. Krantz had imbibed poison hemlock in a cup of tea; tests on a small amount of residue found in a broken cup found lodged beneath his body proved conclusive. While searching for possible sources of the poison – prior to it being established it was in his tea – we also discovered human remains." Pelletier paused, and took in the faces surrounding him. "It has come to our attention that there have been a great number of rumors circulating about the discovery of human remains on the Krantz property – *these* are the facts. One set of remains was located not far from the house where Mr. Krantz made his residence; those remains were of a female, identity unknown. Another set of female remains – also of unknown identity – was unearthed a little further from the Krantz house. A third set of remains – of a male – were discovered close to the cabin that used to be Mr. Krantz's original dwelling. There have been no further discoveries, nor do we expect there to be any."

The room erupted; everyone was speaking at once, and I did my best to take in the expressions, body language, and outcries of all those present. Only the lawyers were unmoved, as well as Bud, myself, and Pelletier.

"Dear God!" exclaimed Colin Evans, and his wife echoed his words.

"*Three* bodies?" Maddie and Janice Dumas stared at each other in amazement, as Max Muller held Maddie's hand tight; I guessed Maddie had told her mother about the discovery of the remains of the male, but the news about the two unidentified women was news to even them.

Tom White pressed his hand to his forehead, his eyes squeezed shut, while his aunt sat shaking her head mouthing, "No, no, no."

Dayton Woodward looked baffled, and was catching anyone's eye with the word, "What?" on his lips, while Louise North nibbled on her bottom lip, her eyes darting around the room.

Again, Pelletier waited until silence fell. This time the atmosphere in the room was jagged, uneasy. Faces were filled with expressions of hope, hopelessness, and anticipation as eyes turned to the man they believed had all the answers.

"You don't know who any of these dead people are?" Louise North's gravel voice cut through the silence like a buzz-saw. Heads swivelled to her, then back to the cop.

"I shall cede the floor at this point, and invite Professor Cait Morgan to address you." Pelletier literally stepped back, until his rear end touched the wall, and I regained everyone's attention. Jacques Pelletier began to inch toward the meeting room's only door.

I remained in my seat and took a deep breath. "Thanks, Jacques." I nodded and smiled; I felt I'd earned the right to use his name as I had because of what we'd already worked through together that morning. "It's only fair that I tell you now that Bud and I were made aware of the possibility that Gordy had been poisoned as soon as his lawyers, Ms. Singh and Mr. Oishi, were told; this allowed them to fulfil another of Gordy's last wishes – which was to ask us to do whatever we could to ensure that the right justice be meted out to the right person or persons should Gordy's death be thought to be 'unnatural'. I think we can all agree that dying by poison is quite unnatural, though I'll also tell you Bud and I didn't immediately decide that Gordy had been poisoned by someone else, not even when we knew he'd drunk poison hemlock in tea…which was only confirmed yesterday morning. I think everyone here knows that Gordy was given a preliminary diagnosis of Parkinson's disease about nine months ago, with a confirmation a few months later. Bud and I talked through the possibility that Gordy had, in fact, chosen to take his own life, rather than live through the debilitation the disease causes. I dare say you're all now thinking through that concept in the same way we did; it might be seen as an understandable decision, but was Gordy the sort of person who'd make it?"

I paused and watched; I thought it was fascinating that – of everyone there – a telling glance passed between Louise and Oishi; the two oldest people in the room.

"That's terribly sad," said Maddie quietly.

Max had tears in his eyes. "He saved me. I could maybe have saved him…but maybe not."

Maddie comforted him, and passed him a tissue, while her mother rolled her eyes and checked her nails.

Dayton asked, "Did he kill himself? Or did someone kill him? But who would do that? It must have been someone he trusted, if the poison was in his tea."

"Exactly, Dayton," I replied. "I think we can all agree that everyone Gordy trusted is in this room, which is why we're particularly grateful you all came today."

"One of *us* killed Gordy?" Colleen scanned the room looking terrified, and was half out of her seat before she noticed Pelletier was standing in front of the only exit from the room.

"Sit down, Auntie," said Tom quietly. "Just sit." He sounded exhausted. Resigned. Hopeless. Knowing what he'd been through a couple of years earlier in Vegas with Tanya, and understanding how his current situation must be reopening deep, psychological wounds associated with being stuck in a room with a ruthless killer for hours on end, my heart went out to him – but I'd had to do it this way, for the sake of others involved.

I continued, "As I mentioned, we didn't know until yesterday that it was a cup of tea that had poisoned Gordy, so – until we were clear about how the poison had entered his system – Bud and I were on a mission to try to work out who might have wanted to cause his death." Shoulders were squared, and a few jaws took on a firmer setting, as people realized I'd been scrutinizing them, not merely trying to put together Gordy's eulogy.

I could have predicted that Janice Dumas would be one of the first to blow, and she did. "I invited you into my home out of the kindness of my heart. You were just there to pry into my private life. It's unconscionable. You should be ashamed." She stared daggers at me, and Maddie flushed beside her.

"Mom, I know it's not pleasant to think of, but I'm sure Cait was doing what she thought was for the best." Maddie was using a soothing voice, but it didn't seem to be working on her mother.

"Goddam woman. Digging up painful old memories. Poking about. It shouldn't be allowed. Did you know about this?" Janice turned her attention to Pelletier. "Because if you did, you should be investigated – you can't use private individuals to take advantage of a situation and get around the need for search warrants and the like."

Pelletier shifted on his feet and I decided I'd better rescue him. "Jacques had no idea, Janice, and I wasn't poking my nose into your business, I was poking my nose into Gordy's. Though I do have a question you might want to answer: how long after your wedding did your affair with Gordy end?"

Janice clamped her mouth shut, her eyes aflame with hatred, her nostrils flared; she looked like a wild horse, trapped, and about to have a saddle thrown onto its back for the first time. Her upper body moved sporadically, and she couldn't meet her daughter's stare of amazement, and horror.

"What are you saying, Cait?' Maddie sounded almost as angry as her mother looked.

I tried to be gentle. "The wedding photos? Your mum looking radiant, the design of the wedding dress, the way she was beaming in all those snaps – when Gordy was behind the camera. Let's not forget the complete break in the relationship between Gordy and your family soon after the wedding, and remember what you told me about the way your father always referred to Gordy?"

I could tell Maddie was reassessing everything I'd mentioned.

"Mom? Did you? Did you and Gordy…oh my God, no! Did you…am I…am I…Gordy Krantz's daughter? Is that why he and Dad had that great falling out? Is that why Gordy all but lost it when he found out who was delivering his meals? Mom? Answer me. Was Gordy Krantz my father?"

The glare of the lighting made the beads on Janice's upper lip glisten; the throbbing vein in her neck told me she was seething. She looked at each and every face in the room before she answered. "Gordy was not your father. Terry was your father. Terry loved you, and raised you, and you were the apple of his eye. What happened between Gordy and me was…a mistake. Your father never knew about it, though…though Gordy threatened he would tell him, at one point, unless I supported his demands that Terry gave him a five percent cut of the K. Dumas annual profits."

It was starting to become difficult to work out what exactly was producing the emotions in the room, there was such a variety of them. I did, however, manage to share a meaningful glance with Rylan Oishi – now we both better understood why Terry Dumas had agreed to split his company's profits with Gordy.

Dayton said to Janice, "Gordy did that? He *blackmailed* you?"

Janice was on the verge of tears. She nodded, her anger almost evaporated. "I was a bride, I didn't want there to be any trouble." She touched her daughter's arm. "Yes, I was pregnant with you at the time, that's why I looked fat, and I couldn't believe Gordy would have said anything, but I didn't want to take the chance. It would have broken your father's heart. I was weak, Gordy was…intoxicating."

"He was, when he wanted to be," said Louise. Every single person in the room looked surprised by her comment.

"Maddie looks a bit like Gordy," whispered Colleen to Tom – loud enough that everyone could hear.

"She's *Terry's* daughter," repeated Janice.

Max was staring at Maddie, nibbling his non-existent thumbnail; I could tell he was re-evaluating the way she looked, and held herself, as were a few others in the room.

Poor Maddie, I'm so sorry to do this to you, was what I thought. "Let's move on," was what I said.

"Wait," said Colleen, holding up her hand like a schoolgirl. "Is she, or isn't she? Gordy's, I mean. Did you know?" Colleen was asking Maddie, not Janice.

Maddie's eyes were wild. "I...I don't know. When I met Gordy I felt...something. It was like meeting an old friend, or someone you've dreamed of. I felt comfortable with him – but I thought that was just because Gordy had known Dad back in the day, and I was trying to find a way to connect with Dad through him, somehow. I...I don't know what I felt." As I judged her to be hunting through all her memories of her times with Gordy, Maddie's eyes darted around the table, not focusing on the people in the room. She repeatedly pushed away her mother's hand, which was reaching out to her.

Colleen turned her body away from the Dumas women and folded her arms, then she caught Louise's wicked grin and wink, and stared determinedly at the table; I suspected jealousy on Colleen's part, that Gordy had never shared his passionate nature with her at any time.

I knew I had to press on, because I suspected I was about to give both Louise and Janice second thoughts about the man they'd shared a bed with – and hoped Colleen would regain her self-respect.

"I'm sorry to have thrown that particular rock into your pond, Janice and Maddie, but now I need to address the discovery at the Krantz property of the remains of two females found there." Unsurprisingly, I regained everyone's attention. "Colleen," I said; the woman jumped in her seat. "When you first phoned me, on the day Gordy was found dead, you mentioned the disappearance of a redheaded woman at some point in the previous few decades. Thanks to Jacques and his team, and their diligent efforts, it is now believed that the person to whom you referred was a doctor by the name of Cymbeline Wright, who migrated from the USA to Canada in the 1980s."

Not much of a reaction from anyone except Colleen. "That's right – a doctor, not a dentist. I remember now."

I said, "Louise." Everyone looked at her, then at me – she raised her almost invisible eyebrows, accordioning the wrinkles on her forehead. "I think this is going to be hard for you to hear, because it happened when you were married to Gordy." She shrugged; the rest of the people in the room each expressed shock in their own way, but they all had one thing in common – every single mouth hung open as they looked again at Louise, who'd adopted a coy smile.

I continued, "Cymbeline Wright, a junior doctor, migrated to Canada and took up her post at the local hospital where she'd been hired as a specialist in orthopedic trauma. She disappeared a few weeks later. I don't know if you remember her, Louise, but she was certainly there when you were still nursing. In fact, she'd possibly have been the doctor who'd have treated Gordy's broken arm, which you mentioned he'd sustained at a significant point in your relationship."

Louise's monkey face scowled. "No, I don't recall her, but I do remember he talked about the doctor who fixed his arm as being good at their job. I had a lot on my mind at the time."

"As I said, she wasn't there very long. Jacques' team, using files from the original inquiry into her having been reported missing, have established that one set of remains found on Gordy's property are hers. Dr. Cymbeline Wright was buried quite close to Gordy's house. The other set of female remains? Again, thanks to Jacques' team, we now know they belong to a woman by the name of Rachel Summers, who disappeared in 1961. She was a girlfriend of Gordy Krantz; he wrote about her in his diaries, which I have read. He referred in his diaries to having 'dumped her'; I took it at the time of my reading to mean he had ended their relationship. I now believe – as do Jacques and his team – that Gordy did, in fact, end the relationship, but that his 'dumping' of her refers to the fact he buried her on his property. I understand there's still work to be done to establish beyond doubt how each of the women died, but initial examinations have found that both had broken hyoid bones, suggesting some form of strangulation."

I looked over at Pelletier who added, "Further forensic investigations are pending, but initial findings are as you say."

It was as though all the air had been sucked out of the room. The hum of the baseboard heaters was the only sound, and I could see everyone was grappling with the idea that Gordy Krantz had murdered two women, then hidden their bodies on his land.

"You're certain of this?" Dayton sounded incredulous.

"Gordy did that?" Maddie clearly couldn't believe it. She turned to her mother. "Mom? Could he have done that?"

Janice's brow was furrowed; she didn't reply, but snatched a frightened glance at Louise, who was tapping a broken nail on the table.

Louise said, "Killed one of them while we were still married, eh? Were they redheads?"

I nodded.

"Me too," she replied. "Bottle variety, you know, but vanity wins out sometimes, right?"

Colleen was grey in the face, grasping for Tom's hand, which he gave to her. He was shaking.

"I cannot believe it," snapped Colin Evans. His voice trembled. "There is absolutely no way on God's earth that Gordy Krantz strangled two women."

His wife snapped at him, "I always said he was too pious. Guilty, that's what he was. Trying to make up for having done such dreadful things. Couldn't spend enough time on his knees, could he? And you thinking he was so holy. Well listen – learn – he wasn't perfect. He was the worst of the worst, that's what he was." She sounded triumphant – which was something of a shock to the others in the room.

"God forgives," said Colin plaintively. "He does. If we truly repent of our sins, he can wash us clean, we can start again. If…if Gordy did what you say, and he then gave his life to God, God would have forgiven him. We should too."

"Killing two young women? Why should we forgive that?" Colleen White sounded outraged; I suspected she was having an Old Testament moment.

"That's a terrible thing to hear," said Max quietly. "He didn't seem to have that sort of hatred in him. I only saw compassion."

"If you accept Jesus as your Savior you can heal others," said Colin.

"Grow up," snapped Ann. "This is the real world, Colin. People do horrible things to each other all the time. Come and see what I see in the emergency room – fights, stabbings, people not knowing what the word 'mercy' means. You? You chatter away with a bunch of old people, drinking tea and gossiping when you work, and do much the same thing at church. That's not the real world. Gordy throttling the life out of two women is the real world. Wake up."

Colin shook his head, his shoulders drooping, real despair on his face.

"But that's not what Gordy was like." Dayton sounded frustrated. "I'm a pretty good judge of character, and I cannot believe Gordy did the things you've said."

"Mr. Oishi himself had personal experience of Gordy's wild nature," I said. Rylan nodded, looking grim. "And Louise will more than suggest he had few inhibitions."

Louise croaked, "He had the best weed in the area, Dayton, thought nothing of jumping into his truck after a long night of drinking and smoking. I was young, and pretty inexperienced, when I first met him, and he took me more forcefully than was necessary, let's just say that."

"Me too," said Janice quietly. "He very much wanted our…fling. I…always believed I could have put more obstacles in his way – but Gordy usually got what he wanted."

Maddie dropped her head into her hands.

"Why'd he turn over a new leaf, then? Killed a second time and finally felt guilty?" Colleen's tone was gruff, unforgiving.

"In 1994 Terry Dumas disappeared," I said. "Not much later, Gordy sold a plot of land to the folks who built the house where Bud and I live now, and built the house to which he moved, from his cabin. He became an active – some might say too-active – member of St. Peter's congregation, though he left the church in 2000, having been hounded out by a whispering campaign that hinted at improprieties with youths at the various groups he organized."

Colin Evans was on his feet. "Okay, that's enough. This is something of which I am absolutely, one hundred percent certain – Gordy was not interested in young girls, or boys. I spent a great deal of time with him. *That* was not Gordy

Krantz." He stared at Mahera Singh and Rylan Oishi. "You're Gordy's lawyers – isn't this libel, or slander, or something? Can't you shut her up?"

Mahera answered softly, "Mr. Evans, we have been briefed by Professor Morgan, and this is not a public place – this is a confidential meeting."

Colin sat down, his wife pulling at his jacket.

I said, "I don't believe for one moment that there was anything amiss – I believe Gordy was, in fact, as innocent of this as you say. But the whispering campaign was real, wasn't it, Colleen?"

"Like I said, you're talking garbage," snapped Colin.

"And I was asking Colleen, not you, Colin," I replied.

Tom White stared at his aunt, who had the good grace to blush. "It was real, I'm sorry to say. Once your parents pulled you out of those groups, Colin, the rumors began. And they did nothing to put a stop to them, in fact, they were only too happy to see all the groups you'd belonged to gradually fizzle out. They wanted you to study harder, thought you were spending time at church that you should have been putting into doing better at school. Gordy…well, he didn't speak up, so people thought your parents had a point. Other parents stopped their children from attending, then Gordy stopped coming to church altogether." She'd studied the backs of her hands, which lay flat on the table, as she'd spoken.

"My parents did that?" Colin's voice jagged. "My father, you mean. Mom was so weak, he bullied her every single day. He bent her to his will; she never stood up for herself. I vowed I'd never let another person dictate to me the way he did to her." He glanced at Ann, and added, "That's why, however much you nag, I will not be told how to spend my time. Dad never listened to Mom, so she stopped talking. You never listen to me…you didn't even let me get a word in when we went for the counselling Gordy talked me into asking you to attend. So I'll say it now, here, in this 'confidential' meeting, where everyone's dirty laundry is being aired – if you want us to stay together you have to start listening to me, not just making up your mind about what I mean when that's not at all what I'm saying."

Ann looked devastated. "I do listen, Colin. But you never seem to know what you want. You change your mind all the time."

"Not a crime, as far as I know," replied her husband. "But gossiping about someone until they have no choice but to leave a community they love, that's something that should be. My parents had no right to do what they did. I had no idea that's what had happened, that Gordy had been hounded out of the congregation. He…he never once mentioned that to me. All he did was try to suggest how Ann and I could start to heal the rifts that were beginning to show in our marriage. That's the sort of man he was."

Ann didn't reply.

Dayton was quite agitated when he said, "Hang on, Cait. Let's get back to what you said. Are you telling us that Gordy not only killed two women, but that he also killed Terry Dumas?" Dayton was clearly putting the whole picture together. He turned to Maddie. "Is the male body they found at Gordy's place your father?"

Maddie shook her head, as did Janice and Max, and she replied quickly, "No, the police have established beyond all doubt that Gordy didn't kill my father. That's right, isn't it?" She looked at Pelletier, as did everyone else.

"I can confirm that the remains of the male we found buried on the Krantz property are not those of Terry Dumas," he said.

Everyone returned their attention to me.

I said, "Bud and I recently had a conversation about how psychologically challenging it is for a person to work as an undercover detective for a long period of time. Bud said something very telling; if you're living a lie, the best way to get through everything you have to do and face, is to believe the lie yourself. I would suggest the same is true if you're seeking redemption – you have to *believe* redemption is possible to even bother to make an effort to achieve it, then you have to live your entire life in such a way that you believe you're worthy of it. There are the big things you have to change – for example, look at the way Gordy lived in general terms after Terry's disappearance: no longer wild, aggressive, domineering, blackmailing, womanizing…but almost hermit-like, church-going – until he was no longer wanted there – then always giving the few people he encountered within his small life the support, direction, and motivation they needed to help them find their way. He stopped being the person known and described by Janice, Rylan, and Louise, the man who killed those two poor women; he became the person Bud and I knew – that the rest of you knew. He'd changed."

Colleen's face betrayed her consternation. "You're saying the guilt Gordy felt because he killed those two girls and that man, whoever he was…did he kill that man?…you're saying Gordy changed his life completely because of this? That he was seeking redemption?"

"In a way." I replied. "Sometimes, it's the little things that make us truly who we are; how likely we are to act a certain way, to take a certain chance, how we present ourselves to the world. When people are trying to hide, or remake their identity, sometimes there are little 'tells' they cannot rid themselves of. Often these signs are not picked up on by those around the person in question, especially if the person is in a new environment, or if they change their habits significantly. I examined everything I found out about Gordy's life and lifestyle prior to 1994, then considered how he acted after that, and I could rationalize some of the changes under the heading of 'seeking redemption'. Then there were other changes I could also find an 'excuse' for. For example, was it the effects of the Parkinson's disease that made Gordy choose to write all his shopping lists, as well as all our letters, in block capitals rather than the cursive he'd used in his diaries? Louise claimed Gordy made fun of her love of books, and yet his own house was stuffed with them – was that because he now had so much more time on his hands? Did he no longer use marijuana and alcohol because they didn't mix with his medications? Yes, I managed to come up with reasonable explanations for all these small changes in Gordy's habits based upon age, illness, financial ability, and possible guilt. I could also rationalize his shift from his Roman Catholic upbringing to his involvement in an Anglican church – it's a shift many people make, for a variety of reasons. But he also stopped working with plants. What of that choice? Gordy's life had been a passionate one in many ways – not least in the way he interacted with the plant kingdom, seeking to alter its course by the intervention of his own hand, creating hybrids that would never have existed without his efforts. Then he gave that up, and became known for his love of nature when it was working in harmony with itself. As a psychologist I know humans are capable of changing; everything we experience changes us just a little – it's how we grow and develop. But this was a seismic shift, and it led me to an inevitable conclusion, which Jacques and his team were able to confirm when they checked Terry Dumas's dental records again this morning. Jacques."

Everyone turned to face Pelletier. "We took another look, as you suggested. There were several teeth missing, but those remaining were a match."

"You said it wasn't Dad." Maddie spoke softly, her voice forceful, but quivering.

"Maddie, your father took a hundred thousand dollars out of the bank, stuffed it into a much-loved old flight bag, and went to do a day's work. I believe, at the end of that workday, he visited Gordy Krantz, and that the money was to pay Gordy off; the drain of twenty percent of annual profits having to be funnelled to Gordy every year – yes, twenty percent, Janice, not the five percent you thought it was…which is why finding the papers you were asked to hunt out would have proved illuminating – that could not have looked good for a firm that Terry was trying to grow. A sensible businessman – which is very much what your father was – might well have tried to bring an end to such an arrangement with the offer of a one-off lump sum payment. In any case, whatever the reason, Louise was able to look down from her home to Gordy's cabin, and see the arrival of your father in his truck, witness Gordy and your father fighting, and then – the next day, noted that your father's truck had gone. No one ever saw your father again."

"Stop it, stop it, stop it – you said the skeleton, or whatever it was, wasn't my father!" Maddie screamed, making people jump in their seats.

I pressed on. "Terry Dumas's dental records were in his missing person's file. They didn't match with the remains found, no, but they did match with the body of the person many of us here today knew as Gordy Krantz. Louise saw two men fighting in 1994, and one of them was never seen again. I believe what *really* happened was that, somehow, Gordy Krantz died in that fight, and Terry Dumas adopted his persona thereafter. *Terry Dumas* died eleven days ago. *Gordy Krantz* died twenty-seven years ago."

I'd expected an uproar, but there was silence. It was fascinating to watch people's minds working. Tom's direct stare at me was especially telling; a mixture of horror, and relief.

I knew I had to plough on.

"Gordy – the 'real' Gordy – was the weed-smoking, heavy drinking, womanizing murderer…who also happened to be a gifted breeder of plants. Some of you here knew that man – but, think about it, none of you who knew 'the old Gordy' mixed with him, or even ran into him after 1994, did you? And if you had – who, or what, would you have seen? A tall, well built man, with a number three buzz-cut – Gordy's only hairstyle since the 1950s – but now sporting a bushy beard. It's amazing how a beard can alter the perceived shape of a man's head – you've grown a beard and moustache quite recently, Tom, have many people commented upon how different you look like this?"

Tom shrugged. "Not really. Most of them saw me grow it, or they just say something like, 'Nice beard'. That's it."

"Exactly. It's just there – men grow beards. So what? But Terry used a beard to great effect as a disguise that most people wouldn't think of as such." I turned to Janice. "Your husband's cleft chin must have been something with which you were very familiar. Maddie told me how she would play with his distinctive dimple when she was a child."

Janice shrugged – she looked oddly bemused.

I continued, "Terry – disguised as Gordy – built the new house, became a church warden, helped and supported people, and gave them a second chance. Those aspects were pure Terry, weren't they? The man who gave retired racehorses another lease of life, who specified certain amounts of money be set aside in his will for charitable uses – he was a thoughtful, well-organized, meticulous man. I was pleased to be able to establish, through Mr. Chan who represents Terry Dumas's lawyers, that Terry's last will and testament was a very specifically worded document, carefully thought through, and lodged years before he disappeared. The will held by Oishi and Singh on behalf of 'Gordy Krantz' is a similarly detailed document."

Janice leaned forward, "Hang on a minute, that Chang guy isn't Terry's lawyer. That's Don…Don Sweetly. Who's Chang?"

"Mr. Vince Channnn" – I emphasized the name – "is the lawyer who has taken over the Dumas files since Don Sweetly's retirement, five years ago." I was absolutely gobsmacked that the woman had focused on her lawyer having a different name rather than on her husband having only died eleven days earlier.

Janice looked nonplussed. "Don retired?"

Vince Chan said, "I have been writing to you for a few years, Mrs. Dumas, though I mainly have dealings with Miss Madelaine, who replies to my letters."

Maddie sighed, and shook her head.

Janice looked insulted, and folded her arms.

Maddie spoke softly, "Are you telling me that I've been delivering meals to my *father*, Terry Dumas, who's been pretending to be Gordy Krantz, all this time?"

I nodded. "It must have come as a great shock to him when Max told him your name."

Maddie nodded. "I…how I felt about him…I recognized him, deep down, didn't I? But I didn't know what I was feeling…"

Max seemed to be processing everything, carefully. "Gordy was really Terry, your father? This is…this is…good? Bad? I don't know any more."

I continued, "Terry, to be able to live as Gordy, made sure he avoided Louise, and anyone from Gordy's previous life, and he built a new life for the 'new version' of Gordy. He had a lot of cash – the bag containing the money he'd taken out of the nursery business – so he built a home for himself, where he wasn't overlooked by Louise. Of course, this being Terry, he had no idea he was building his new home so close to the burial sites of two women Gordy had killed…Gordy had buried them well away from his cabin, where he lived when he killed them. All Terry knew was that he had to get away from the place where he'd buried Gordy's remains – close to the cabin. Jacques' team is hoping they'll find Terry's old truck in the bramble-covered debris of the dilapidated old roadside store that was used by Terry and Gordy – in better days – to sell their plants to the public, when they were co-owners of a company called D. Krantz."

"D. Krantz? Don't you mean K. Dumas?" Maddie sounded understandably confused.

I shook my head. "D. Krantz was the original business Terry and Gordy set up – with the help of Mr. Oishi – back in the 1960s. It was the business Gordy hung onto when he and Terry's relationship fractured, and it was the business into which Terry had been paying a part of the profits from his 'new' business, established when you were just an infant – K. Dumas. When he felt secure in his role as Gordy, I think Terry looked into Gordy's life in detail – he had access to all of Gordy's records, and could even interact with his accountants and lawyers, as Gordy. D. Krantz is a successful entity; your father – as Gordy – put all the proceeds from a successful uranium mine into creating, and supporting, a significant center of excellence for environmental studies at the University of Vancouver, Krantz Hall."

Maddie leaned forward, tears rolling down her face. "But why? Why would Dad leave us like that? You're saying Dad killed Gordy, in a fight, and…what? Just decided to abandon me and Mom and live his life as Gordy, not thinking how that would affect us? Why didn't he just own up, and come home?" A sob wracked her entire body.

I spoke softly. "I can't be certain of exactly what happened, none of us can, Maddie, but if the fight Louise witnessed led to Gordy's death, and Terry didn't report that fact immediately, then as the hours, then the days passed, possibly he feared it was too late to own up to what had happened. Maybe he felt that 'hiding out' at Gordy's place in the short term was the best of the bad ideas he could come up with…and the 'short term' ended up being forever. I wish I could tell you I know, but I don't. And I don't think we ever will."

"I might be able to help," said Tom.

All eyes in the room turned to him. He gulped. "Some of you know I felt a great warmth for Gordy…well, Terry, I guess…so, that's why I did what I did. Though I didn't know about the cup."

Puzzled looks, especially from his aunt, were Tom's only reply.

"You found him, didn't you?" I said. Tom studied the tabletop again. "You'd arranged to meet him before dawn that morning, for him to show you a good mushroom foraging spot; he knew you'd be on time, and he also knew you wouldn't bring your vehicle along his drive, parking, as was your usual habit, on the lower road. He left the door un-bolted so you were able to get into his house, and I think you even put a few logs into his woodstove before you left – his stove would have burned out completely before Bud and I arrived, otherwise. He wrote a suicide note for you, Tom, didn't he? Explaining why he'd taken his own life."

Tom finally raised his head. Tears streamed down his face – he ignored them. "An envelope was pinned to his front door. I opened it and read it before I went in – I thought it might be some sort of foraging map, or something like that, you see. But it wasn't. It was Gordy asking me to clear away his tea, which I did. I rinsed the pot, made sure there were no bits left in the sink…but I couldn't find a mug or a cup or anything. That must have been because he was lying on it. And, yes, I put some logs into his stove. I guess it sounds weird, but…I didn't want him getting too cold." Tom shook his head, and wiped away a tear. He sighed, then continued, "He said in his note he'd chosen to fall asleep and not wake up, rather than becoming a burden to more and more people. He said I wasn't to tell anyone, unless it looked like someone would get into trouble because of him killing himself. He didn't want anyone to know what he'd done…he hoped everyone would think he'd just died in his sleep. He didn't want to be a bother."

"Did you keep that note?" Pelletier's voice was grave.

Tom did his impersonation of a deer in headlights, and nodded. "Yes, I've got it with me. I've had it in my pocket ever since. I couldn't bring myself to destroy it, like he asked me to. But, you see, I didn't know anyone had worked out he'd been poisoned until today. If I'd known, I'd have taken his note to the cops…and this one, too."

Tom pulled a crumpled piece of paper and a sealed envelope out of his jeans' pocket, and slid them across the table toward me. "This says, 'TO BE OPENED IF MY SUICIDE IS DISCOVERED'. I haven't opened it."

I got a nod from Pelletier, and opened the sealed letter. I read it aloud.

Here's the truth of me, for anyone who can stomach it.

I am Terry Dumas, a coward.
I was a coward when I let Gordy Krantz talk me out of the business I'd set up with him.

I was a coward when I let him bully me into promising to pay him money that should have gone to support my family.

I was a coward when I tried to buy him off. I should have known he'd laugh in my face.

I was a coward when I didn't call for help after Gordy hit his head on a rock when we fought – I didn't think anyone would believe me.

I was a coward when I didn't get in touch with Janice, and my beloved Madelaine, after that. I was too frightened to go to prison. I didn't think Janice loved me enough to wait for me.

I was a coward when I hid for years living as another man.

I was a coward when I left St. Peter's instead of defending myself.

I was a coward when I met my daughter again – I should have told the truth then, and at least she'd have known I'd always loved and missed her.

I'm taking the coward's way out now by sipping poison hemlock tea, instead of facing this disease, and its pain, and because I don't want anyone to see me weak and feeble and useless.

I am carrying out my own death sentence – this poison was good enough for Socrates, it will do for me.

I am Terry Dumas – a coward.

My epitaph.

The silence was broken only by Maddie's sobs, and Max's attempts to comfort her. "He left me behind again," she said, before she buried her head in Max's shoulder.

I knew there was more. "So, Terry Dumas died eleven days ago. Gordy Krantz died twenty-seven years ago," I said, "which makes for an interesting legal situation."

"What the hell do you mean?" snapped Janice. "Stop with all the riddles."

I squared my shoulders. "Very well, Janice. You had your husband's last will and testament enacted as a result of his declared date of death twenty-seven years ago. We've all been receiving letters and instructions from him now, in his disguise as Gordy, which means 'Gordy's' last will and testament isn't his at all – it was drawn up at the request of Terry masquerading as Gordy. It's invalid."

"We're never going to get what we were promised in those letters, are we?" Louise sounded disappointed. "My letter said all I had to do was show my *trousseau* to the lawyers, and I'd get fifty acres of trees. Gordy promised me that when we got divorced, too. So, if *Terry* wrote all those letters, how'd he know about the fifty acres *Gordy* promised me?"

I replied, "Bud and I found about forty years' worth of Gordy's diaries hidden in his old cabin. I've been able to read through them all, and now the police have them for their use. But there were three years' worth of diaries missing – 1988 to 1990. Those were the years when Gordy and you were married, Louise. I believe Terry found those diaries originally, read them, and found out about you, and Gordy…and so on." I decided it was best to not mention the miscarriage. "If Terry had noted the fact Gordy had promised you fifty acres, then I think it's likely Terry would have been trying to deliver that promise when he wrote the fake-Gordy will."

Louise shrugged.

I continued, "Even before you got your letter from 'Gordy', you wanted to get your hands on that *trousseau*, didn't you? You thought it was at the new house, so you tried to break in there, but you failed. Then you found it in the cabin, and took it, correct? You used your motor scooter at the house, didn't you?" I asked.

Louise looked up, a twinkle in her eye. "I'd never dared ask Gordy for it. Then he was dead. Gone. Couldn't get into the new place that night – came all the way around the mountain with my mobility scooter in the back of my van, then rode it up the drive; it's a whole lot quieter. But you two started flashing lights, and making a noise, so I booked out. After that the cops were all over the place, like food on a plate, so I didn't stand a chance. I wondered if it might be in the cabin – that's where Gordy had been living when we were married in any case, but the thing was always locked up, and the window was too small for me to get through – not that I'd be much good at getting through a window these days. I saw you from my house when you went to the cabin – first you" – she nodded at Bud – "then the two of you, together. I can still see the cabin from my place, through the trunks of the trees, though not as clearly as I once could. I know I'm not too good on these old legs, but I can be a determined woman when I choose, and that day I was. Took me a while, but I managed to get it all back to my place. Mom started making that *trousseau* when I was born; put her heart and soul into it, she did, so – of course – I brought it with me when I left the good old US of A. Hell, yes, I wanted it back but, like I said, I didn't ever ask Gordy for it. Then I got that damned letter, so, yes, I guess Terry must have read Gordy's diaries, and probably knew some stuff about me I thought was private."

She sighed as I said, "Sorry Louise, no fifty acres."

Louise shrugged. "That's a real shame. I'd been thinking of sheltered accommodation – I could have sold that land to be able to afford a place. Never mind, I'll put my five acres on the market, it might sell."

"What now?" Colleen was looking around, seething. "Is that it? Gordy was really Terry, and Terry killed himself. And the real Gordy was the one who killed two girls back in the day, then Terry killed him, and pretended to be Gordy. Right?"

Tom snapped, "It's not that simple, Auntie Colleen. Terry was Maddie's father – think about it...she's lost him *twice*, now." He smiled sadly at Maddie, who managed a weak smile in return.

"There's a little more," I said. "I had a chance to discuss the legal situation with Oishi, Singh, *and* Chan, and it's clear that, because Gordy Krantz in fact pre-deceased Terry Dumas, and Terry killed him, the record needs to be set straight."

"So?" Janice was pink in the face. "That's got nothing to do with Terry's will – Terry's last will hasn't changed, has it? It's still what it was back when we read it."

I wasn't surprised that Janice Dumas's focus was on how her property and possessions were affected. "True" I replied, "but the real Gordy's will, lodged with Mr. Oishi's firm in the 1980s, was still current when he died in 1994. According to Mr. Oishi, Gordy left everything he owned to Terry Dumas. I'm sorry, Louise, Gordy didn't gift you fifty acres in his real will either."

"Huh! Not surprised," said Louise angrily.

I continued, "Gordy Krantz's legal will relates to all of his property – which, just to be clear, includes the entirety of Red Water Mountain, the Charity Uranium Mine in Saskatchewan, a raft of lucrative global cultivation deals for many hybrids of plants, as well as the house and cabin – and all of this was willed to Terry. And Terry's will – as of 1994, which he never legally changed – still stands."

The way Janice Dumas perked up made me feel ill. "Really? I get the lot?"

"Mr. Chan," I said, "would you remind Janice and Maddie of the terms of Terry Dumas's will, please?"

Mr. Chan spoke quietly, "Certainly – the will required that whatever his net worth at the time, ten percent or one hundred thousand dollars, whichever was the greater, should be set aside to facilitate the stabling of as many retired racehorses as could be reasonably accommodated. It further stipulated that the same amount be set aside to support charitable works performing outreach to benefit the community at large. The land upon which the family home sat, as well as the family house itself, were to pass to Janice. Also, all matters pertaining to the business of K. Dumas – including liquid assets, properties, stocks and possessions, as well as the rights to operate the business – were left wholly to his wife, Janice. All other property in his possession at his death was to pass to his daughter, Madelaine, or be held in trust for her until she reached the age of twenty-one. At the time, this consisted of only the stables on the family property. This will and these terms were agreed upon as being the legal last will and testament of Terry Dumas upon his declared date of death, which was given as 3rd October 1994. No further legal filings of wills for the person of Terry Dumas have been made, nor would they be accepted without proof of life, after that date."

Janice was starting to turn pink. "Does that mean…no, it can't. I don't get anything more? She gets the lot?" She glared at the lawyer, then turned her venom on her daughter. "You don't deserve it." She banged her little fist, with its jangling bracelets and perfectly manicured fingers, on the table.

Maddie stared at Mr. Chan. "Is Mom right? Do I get the mine, and the mountain, and everything Gordy left my father?"

Chan, Oishi, and Singh all shook their heads, silently.

I replied, "The common law 'Slayer Rule' is enforced in Canada – as well as in many other countries; it means that no one can inherit from a person they kill. If that were possible, it could lead to some dreadful situations. So, because Terry killed Gordy, Gordy's will has to be enacted as though Terry predeceased him."

"What?" Janice was on her feet. "This is ridiculous – who gets all Gordy's stuff? That's what we all want to know, right? If Terry killing him means I don't get it, then who does?"

Her eyes and cheeks shone as she looked around the room. I could only wonder if she had any idea just how full of disgust the expressions were that met hers.

I said, "Mr. Chan, could you please explain the situation, in full?"

The look the lawyer gave Janice was one of pure disdain, then his expression softened as he shifted his attention to Maddie. "Although your father could not inherit from Gordy Krantz, you, Madelaine Dumas, are specifically named as the person who should inherit Gordy's estate if your father has pre-deceased him, and the law says we must act as though that were the case." Maddie looked dumbstruck. The lawyer cleared his throat and added, "There is a specific clause which stipulates that" – he looked down at his notes – "Mrs. Janice Dumas be 'not allowed to directly benefit from my estate to even the sum of one cent'."

Maddie looked as shocked as her mother, but rallied faster. "May I give fifty acres of the Red Water Mountain to Louise, as both Gordy *and* my father promised her?"

Mr. Chan answered, "The mountain is yours, you may do with it as you wish."

"You'll get your acres, Louise, don't worry, we'll sort it out. And what else was promised to others here? Did your letters tell you?"

Everyone shook their heads – it appeared only Louise had received specific information about the nature of her "gift from Gordy".

"We know what all the gifts were supposed to be," said Mahera Singh.

"Good," replied Maddie. "I want everyone to get what my father, when he was writing as Gordy, planned for people to have. Can we work together to make sure that happens?"

Mahera nodded. "It might take a little while, because now there's even more paperwork involved. But we'll happily work with Mr. Chan and his colleagues to ensure a smooth transition of ownership, with every legal challenge dealt with."

"Thank you." Maddie acknowledged the lawyers. "Is there anything else?"

I looked at Pelletier before I spoke. The slight tilt of his head told me I was finished. "No, I think everything is explained. I'm so sorry for your loss, Maddie. Again." I couldn't bring myself to console Janice.

"So, Tom, who did I have lunch with when the bishop came?" Colleen was fussing with her wrap as Tom helped her from her seat.

"Terry Dumas, Auntie – you only ever knew Terry Dumas. You probably never even met Gordy Krantz."

"But your grandmother used to buy all her plants from them, at the roadside. I must have met him then. Just think – I've met two killers. What a surprise." Colleen was twittering. "Wait till I tell them all at church…"

"Hang on, Auntie, you've promised you won't say anything about what we've heard today. Remember the trouble you caused when you gossiped about Gordy?"

Colin and Ann stood wearily, and I wondered if they'd ever manage to heal the deep wounds they'd obviously been inflicting upon each other for years…I hoped so. Dayton Woodward seemed relatively unscathed by all the events, though he did comment, "People are so complicated. I prefer trees."

I finally reached the door, where Bud hugged me. "Good job, Wife. You were right about everything."

I returned Bud's smile. "No, not everything. I was wrong about the choice of poison being of no consequence – it was a considered choice, with a specific meaning."

Jacques Pelletier was beaming. "You've done a great service to this community. Giving me the tips about those women's identities will allow us to help two families find some sort of peace, and the notes in Tom White's possession make it clear suicide was intended, so I'll get those to the coroner. Bud was right – you're quite a woman. You see things...differently."

"I'm sure your team would have got there, Jacques," said Bud, smiling at me.

"Not in this timeframe, Bud. She's like a whole team in just one person...treat her well." He leaned toward me and kissed me on each cheek. "And you look after him...he's golden."

"You're right," I said. Pelletier winked.

We were all happy to leave the lawyers' place, and I was even more delighted when, as Bud and I drove toward our sanctuary – our home – he offered to stop at my favourite fish and chip shop on the way. The shop's run by a Scottish family who make chips exactly the way I like them; they even have giant bottles of malt vinegar on the counter.

The smell of our supper had filled the truck by the time we got home, and Marty was deliriously happy to see us...though maybe the chips had something to do with it too – he likes chips, though he's only allowed a few.

The golden hour trickled past, and we managed to have a conversation about something other than Gordy, and Terry, and all those who'd been affected by both men's lives, and decisions. Then, as the day ended, we snuggled on the sofa with Marty, to watch an hour of television – nothing featuring dead bodies at all, but instead the terror associated with a fatless sponge not rising enough to create a three-tiered showstopping cake.

Thanksgiving came and went, and we'd just finished the last of the turkey curry when we received an email from Maddie Dumas.

Hi Cait and Bud, I will phone, but I need there to be a digital trail for future reference.

I don't know if you've heard, but Louise is all set up at a nice place where she has her own apartment; she's even got a rescue dog from the pound – they're allowed at the place Max and I helped her hunt down. She sold her fifty acres to a consortium that's going to make sure the old-growth trees stay exactly where they are – she could have got more money, but she reckons she's got enough to be comfortable for the rest of her life.

She also sold her five acres to Tom White, who's tearing down her house, and building a new place for himself; he's sinking the rest of the money my father wanted him to have into new, larger premises for his restaurant in what used to be the Shakemakers Taproom – remember that old, log-cabin-style bar that closed down just off the highway? It'll be great.

Mom's gone off with Andrew on their cruise, still bitter. Maybe she'll get over it, I don't know. She still won't tell me whether Gordy or Terry was my biological father – I'm not even sure she knows. Maybe one day I'll get a DNA test done, but – for now – it's enough to know Terry raised me, and loved me. He'll always be my father, whatever the source of my genetic code.

I've sorted it so that Krantz Hall continues to get its funding, because that's what he wanted, but I'm selling the uranium mine, making sure I have good plans for that money. The income from all the hybrids into the center for environmental studies, and the uranium money will be used for the other things I'm planning.

To start with, our community meal program is going to expand dramatically, and Max will have a much bigger team who can use recipes he develops, so he's happy. As am I, because it turns out he's as keen on me as I am on him. We'll see how that goes.

My Dad's will – when all's said and done, that's what it was, really – also left money for Dayton, who's going to expand his business and focus on training up more arborists and lumberjacks; for Colin and Ann, who have apparently agreed he'll use it to get his nurse practitioner qualifications; and even for Colleen, who's giving it to the church, to have the old church bell fixed.

As for you – well, I can now tell you what it was Dad wanted to gift to you both. He wanted you to have your mountain. The lawyers have a map, and it amounts to several hundred acres, excluding the five acres Tom now owns, and the fifty I set aside for Louise. You'll have your own haven, forever. (Don't panic about the taxes, they're covered.) I know it was my father who built the house next to yours, but, honestly, it doesn't hold any real memories for me, so that's yours too. However, I'd like to spend some time there, looking through what I now know to have been my father's possessions, if that's okay with you. Maybe we can spend some time together, too, so you can tell me a bit more about what he was like?

I'm just off to meet with a realtor who's taking me to see a thirty-acre property down at the border, on Zero Avenue; it's already set up for horses, and I'm hoping it can become a new, self-contained retirement home for animals who've given their all on the racecourse. I have a plan to staff it with people who've also come to the end of their earning potential in that career – the stable hands and jockeys who still want to be with the creatures they adore.

I'll phone soon, and wish you both well. The map of your new property is attached. The lawyers will be in touch regarding title documents soon.

Regards, and unending thanks, Maddie xx

Bud and I sat quietly for a few moments, with only the thumping of Marty's tail breaking the silence.

"We own a mountain, Husband," I said.

"So I see, Wife," said Bud, sounding a little stunned. "I never imagined I'd ever be responsible for an entire mountain. I guess…well, I guess we'll have to have a think about how we make sure it's well taken care of – whatever that might mean. I thought five acres was a lot. Now…hey, I'm sure we'll cope. Right?"

I hugged him. "You know we will. But you know what else it means, don't you?"

Bud looked puzzled. "What?"

"Clearing out next door will be our responsibility, after all."

Bud rolled his eyes heavenwards. "Good grief. You're right."

Acknowledgements

There are always so many people an author wants to thank when a book finds its way out into the world; this time, things are a little different…for this author, and the world. I don't know when you're reading this book, but it was written at a time when most of us were at home, unable to be with all those we love, even for important celebrations, or the most critical, or tragic of situations.

Many authors have debated how they'll represent the world with Covid 19 in it, as opposed to the world before we knew what "pandemic" really meant. I've chosen to take Cait and Bud to their home, which is something we've all been faced with; while there'll be no pandemic mentioned in any Cait Morgan Mysteries, I wanted to take the opportunity to consider concepts such as home and community through the eyes of my characters, which is why *The Corpse with the Iron Will* is the book it is.

Throughout the time I was planning, writing, and editing this book, I was mindful of the various communities to which I belong; the community where I grew up, the community where I live now, and the "crime fiction" community. That inspired me to ask certain people within them if I might use their names for some of my characters. No one said no, which is wonderful. Thank you to everyone.

Janice and Maddie Dumas: you've been stalwart supporters of my work since Day One…thank you for being at all my signings, and for your unending kind words. Until her recent departure, Janice was an enthusiastic and knowledgeable bookseller in BC, championing my work, and is a valued early reader; she's the polar opposite of the character for whom I used her name, and about to start an exciting new chapter in her life…I have every expectation she'll enjoy it. The *real* Maddie is a delight, and her smile lights up any room. Thank you both, for everything.

The Oishi family is well known in our area for many reasons – all of them good – and they've been supportive of our family, as well as the broader community, especially the 4H folks, in myriad ways. We're fortunate to have our families' lives intertwined across three generations.

Tom, Dayton, and Rylan Van Der Pauw are nothing like the people in this book who run nurseries; they've helped my husband and I create a little paradise here at our home. We both thank them for sharing their knowledge of plants, and for inviting me to launch one of my books several years ago at their wonderful Triple Tree Nursery.

Without the delightful Colleen White, I would not have been able to travel as I have – thank you for loving our dogs as much as we did, and for staying in our home when we needed to be away…and hugs to Auntie Ann, in Scotland.

Colin and Ann Evans live in Swansea, and I thank them for their wonderful support of my writing, my family, and my community back there.

The late David Shantz inspired both my husband and I with his encyclopedic knowledge of rhododendrons and maples, and our garden bears testament to the fact he shared his passion, knowledge, and plants with us over almost two decades. The nursery he and his late-partner Milton Wildfong created together in Mission, BC was rightly lauded by the American Rhododendron Society, and we continue to do our best to fulfil our promise to keep all the plants he gave us well-tended. We think of him every day, and are grateful we got to share the last couple of decades of his life. He died aged 93, and had only stopped climbing trees to limb them a few years earlier (because we nagged him).

Charlotte Louise Prevost Lycett Davis was a legend in our community; born and raised in Philadelphia, she enlisted when World War Two broke out, served as a navy nurse, then gained her PhD and was instrumental in establishing the University of the US Virgin Islands and St. Thomas. She was the most-travelled person I've ever met; she eventually settled in Canada. Over 70 years she had as big an impact upon the Golden Retriever breeding and training community here as she had in the USA. She was a Charter member of the Canadian Dogs for the Blind and Pacific Assistance Dogs. Our conversations were always spirited, and I was grateful her final months were spent comfortably. She was 98 when she died.

I have dedicated this book to the memory of David, and Charlotte, but whilst you might see shades of them in characters in this book, please be assured that the real-life people *were not* the characters you might think they are in this work of fiction…I have *created* all the characters in this story to be what they need to be to tell this story. That goes for the characters who bear the names of the other real people I've listed, too.

Of course, my closest family were all instrumental in this book coming to be: my husband is my constant and total support; my mother listens to me talking through plots for hours, is an avid and hugely experienced reader of mysteries (it's her fault I started reading them!) and is the best word-of-mouth salesperson I have; my sister is so valued as an early reader, and then plays so many critical roles as my books near completion. Without them and their love – no books, ever, it's that simple.

Anna Harrisson is a professional editor, but – like so many others – she's also had to juggle an entirely different concept of motherhood while she's continued her work; my thanks to her, and her family. Sue Vincent checks the proofs with vigor, and that hasn't abated even during lockdowns; my thanks to her.

Finally, in these still-unprecedented times, what of the members of our community who've played a slightly more direct role in this book finding its way into your hands? To early readers (SA, JD, KA), bloggers, Facebookers, Tweeters, Instagrammers, reviewers, librarians, booksellers, organizers of online events, and (one day to be in-person again) festivals and conventions – thank you for doing whatever you did that helped this reader find this book. And to you, dear reader, thanks for choosing to spend time with Cait Morgan…and her community.

Community is what *we* make it.

Community is stronger when *we* make it stronger.

Community starts at home, but gains strength as it grows beyond self.

I am fortunate: I belong to a great family, and a wonderful local community where I live; I'm still connected to the community where I grew up, and I'm part of a global community of book lovers.

Thanks to all of you for sharing your support.

About the Author

CATHY ACE was born and raised in Swansea, Wales, and now lives in British Columbia, Canada. She is the author of *The Cait Morgan Mysteries*, *The WISE Enquiries Agency Mysteries*, *The Wrong Boy*, and collections of short stories and novellas. As well as being passionate about writing crime fiction, she's also a keen gardener.

You can find out more about Cathy and her work at:
www.cathyace.com